About t.

Award-winning author Heather Peck has enjoyed a varied life. She has been both farmer and agricultural policy adviser, volunteer covid vaccinator and NHS Trust Chair. She bred sheep and alpacas, reared calves, broke ploughs, represented the UK in international negotiations, specialised in emergency response from Chernobyl to bird flu, managed controls over pesticides and GM crops, saw legislation through Parliament and got paid to eat Kit Kats while on secondment to Nestle Rowntree.

She lives in Norfolk with her partner Gary, two dogs and two cats.

See more and sign up for Heather's free monthly newsletter at
www.heatherpeckauthor.com

Also by Heather Peck

THE DCI GELDARD NORFOLK MYSTERIES

Secret Places
Glass Arrows
Fires of Hate
The Temenos Remains
Dig Two Graves
Beyond Closed Doors
Buried in the Past
Spinning into the Dark
Death on the Rhine (novella)
Death on the Norwich Express (novella)
Expedition to Death (novella)

Milestones (Winner, Page Turner Book Awards 2024 best crime novel)

BOOKS FOR CHILDREN

Tails of Two Spaniels
The Animals of White Cows Farm
The Pixie and the Bear

WELCOME TO THE DCI GREG GELDARD NORFOLK MYSTERIES

Previously in the series:

When Greg's team stormed a quiet village home to rescue two missing children, they uncovered a far darker secret — two hidden bodies.

As the cold trail of a decade-old murder began to warm, a new nightmare struck: cyclists were vanishing from Norfolk's peaceful lanes. Balancing the hunt for a ruthless predator with an unexpected offer of promotion — and the looming arrival of his first child — Greg found himself fighting to hold his world together while chasing a killer who always seemed to be one step ahead.

Last Act

DCI GREG GELDARD BOOK 9

Heather Peck

Ormesby Publishing

Published in 2025 by Ormesby Publishing

Ormesby St Margaret

Norfolk

www.ormesbypublishing.co.uk

Text copyright © Heather Peck 2025

Author photograph by John Thompson 2021

This is a work of fiction. Names, characters, places and incidents either are products of the author's imagination. Or are used fictitiously. Any resemblance to actual events or persons, living or dead, is entirely coincidental.

British Library Cataloguing in Publication Data

A CIP catalogue record for this book is available from the British Library.

Page design and typesetting by Ormesby Publishing

Acknowledgments

My thanks to Gary for everything

and many thanks yet again to my beta readers Geoff Dodgson,
Alison Tayler and Gary Westlake for their constructive
criticism and comments.
This book is all the better for your help.

Particular thanks go to Clive Myhill and Neil Mace for their
specialist advice and guidance on all things involving police
dogs. Any mistakes are mine!

And finally, thanks also to Sharon Gray at CluedUpEditing for
her meticulous and knowledgeable proof editing.

Contents

Key Characters

Norfolk Police

Chief Constable Ralph Thornfield
Major Crimes team:
Detective Superintendent Greg Geldard
Detective Chief Inspector (DCI) Ram Trent
Detective Inspector (DI) Jim Henning
DI Chris Mathews
Detective Sergeant (DS) Jill Hayes
Detective Constable (DC)s Bill Street, Jenny Warren and Graham 'Gray' Clarke
In King's Lynn
DCI Helena Bell
DI Glyn Roberts
DCs Colin Waterton and Ian Challinor
Geraldine Dennis and Chas Young (civilian staff)
In Great Yarmouth
Chief Inspector (CI) Richard 'Rick' Lake
Sergeant Briscoe

Specialist Services

Ned George — Lead crime scene investigator

Yvonne Berry — Deputy crime scene investigator

PCs Rogers and Scouller — Dog handlers

Police Dogs (PD)s Nell and Digby — German shepherd general purpose (GP) dogs

Legal services

Frank Parker — Crown Prosecution Service

Henry Fell, Mr Hempstall and Mr Gregson — Solicitors

Sir Frederick Seymour — Prosecution barrister

Mr Fordyce — Defence barrister

Medical experts

Dr Paisley — Police pathologist

Other participants

James 'Jamie' Gregory Simon Geldard — guess who...

Mr Geldard, senior — Greg's father

Bobby — Greg's cat

Tally — Chris's foul-mouthed parrot

Jane Mathews — Chris's mum

Bob Fisher — Fire service commander

Northfolk Players — *currently rehearsing* Kiss Me, Kate

Leonard Ware — Fred/Petruchio

Louise Lacon — Lilli/Kate

Dean Mason — Bill

Myrtle Harris — Hattie

Josie James — Lois

Barry 'Aubrey' Sinclair — Producer

Pop	Doorman
Marie Leakey	Masseuse
Nick Atkinson	Garage owner
Sharon Jones	Hairdresser
Sam Jones	Sharon's husband
Anthony Newell	Vicar in Martham
Warren Thorne	Tree surgeon
Joseph Andrews	Retired solicitor

Glossary

HDU   high dependency unit
ICE   in case of emergency
ITU   intensive therapy unit
N&N   Norfolk and Norwich Hospital
RTA   road traffic accident

1

---

19 July 2021: the curtain rises on The Garage, Norwich

Chalk lines on the rehearsal room floor marked the actors' entrances and exits. A row of chairs indicated where unpainted scenery flats would be propped, and more chalk announced the edge of the stage. The first rehearsal of *Kiss Me, Kate*, as interpreted by the Northfolk Players, was underway.

Most of the cast, jubilant about rehearsing after the long period of lockdowns, were celebrating their reunions and the return of drama to their lives. Sitting in the centre of a row of chairs, as far away from the chalk stage as possible, Aubrey Sinclair was clutching his head in his hands.

'No, no. Nooo,' he howled at the lady, very much of a 'certain age', holding centre stage. 'OK, I said come down to centre stage, but I also said keep all gestures light and airy. Which bit of "light and airy" didn't you understand? I said keep all gestures at shoulder level, so they're dramatic and flamboyant. And what do I get? Someone who looks as though they're shovelling coal! I really don't feel you're channelling this part, dear. Come on, darling. This is the opening scene. It sets the, the...'

'Scene?' suggested Hattie helpfully.

'All right, yes, it sets the scene for the drama to come, and for an evening of hilarious entertainment for our audience. At the moment, the audience will be either anticipating hemlock shots all round or leaving in droves.'

Hattie marched to the chalk line with determined steps. Given that she weighed north of one hundred and twenty kilos, the sound on the echoing wooden floor was impressive.

'Look here, Barry,' she snapped. 'Just give it to me straight. If you want louder or softer, say so. If you want me to come forwards or move back, say that. I just don't get all this highfalutin poncing about. Tell me what you want in words of one syllable and I'll deliver it.'

'Aubrey,' corrected Barry 'Aubrey'. 'I don't use Barry now.'

'Humph,' said Hattie, and retired to the back of the stage before her impulse to bluntness overcame her again.

'Let's leave the opening scene for now,' said Aubrey, knowing when he was beaten. 'Where're Lois and Bill? Let's go through "Why can't you behave?", and make sure Fred and Lilli are ready to block "Wunderbar".

'OK, Maggie,' he said to the long-suffering pianist, who had seized the opportunity to open a packet of wine gums and shovel a few in. She could see this was going to be one of those evenings when a high blood-sugar level would be a prerequisite. 'From the top, and speed it up a bit.'

'OK, Aubrey,' she spluttered through the sweets and set off at a merry gallop. But as the introduction ended, there was a marked lack of Lois.

'Cut,' shouted Aubrey, forgetting for a moment that he was producing an amateur theatrical company not a film. 'Where the hell's Lois?'

There was a scuffle, then a teenager dressed all in black emerged with some difficulty at the back of the stage. 'Sorry, Aubrey,' she gasped. 'I parked my bike in the alley, and then I couldn't get up the back passage.'

There was a snort from Hattie, still hanging around stage left, and an outright guffaw from Bill, waiting his turn for some dialogue. Aubrey decided to rise above it.

'No problem, Lois,' he said to the girl. 'Take it from the top, Maggie, and, Lois, remember what we said last week about singing to the audience, not to Bill. She's a nightclub singer, remember?'

'Oh, yes,' said Lois. 'Right. OK.'

Maggie set off again, and this time Lois managed to take her cue. Aubrey began to relax and Bill got ready for his line. The Northfolk were up and running again. At least, until the next interruption.

'Aubrey,' shouted a voice from the room next door. 'Aubrey, we've got a problem.'

Aubrey clutched his head again, Maggie came to a sudden stop and Lois, warbling in a throaty alto, trailed off in the sudden silence.

'What now?' demanded Aubrey.

'More congestion in the back passage?' asked Hattie with another snort.

The voice came round the door, turning out to belong to the old chap cast as Pop, the *Kiss Me, Kate* doorman. 'Leonard's been run over,' he said with all the relish due to the bearer of bad tidings. 'Just out here, in front of the theatre.'

There was a concerted dash for the door and Lois was left alone onstage.

2

The following day: by the Bure, near Acle.

Greg was peering at himself in the full-length mirror, brushing imaginary flecks off his dark jacket. Watching him, their five-month-old son, James Gregory Simon Geldard (named for his father and his two grandfathers), was hiccupping gently over Chris's shoulder. She reckoned she could count on the fingers of one hand the number of times she had seen Greg preening in a mirror.

'You're nervous,' she said accusingly. 'Whyever? You've been assured it's a shoo-in and you're not even sure you want the job, so what's to be nervous about?'

Greg looked into her eyes reflected in the mirror and grinned sheepishly. 'I guess I do want it after all,' he admitted. 'More than I thought.' He turned round. 'Do I look like a good candidate for detective superintendent?' he asked.

Chris surveyed the dark suit, white shirt, just ever so slightly outré tie and highly polished black shoes. 'Show me your socks,' she demanded. Greg laughed and hoicked up his trouser legs to reveal impeccable black socks.

'I did consider taking a leaf out of your book and wearing those pink ones you got me for Christmas,' he said. 'But I decided against it, just in case the panel have no sense of humour.'

'You pass,' said Chris. 'Now give us a kiss and be on your way. You don't want to be late.'

'Give me my son and heir then,' he said and held out his arms.

'Not on your nelly,' she exclaimed, holding the baby out of reach. 'Guaranteed he'll barf all down your best suit. Just blow him a kiss for luck and get off with you. Break a leg,' she added as he went down the stairs.

'Your dad is looking damn good,' she said to the uncomprehending baby. 'I could even fancy him myself.' She jiggled the baby and went downstairs to feed the indignant cat and parrot awaiting, with varying degrees of patience, her ministrations.

Their cottage was sited on the banks of the River Bure, not far from the market town of Acle. Succumbing to the temptation of a wander in the garden, Chris could still hear Greg's car bouncing over the long, rough track that led down the side of a field to the main road. For March, the day was sunny, and the wind had dropped, so it almost qualified as warm. The river was flowing swiftly, swollen by recent rains, provoking the thought in Chris's mind that they really must arrange for the garden to be fenced off from the river before the baby started crawling. She turned to carry the baby back into the house, almost tripped over Bobby, their cat, and suppressed the words that came to mind.

'No swearing in front of you, either,' she said to little Jamie; and to Bobby, 'Come on, you. I'll feed you now.'

By the time the whole menagerie had been fed – cat, parrot and baby – Chris was more than ready to sit down with a mug of coffee and her laptop. Jamie had, for once, deigned to go to sleep promptly on being put down, and she clicked on the Norfolk Police link with a sigh of relief. She wasn't due back at work for some weeks yet, but to Chris, a career detective inspector, work wasn't a chore; it was both safe haven and, after Greg and Jamie, reason for living. She dived into the website like a salmon leaping upriver.

The drive to Wymondham was, for once, pleasantly free of roadworks and Greg arrived so far ahead of his scheduled interview he had time to waste. He decided against an extended coffee stop, on the grounds that he didn't want to spend his interview with his legs crossed as well as his fingers, and dropped in on Jim Henning instead. Jim was, as usual at that time in the morning, tonsils deep in a bacon butty.

'How you can keep eating those and still get through the door beats me,' said Greg in greeting.

DI Henning surveyed him in a silence which owed a lot to the fact that his mouth was full, swallowed, cleared his throat and said 'Woohoo! Look at the supermodel. Anyone can tell you've got an interview this morning!'

'Can it, Jim,' responded Greg, sitting down in the chair opposite. 'Anyone would think I usually come in scruffy.'

Jim leaned over to survey his boss's feet. 'Even the shoes are polished,' he remarked, then took pity on his superior. 'Joking apart, Greg, the whole team is rooting for you. Best of luck from us all.'

'Thank you,' said Greg. 'I'm still not sure it's the right time...'

'Of course it is,' Jim replied. 'With Margaret on her way out, it's the only time. We're all just glad the bosses apparently see it that way too.'

***

An hour later and Greg was wondering if they did indeed see it that way. He'd been grilled on his leadership style, asked to outline a difficult decision and how he had reached it, challenged on why he wanted the job, and quizzed on his understanding of Norfolk Police, its structures and policies. The independent panel member had asked him about his involvement in the local community, and he had begun to feel he might be on the home straight, when the panel Chair bowled him a googly.

'You must be aware of the murder in March that was in all the headlines and the subsequent arrest of a serving officer. How would you deal with a case like that involving a member of your team?'

Greg thought quickly, vaguely conscious of the multiple procedural shortcomings in the appointment of the officer in question and very mindful of the likely sensitivities of some of the panel members. In seconds he considered and rejected a diplomatic reply, deciding that if he couldn't do the job his way, he didn't want to do it at all. *If they don't like my answer, they can stuff the job.*

'I think I can best answer that by describing how I dealt with a similar case,' he said slowly. 'It wasn't as serious as murder, thank God, but it was bad enough. I was sent a transferee from the Met as a new team member. I had cause to pull him up for poor behaviour in his first few days. Specifically, misogynistic attitudes and a failure to respect both female colleagues and members of the public. Then his negligence led directly to violence against a member of the public and the abduction of a serving officer. On top of that, I caught him sharing inappropriate images of the colleague who had been taken hostage via a *WhatsApp* group. I took immediate action to suspend the officer pending dismissal.

'If I was to extrapolate from this case to the one currently being reported, I would argue that the failings started much further back in time than the recent tragic incident, and the solution is to ensure that the perfectly good procedures that are in place are followed robustly.'

'So you would argue that the current procedures are adequate?' asked the Chair with a raised eyebrow.

'Yes, sir, I would,' said Greg stoutly. 'If they're followed. I have always followed a policy of zero tolerance for the sort of behaviour that we are discussing. And I have never had a problem deploying the policies already in place. The problem, as I see it, is not the policies; it's the failure to adhere to them.'

***

Recounting the discussion to Jim, Greg said, 'It's in the lap of the gods. If they liked what I had to say, I'm in with a chance. If they didn't...' he shrugged. 'But if they want a politician in the job, they don't want me and I don't want the job, so we'll just wait and see.'

Privately, Jim thought that the interviewer had probably provoked Greg deliberately, knowing that he held strong views about police behaviour and attitudes and his likely response. He wondered which of the panel members the Chair had particularly wanted to hear Greg's speech.

'Let's forget about it for now,' said Greg. 'Back to the real world. Anything I need to know about?'

'A couple of things,' said Jim, rootling through the paper on his desk. 'As you know, our homicidal tree surgeon, Warren Thorne, was transferred to the secure psychiatric unit at Rampton. Last week it seems he attempted an escape, but the Serco team took heed of our warnings and didn't fall for his *Oh dear, I'm having a heart attack* routine. They had him checked out by medics and there was nothing materially wrong. Hopefully they'll continue to keep him safe until he comes to court.

'The county lines investigation has run into the buffers again, and we have a suspected murder attempt outside the Theatre Royal in Norwich yesterday.'

'Who was the victim?' asked Greg.

'The intended victim,' corrected Jim. 'He survived, luckily. It was the leading man from an amateur dramatic society. They were apparently rehearsing *Kiss Me, Kate* in The Garage, just down the road from the theatre. The man in question, a Mr Leonard Ware, is playing Fred Graham and Petruchio. He was a bit late for the rehearsal and was rushing from the Chantry car park. When he crossed the road to The Garage, he was hit by a dark car heading towards the city centre. It didn't stop.'

'Anything on CCTV?' asked Greg.

'As luck would have it, the camera on Theatre Street was out of action, and without a better description than "a dark car", it's been a bit difficult to pick out one among the many in the city centre. That's where we're at so far.'

'Why are we not regarding it as a simple hit and run?' asked Greg.

'Because the intended victim insists the car started up as he crossed the road and drove straight at him. He's in the N&N with a dislocated shoulder and possible heart attack.'

3

Morning of 20 July 2021

When Detective Sergeant Jill Hayes arrived at the bedside of their possible attempted murder victim, she found him holding court to two ladies and a gentleman – in blatant breach of the rules on visitor numbers. A staff nurse who had been trying to dismiss at least two of the entourage greeted Jill's arrival with a sigh of relief.

'If you can help me get rid of this lot,' she said quietly, 'I'll make sure you have time for a quiet chat with our Sir Laurence.'

'I thought his name was Leonard something,' said Jill.

'It is. Sorry. We christened him Sir Laurence after the famous actor. He's been boasting of his dramatic triumphs ever since he got here. Mind you,' she added, 'personally, I think he could list his performance after the accident as one of his most convincing successful roles.'

'You don't buy the near-death-experience-and-heart-attack narrative then?' asked Jill.

'No idea about the first,' replied the nurse cheerfully. 'Glad to say sorting out fact from fiction on that is your problem, not mine. But the so-called heart attack wasn't real. More panic attack, if you ask me. Right. Let's get shot of the fandom.'

She approached the bed and clapped her hands sharply. 'Enough,' she said. 'I insist on you leaving now. Mr Ware has to give a statement to the police and then he needs his rest. Moreover, you're disturbing other patients. So say your goodbyes and be on your way.'

Waving her arms as though herding a flock of sheep, she edged the trio away from the bed. The man, a middle-aged gent in red corduroys and sporting a cravat, went happily enough. The two ladies were more reluctant, mainly because neither wanted to leave the other in control of the field. Eventually they drifted away with much blowing of kisses and 'darlings', leaving Jill reviewing her interviewee.

The man in the bed was florid and thickset, with a head of hair that seemed to have been expensively augmented by surgery at some point. He had been made victim of the health service's obsession with overly revealing standard-issue nightwear but had covered the loosely tied gown with a tweedy jacket and silk scarf. As she approached, he lay back on his mounded pillows with a faint sigh intended, Jill surmised, to be redolent of major trauma bravely borne.

'Mr Leonard Ware?' she asked, taking out her notebook. 'I'm DS Jill Hayes. We're investigating last night's events. Can you talk me through what happened to you after you left the Chantry car park?'

'I already told a police officer last night,' grumbled Ware.

'Yes, I know and I've seen his report,' Jill reassured him. 'But you may have remembered more this morning. It's amazing how often that happens. You presumably paid your car park fee and put the ticket inside your car. What time was that?'

'About ten past seven,' replied Ware, screwing his face up to assist his memory. 'I was running a bit late. I had a phone call just as I was leaving home that held me up a bit.'

'Then what?'

'I walked up the hill towards the Garage. We're rehearsing *Kiss Me, Kate* there,' he explained. 'I'm playing the male lead.'

'So I understand,' said Jill. 'Which side of the road did you walk?'

'The side next to the Theatre Royal,' he replied. 'I didn't start to cross until I was past the theatre.'

'What happened then?'

'As I started to cross the road, a car pulled out from the parking spaces on the other side. By the time I was in the middle of the road it had speeded up a lot, and I suddenly realised it was heading straight for me. I shouted something, I think, and jumped for the side of the road, but there were cars parked there too. I tried to get between two parked cars and just before I got there the car hit me and drove off.'

'How did it hit you?' asked Jill. 'I mean, did it hit you head-on, or a glancing blow?'

'I suppose it was what you'd call a glancing blow,' Ware admitted. 'I nearly got away, but the wing, or maybe the mirror, hit me. I have bruises,' he added, and went to pull up his gown to show her.

'You're OK,' said Jill hurriedly. 'I'll have a detailed report from the doctor, don't worry, and we may send someone to take photos later today. Did you see the driver of the car?'

'No. I had my back to it by the time it was close to me.'

'And what about the car? I gather you described it as dark. Can you tell me anything about the make or colour?'

'No idea about the make,' said Ware. 'As to colour, it must have been black or dark blue. Maybe dark green.'

'Was it a normal saloon car, or a people carrier, or four-by-four?' persisted Jill.

'Just normal, I think,' replied Ware. 'It might have been a hatchback, I'm not certain.'

'Did you get a look at the number plate?'

'No, sorry,' he said. 'I'm not doing very well, am I?'

'It's understandable,' said Jill. 'But it's true, we don't have much to go on. An ordinary car in a dark colour which may or may not be a hatchback doesn't rule much out. What about other witnesses? At that time of night there must have been loads of people about, heading for the Theatre Royal.'

'Unfortunately not,' replied Ware. 'The theatre's still dark at present, until the next big show starts in a few days. There was no one about except Pop sneaking a crafty fag outside the Garage, and he's so shortsighted he needs a white stick to find his flies!'

Jill suppressed a grin and paused for thought. 'We'd better have a word with him anyway,' she said. 'Is there anyone you think might want to harm you? Anyone with a grudge, or reason to be resentful?'

'No, no one,' he replied with what she thought was his most genuine reaction of the morning. 'I can't think of any enemies, really I can't.'

'What about at work?' she asked. 'What do you do when you're not acting?'

'I'm an accountant,' he replied. 'I do pretty low-key company accounts. No involvement with anything dodgy. Most of my customers are sole traders, running restaurants or shops. Nothing there to paint a target on my back. And while there may be a little bit of jealousy from fellow thespians about how often I get cast in the lead, there's nothing serious.'

'And family?'

'I'm single. My ex and I divorced nearly ten years ago, and, while I wouldn't say we're close friends, we are still polite. No issues left over there. No children.'

'No one special in your life?' she asked.

'Just friends. No one like you mean. My closest friends are in the Northfolk. Louise, who's playing Lilli, Myrtle Harris, who's playing Hattie, and Dean Mason, who's been cast as Bill. They're probably my closest friends. We've played together in two productions a year for the past four years at least. You grow close to people like that.'

***

Reporting to Greg later, Jill was, while not exactly dismissive, not particularly engaged with Mr Ware's theories. 'There's no real evidence of anything other than an RTA,' she explained. 'And not much chance of catching up with the driver, to be honest. I think this is one to note and put on the back burner. I'm sure we have higher priorities at present.'

'Too true,' replied Greg. 'Let's get our heads together with Jim and review exactly what we've got on. I think—' He was interrupted by a buzz from his phone and a message popped up on the screen. 'Sorry, Jill, I'll need to postpone,' he said. 'I have to go and see the All—' He stopped himself. '...the Chief Constable, I mean.'

'Good luck, Boss,' said Jill. 'I guess this is it?'

'Maybe,' said Greg. 'Maybe.' He was scrabbling in his desk drawer. 'I'm sure I put my tie in here somewhere...'

Greg paused in the corridor to get his breath back and straighten his tie. Then he went into the outer office. The PA looked up, gave him a warm smile and said, 'Go straight through. He's expecting you.'

The tall man in pristine uniform got up from behind his desk and held a hand out as Greg came in. 'I'm delighted to say that congratulations are in order, soon-to-be Detective Superintendent Geldard,' he said. 'Take a seat. Strictly speaking, I'm jumping the gun slightly,' he added as Greg stuttered his thanks. 'You won't hear formally from the HR team for a day or so, but I wanted to be the one to tell you.'

'Thank you, sir,' said Greg again. 'I'm very pleased, of course. Especially as I thought my lack of diplomacy might have put the panel off.'

'Your plain speaking did rock a couple of them back on their heels,' agreed Thornfield. 'But I liked it. A few people who think more like police and less like politicians would be a good thing. Anyway, you can leave the politics to me, and I'll leave the detecting to you. Is that a deal?'

'It certainly is a deal,' said Greg with some relief.

'Righto. To be plain, Geldard, I don't mind bad news. Things can't always go smoothly. Just make sure I always hear it from you first. Never blind-side me.

'The other thing I need to tell you is that you'll have a new DCI under you. It's someone you know – DCI Ram Trent. One thing to be aware of, however, is that he too applied for the superintendent role.'

'Ah,' said Greg. 'Tricky. Why didn't he get it? If I might ask.'

'Lack of experience in leadership. No fault of his, but he's spent a lot of his career as a lone expert. Anyway, I'm sure you'll cope. He's too good a DCI to allow that sort of issue to get in the way, once he's got over his disappointment. And he'll complement you and the rest of your team. He has strengths in fraud and finance, where we're weak at present. And perhaps you can teach him more about leading a team.'

When Greg emerged from the CC's office, he was met by another broad smile and this time 'Congratulations,' from the PA, who clearly was fully au fait with recent developments. He seized the opportunity of an empty stairwell to ring Chris, then headed down to the incident room and Jim's office.

'Well?' demanded Jim before he'd fairly got through the door. 'Did you get it?' Then he read the expression on Greg's face correctly and added, 'Great. So pleased. You can buy me a pint this evening. No getting out of it now the pubs are open again.'

'I'd be delighted to,' said Greg. 'How about the Kings Arms? But I have another piece of news and I'm not so sure you're going to welcome it. I'm afraid there isn't going to be a vacancy at DCI level, Jim. I'm sorry.'

'Good Lord, don't even think of it,' interrupted Jim. 'I'm not planning on promotion, not at this stage in my career. Who are they going to post in? Do you know?'

'Ram Trent,' replied Greg, keeping the rest of the CC's news to himself.

'That sounds OK,' said Jim. 'He knows us and we know him. He's not you, but he's a good detective. In fact, I thought he might have applied for the superintendent role himself.'

Greg reflected that he might have known Jim would have had his ear to the ground. 'He'll bring some different skills to the team,' he said evasively. 'But I need to go and see Margaret before I do anything else. Can you pass the news on to the rest of the team please, Jim? I don't take up the role for a couple of weeks, but the Chief was happy for people to know.'

'I take it you've told Chris,' said Jim.

'Of course. She'll join us at the Kings Arms this evening.'

***

The impromptu party was in full swing by the time Margaret Tayler, retiring chief superintendent, arrived at the Kings Arms. Greg, mindful of the need for his team to work the following day, had had a quick word with the chef, resulting in an impromptu buffet of sausage rolls, slices of pie and quiche, chips and sausages, bread and cheeses. Pretty impressive, given they were only just returning to normal after all the government restrictions. If the locals were perturbed at their newly reopened local being taken over by a slightly raucous party of celebrating police, it didn't show. A number of those present, including Chris, had taken the precaution of a chat with a local taxi firm, while others were hitting the low alcohol beers rather than risk retribution from the soon-to-be detective superintendent. Most of the core team were there, including the recently redeployed Jenny Warren. Chris was very rapidly relieved of Jamie by a queue of officers wishing to get to know the baby. She relinquished him to Jenny with only slightly mixed feelings, guessing that he'd be returned as soon as he got smelly.

Margaret pushed her way to where Greg was perched on a stool by the bar, a sausage on a stick in one hand, and a pint of Wherry in the other.

'Margaret, so glad you could come,' he greeted her. 'This is down to you after all.'

'You mean, me shoving you into it?' she asked with a grin.

'Partly that. Partly the encouragement, the opportunities and the support when things have been tough,' he said.

She waved a hand dismissively. 'Oh please. Stop,' she replied, 'or we'll be getting the violins out. Mine's a large glass of red, then I'll leave you to party in peace.'

'I can run you home after, if you like,' Greg offered. 'I'm sticking to the half per cent stuff after this one, just in case—' He was interrupted by a vibration in his breast pocket. He glanced at the phone screen with a word of apology, then added, 'Damn. Might have known it. It's the Control Room. I think we've got a callout.' He headed for the door and the relative peace of the car park.

Under the trees that divided the pub area from the neighbouring churchyard, Greg listened intently, one finger in the ear not pressed to the phone. 'OK,' he said at last. 'Leave it with me. I have most of the team here. We'll deploy direct to North Walsham and take it from there. Is the doc on his way?' Receiving an affirmative answer, he put his phone away, glancing round as a movement under the trees caught his eye. He smiled as he realised it was a black cat slinking homeward with a small rodent in its mouth. Then he headed back into the bar.

'Jim!' He backed up his shout with a gesture and once he had his full attention said, 'Collect Steve... Sorry!' He could have kicked himself as he realised habit had caused him to name the colleague killed on duty only a few months before. 'I mean Bill. We've got a shout. Emergency services have attended a casualty in North Walsham and found a body. Believed poisoned. Jill is already on her way there. Ditto the doc and the duty SOCO. Are you OK to drive?'

'Luckily, yes. Barely got started,' replied Jim.

'I'll just tell Chris, Margaret and Ned what we're up to. Then I'll hit the road. See you in North Walsham.'

Chris had already picked up on the change of mood. 'Duty calls?' she asked.

'Yes. Suspicious death. North Walsham. Sorry, Chris.'

'No problem. Wish I was coming with you. Let me know if I can do anything to help.'

'Will do.' Greg kissed her swiftly and looked round. 'Where's the son and heir?'

'Still accepting homage from Jenny, I think,' said Chris.

'She's probably teaching him to "sit" and "stay",' remarked Greg. 'I'll see him on my way out.'

'Let me know how you get on.'

Correctly interpreting this to mean *And let me know when you're coming home*, Greg grinned and said, 'Will do. Take care.'

Along the road by the church, Bill was getting into Jim's car and Margaret into her own.

'Pity your celebrations were cut short,' she said to Greg. 'But that's the job. At least, it's *your* job, since you insisted on remaining operational.'

He leaned over to talk to her quietly. 'To be honest, I'm not that sorry,' he admitted. 'At least this way I know they'll all be sober in the morning!' He waved, climbed into his red BMW and set off across country for the A149 and North Walsham.

4

20 July: North Walsham, a few hours earlier

When Marie Leakey got home from a long day at the massage coal face in the North Walsham spa, she was almost staggering with tiredness. It was great to get back to work properly after the long, boring time spent on furlough. But her muscles weren't used to that level of activity any more, and she ached. Having had her Covid booster the day before probably hadn't helped either. That arm was definitely sore.

She got her key into the front door of her tiny bungalow near the hospital on her second attempt, and only then noticed the parcel sitting on top of the wheelie bin by the fence.

Odd, she thought. *I wasn't expecting a delivery.* Leaving the key dangling in the lock, she went over to the parcel and picked it up, examining it curiously. It looked like a small Amazon box that had been opened, then reused and roughly resealed with sticky tape.

She pushed her front door open over a small heap of rubbish post – leaflets, adverts and the local free newsletter she noticed

– and went through to her galley kitchen. Her first move was to switch the kettle on, assuming that there was sufficient water in it for a cuppa. Then she checked the fridge for supper options and concluded that nothing appealed very much. The options boiled down to eggs – boring but quick. Or she could make the effort to transform the waiting minced beef into bolognaise sauce, in which case she'd probably be too tired to eat it by the time it was done. Picking up her tea, she decided to opt for a takeaway and opened the mystery box while she made her mind up between a Chinese or a curry.

'Problem solved,' she said aloud as she read a typed label on a plastic tub:

Thought you might like a share of this, as you're not used to working!' Laughing emoji, followed by a scrawled letter C.

'Now, is that Catherine or Colin?' she wondered as she took the lid off the tub and sniffed appreciatively at the green curry inside. 'Spinach, mushroom and chicken,' she guessed, and, replacing the lid loosely, put it in the microwave to reheat. She couldn't be bothered with rice but ferreted around in her freezer for a packet of naan bread she thought she'd squirrelled away the last time she'd done a proper shop.

With the naan warmed up under the grill and curry steaming gently in a bowl, she sat down in front of the TV and a Netflix film. The curry was tasty, but the spinach flavour was strongly earthy, so she fetched a rather elderly jar of lemon pickle and added a generous spoonful.

Less than an hour into the film, she felt her attention wander. The curry seemed to be burning rather more than usual. *Bit heavy on the chilli, Catherine*, she thought. *Or Colin*. But the sensation didn't ease, even when she ate a bit more bread. In fact, she began to feel distinctly odd. She was struggling to focus on the TV screen, and the muscles that had ached when she got home were now positively painful. Her mouth seemed to flood with saliva, and she swallowed hard. Once, twice, and began to panic. *The mushrooms,* she thought. *I wonder if there was something wrong with the mushrooms?* She reached for her phone and, with only a minor hesitation: *Am I being ridiculous?* she dialled 999.

'Ambulance,' she said to the operator. 'I need an ambulance. I think I might have eaten dodgy mushrooms.' She managed to get the first part of her address out of an increasingly numb mouth, then she convulsed and dropped the phone. She could vaguely hear the operator's voice in the background. Then nothing.

5

Evening of 20 July: North Walsham

Greg, Jim and Bill, followed by a forensic science van, arrived at the suburb near the hospital at more or less the same time. It was easy to spot their destination, as it was brightly, if intermittently, lit by the blue flashing lights of a first responder's car, an ambulance and a police car. They pulled up behind the trio, effectively blocking the road to through traffic.

'Bill, go and take over the scene management from uniforms and ask them to take over traffic control out here,' instructed Greg. 'Ned,' he added, turning to the tall man emerging from the van. 'Let me check what's happening with the victim, then I'll give you a shout.'

Ned nodded and turned back to his colleagues busy unloading equipment from the van.

At the front door of the small bungalow, Greg was met by the first responder carrying his bag and a folded green blanket.

'Ben!' Greg greeted him. 'Isn't this a bit off your patch?' In most of their – many – previous professional interactions, Ben had been working in East Norfolk.

'A bit,' replied Ben. 'But we're shorthanded again, so I'm covering. I'm afraid I was too late here. She was already unconscious when I got here, and although the ambulance arrived minutes after me, we couldn't get her back.'

He was clearly depressed, and Greg remembered something he'd said some years ago, about *how you couldn't remember all the callouts, but you always remembered the fatalities.*

'Who made the 999 call?' he asked.

'She did, according to the call centre,' responded Ben. 'She managed to give most of her address and say she thought she might have eaten some dodgy mushrooms before she stopped responding to the operator. Luckily there was enough address for me to work out where she was, and the back door was open. There was no one else in the house when I got here, and no sign of anyone either. The paramedics are just clearing up their stuff,' he added.

'Who opened the front door?' asked Greg as he and Jim hopped about pulling on paper coveralls, plastic overshoes and gloves.

'I did,' said Ben, 'to let the ambulance team in.'

'OK. We'll need a statement from you later. You know the routine.' Ben, whose past career had included police officer as well as district nurse, did indeed know the routine. He nodded, then his radio squawked.

'Another callout,' he sighed. 'OK if I go?'

'Before you do, you said there was no sign that anyone else had been in the house?'

'That's right,' said Ben. 'No sign at all. Only one glass and plate on the table and no one else present, unless they're hiding under the bed.'

'OK. Thanks.' Greg gave him a thumbs up and followed Jim into the bungalow.

The two paramedics in green had just packed their equipment away. Their erstwhile patient lay between them on the floor, signs of attempted resuscitation evident in the tube in her throat and the disturbed clothing.

'Leave her just as she is now,' instructed Greg. 'You know I'll need your report asap, but, for now, can you just glance round and tell me if you moved anything in here? – other than the patient of course.'

The taller of the two, a dark man with hair in a ponytail, answered for them both. 'We pushed the sofa and this table' – he indicated a low coffee table – 'to make more room for us to work. Ben had already laid her on her back and begun CPR. We took over, put the tube in and injected adrenaline, but there was no response. We confirmed death at 22.24. It'll all be in the report.'

'Yes, thank you.'

'What about the phone?' asked Jim. 'I think Ben said she was on the phone to the call centre when she collapsed.'

'It's here,' said the shorter paramedic, a ginger-haired, younger man with the beginnings of a sunburn colouring his face and neck. He was pointing to the sofa, where an iPhone could be seen lying on the seat cushion. 'I terminated the call when we arrived, so the operator could move on.'

'So you handled the phone?'

'Yes. But with my gloves on,' he explained. 'I just picked it up, said we'd arrived, then turned it off using the side button.'

'OK.' Jim took out an evidence bag and placed the phone into it. 'Thank you.'

'Can we go now?' asked Dark Ponytail. 'We're needed.'

'I assume we have all your contact details?' Getting nods from both, Greg added, 'Yes, thank you,' and followed them to the front door to beckon Ned over.

'Jim's having a quick look round and he's bagged the victim's phone. Obviously there's been some inevitable disturbance from Ben and the paramedics. Ben says he came in the back way, which was open when he arrived, and let the ambulance crew in through the front. Over to you. Is the doc on her way?' he asked as Jim rejoined them.

'On her way,' he confirmed. 'ETA about fifteen minutes.'

Greg looked at his watch. 'Another late one then. Can you have a chat with the North Walsham team and see who we can let go? We don't need to keep them *and* Bill here, once the body's on its way to the morgue. Has anyone started on the neighbours?'

'Not to my knowledge,' answered Jim. 'I think the locals had their hands full securing the scene until we arrived.'

'Let's see whether we can get any response now. I realise it's getting a bit late, but there are a few nosy parkers about still.'

Jim nodded and went off to set Bill to work knocking up the most immediate neighbours while Greg joined the two constables from the local station on the front line of the crime scene tape. A light rain had begun to fall and, with the departure of the ambulance, the small crowd had started to disperse.

'Anyone here a neighbour?' asked Greg, pointing behind him to the bungalow in question. Most of the few remaining observers shook their heads and the dispersal accelerated. Three lingered: an elderly man dressed in an overcoat over what looked like pyjamas and two middle-aged ladies.

'We live here,' said one of the ladies, indicating the property directly across the road.

'And I live next door to them,' added the man with a jerk of his chin. 'Has something happened to Marie?'

'How well did you know Marie?' asked Greg.

'Just as a neighbour,' replied the man. 'I knew her name and that she worked in the hotel on the edge of town. We'd chat if we met, putting out the bins, that sort of thing.'

'We'd talked to her at the spa,' one of the ladies added. 'She was good with bad backs. Sally here suffers with her back, and she had a massage from Marie two or three times. Before lockdown, obviously. But I wouldn't say we knew her very well.' Her friend concurred with a nod.

Greg turned to one of the constables near at hand. 'This officer will take your details, and we'll need to talk to you, probably tomorrow,' he said, noticing Ned emerging from the bungalow.

'Photos more or less done, and we've sampled and bagged anything that looks likely as a source of poison,' Ned reported. 'Still taking samples and fingerprints from around the bungalow, but the most interesting materials are the remains of her supper. We found traces of what smells like a curry in a bowl and also in a plastic box in the kitchen. The call handlers say she mentioned mushrooms and there's some in the remains of her supper. Can't tell just by looking if there's anything wrong with them, but the appearance of the body is consistent with poisoning. Foam on the lips and pinpoint pupils, for example. Obviously, it's for the doc to determine cause of death,' he added hastily, 'but we'll analyse the materials we sampled for any vegetable toxins.'

'She should be here very soon now, Ned,' Greg assured him.

'We found this too,' said Ned. He held up an evidence bag containing a piece of paper torn in two. 'Found this in the kitchen bin, along with the box smelling of curry and a plastic bag.'

Greg read the note. 'So she may have eaten something cooked by someone else?'

'Seems that way.'

'Another question to ask the neighbours,' Greg was saying when they were interrupted by a car drawing up beside them. Dr Paisley stuck her head out.

'Ready for me?' she asked cheerfully.

As the doctor followed Ned through the front door, Jim came up to Greg.

'No answer from either of the next-door neighbours,' he reported. 'I'd say one lot is out and the other lot not answering. Unless you want us to get assertive, I think we'll have to leave them until morning.'

Greg took another glance at his watch, weighed up the benefits of getting on with the investigation against the fact that they had only a suspicious death at present and the lateness of the hour, and sighed. 'The neighbours across the road are up and about,' he replied. 'Let's see what we can get from them and pick up the rest of the house to house in the morning. Uniform will secure the property tonight and tomorrow, pending sign-off by Ned and the identification of any next of kin. Hopefully her phone will give us some clues there. Has anyone found an address book?' he asked.

'Not so far as I know,' replied Jim. 'Ned mentioned there's a driving licence in her handbag that identifies her as Marie Leakey, aged forty-two, and a pay slip that states she was furloughed from the Walsham Hotel. I'll have a chat with them in the morning too. It's getting a bit late now.'

Greg checked his watch again: twelve forty-five. 'It is a bit,' he agreed. 'OK, I'll leave the hotel and the remaining neighbours to you in the morning. Hopefully the doc will be able to schedule an early post-mortem, and I'll deal with that.' Spotting Ned poking about near the bins, he called over, 'Are we right, that she lived alone?'

'Looks like it,' agreed Ned. 'At least, no sign there's been anyone else in there in the last few days. All the clothes we've found look like hers, and only one toothbrush in the bathroom. Looks very like she lived alone.'

By midnight the doc was done, and the mortuary hearse was on its way to Norwich, bearing the remains of Marie Leakey to her penultimate stop before interment.

'Not much I can tell you tonight,' were the doc's parting words to Greg. 'You know roughly when she died, as she was on the phone to emergency services when she collapsed and the paramedics declared life extinct shortly after they arrived here. The external appearance of the body is suggestive of poison, probably in whatever she ate for her supper, but I'll need to look closer and take samples when I open her up. OK for now?'

'Yes, thanks, Doc,' said Greg. 'I'll see you tomorrow.'

Back on the A149 and heading for home, Greg debated with himself whether to ring Chris to say he was on his way. On balance he decided that the risk of waking Jamie was too great, and he was, after all, less than half an hour away. He poked at the touchscreen in front of him to wake the *Spotify* app and settled to listen to the playlist he and Chris had put together between them. As it reflected both their differing tastes, it was an eclectic mix of folk (Chris), jazz vocals (Greg) and pop ballads (both). 'Can't Help Falling in Love' formed the soundtrack to the last part of Greg's drive home, only changing to 'Always a Woman' when he turned into the rough track that led to their home. At the last minute he remembered an earlier injunction and slowed his approach to their cottage to avoid his habitual spray of gravel. Then tiptoed in. Unnoticed, Bobby slipped in just before the door closed, a petrified rodent in her mouth.

6

21 July

Greg slept heavily and undisturbed by the early morning movement of Chris getting up to Jamie and creeping downstairs to start the morning round of feedings. He was, however, woken violently by two shrieks: the first of horror as a still-alive mouse ran across Chris's bare foot. The second, of rage as her brain caught up with her foot.

'Gregory Geldard,' came the bellow up the stairs, 'what have I said about letting Bobby into the house with live prey? She was outside when I came to bed, so you must have let her in.'

Bobby, sitting on the old kitchen sofa, continued washing her paws, unmoved by the racket created by an outraged human adult and the cries of a frustrated human baby waving his arms in protest at his bowl of mush. Upstairs, Greg clutched his pillow, contemplated a return to sleep then caught a glance at the clock and realised it was time to get up anyway, if he was to get to the mortuary on time.

He bellowed a 'Sorry' down the stairs and headed for the shower. By the time he reached the kitchen, dressed for work and his trusty pot of Vicks in his jacket pocket, Chris had fed

Jamie and was on her knees by the dresser, poking under it with the handle of a mop.

'Dare I ask what you're doing?' he asked mildly.

'Trying to catch that bloody mouse you let Bobby bring in,' she panted, hair all over her face and dust all over her bright yellow chinos.

'I thought we weren't going to swear in front of Jamie,' commented Greg with a lack of caution he instantly regretted.

'You catch the damn thing then,' snapped Chris. 'It's your cat. Ergo, your mouse and your problem.' She handed him the mop, picked up Jamie and retired to a safe distance, muttering.

Greg sighed, looked at his watch, then at the undisturbed Bobby still washing her paws. 'I don't suppose you're going to help,' he remarked. 'I'm going to be late.'

He swopped the mop for a broom, opened the back door wide, then swept dust, furballs, a parrot feather or two and the mouse out into the garden with four determined thrusts of his weapon.

'All sorted,' he said to Chris with a degree of smugness that nearly earned him a clip round the ear, then dropped a kiss on her head and departed in a hurry for the mortuary.

Chris was left juggling Jamie on her knee and ruminating, darkly, on the subjects of men, motherhood and mice.

Arriving almost simultaneously with Dr Paisley, Greg followed her into the mortuary reception then, at her wave of invitation, into her office.

'Sorry, I'm running late,' she said, beating Greg to the draw by a fraction of a second. 'Family crisis. Do you want to come back in an hour or so, or wait here?'

'I'll stay here if it's OK with you,' replied Greg. 'I can get on with some paperwork and phone calls while I'm waiting.'

'Be my guest,' she said, waving at the desk, and whisked away, pulling on a white coat.

Greg made himself comfortable at the desk, conscious of background noises that seemed to indicate another subject was arriving in a hearse while dimly audible voices suggested that distressed relatives were being ushered into the waiting room. He heard muffled reassurances and reflected that in this space, as in many others he visited, the reception staff did a more difficult job than anyone gave them credit for.

He'd chewed through a succession of emails, reviewed a report or two and was just pondering a phone call to Ram Trent when Dr Paisley stuck her head round the door. 'Ready for you now,' she said.

Pulling on a white coat in his turn and applying a smear of Vicks to his upper lip, to obscure any untoward aromas, Greg followed the doctor across an inner hall and into the chilly space occupied by a series of metal tables with drains beneath and bright lights overhead. Only one was currently occupied, by the remains of Marie Leakey, age forty-two, masseuse.

'I can confirm that this looks like death by poisoning,' said Dr Paisley. 'The pinpoint pupils, foam around the mouth and in the trachea and respiratory system are all indicative. The remains of her last meal are in the stomach, and I've found both fragments of a green leafy material and of fungi, probably mushrooms. At the moment I can't say definitively whether the leaves or the fungi were the source of the toxin, nor precisely which toxin was the cause. On the basis that there are indications of muscle weakness, that death occurred comparatively quickly, apparently because of respiratory failure, and that I can't find signs of liver damage, I would say that poisoning by something like hemlock is looking more likely than mushrooms. But I won't be able to confirm that until we have the results of blood and tissue analyses.'

'Ned found a box that seemed to have contained a curry or something like that,' said Greg. 'There were some vegetable remains in the box as well as in a bowl, plus an indication that it seemed to have been given to her by someone else. Samples have been sent for analysis, but should we be looking specifically for hemlock?'

'Tell them to look for coniine,' recommended the doctor. 'I'll drop Ned an email anyway. But that's the toxin in hemlock.'

'Where would someone find hemlock?' asked Greg. 'It's not a garden plant, is it?'

'Not normally,' replied the doctor. 'I'm not an expert, but I know it likes water. I'd be very surprised if it can't be found on the Broads.'

***

At the Walsham Hotel and Spa, Jim was suffering from heat and volubility. He'd already removed his jacket and kept easing his collar in the warmth and humidity that seemed to leak from the nearby sauna. The lady he was talking to, or to be more accurate, the lady he was *listening* to, and had been for – he stole a surreptitious glance at his watch – at least fifteen minutes, was still in full flow. She had an enviable ability to speak without taking breath and a remarkable recall of every client who had passed through their doors in the past three years, which was when Marie Leakey had become a masseuse. Now, seventeen minutes in and they'd only just reached 2019, Jim reckoned he had another quarter of an hour to go if he didn't do something soon. Filling his lungs, he interrupted with a determined, 'So Marie Leakey was well regarded by her clients and had a lot of repeat business.'

Ms Nash took another deep breath and Jim carried on hastily. 'I'd be very grateful for a full list of her clients and also of her appointments, going back to just before Covid, please.'

'There'll be a big gap in the middle, as I was explaining,' said Ms Nash. 'Because of Covid.' Her firmly braced and cantilevered bosom under the spa uniform heaved with disappointment at the interruption.

'I understand that,' responded Jim firmly. 'And thank you very much for your assistance. I think you said that only one of her fellow masseuses is in this morning. I'd like a chat with them now.'

'Oh, well, if you must. But don't keep them from their clients, will you.' Clearly he'd just been crossed off Ms Nash's Christmas card list, Jim reflected as he followed the bustling figure down past the entrance to the swimming pool to the small space that served as a staff room.

'This is Robby Brown,' said Ms Nash somewhat unnecessarily, as the young man who rose from the bench seat along the back of the room was wearing a large name badge.

'Thank you,' said Jim and, as Ms Nash seemed inclined to linger, closed the door firmly in her face.

The space seemed to double as changing room as well as staff room, with lockers by the bench seat and a table bearing tea- and coffee-making kit in the corner opposite to the door.

'Can I make you a coffee?' asked Robby.

'Yes, please,' responded Jim. His reply was heartfelt. Whether it was the volubility or the heat he wasn't sure, but he felt parched.

The kettle had obviously boiled recently as it didn't take long to produce steam and a couple of cups of instant coffee. Robby sat at one of the seats at the table, and gestured Jim to the other. 'I gather this is about Marie,' he said. 'Terrible news. How can I help?'

'Had you known her for long?' asked Jim.

'Not really,' replied Robby. 'I started working here towards the end of 2019, at first as a lifeguard at the pool, later doing sports massages as well. Then Covid and, well, like everyone else I was on furlough and only saw Marie on Zoom for most of a year. We were just getting going again, and business is good because everyone wants their bad backs sorted. Marie and I were rushed off our feet.'

Outside the hospital, Greg rang Jim to bring him up to date with the post-mortem findings. 'It's not looking like an accident,' he concluded. 'We're awaiting the analytical chem, but I think we should proceed on the basis that it's murder. What did you get from the hotel?'

'She's worked in their spa for the past four years, and before that in the hairdresser franchise that operates at the spa,' replied Jim. 'She apparently retrained as a masseuse and was just building a solid clientele when Covid intervened. She's been on furlough for much of the past year and only recently went back to full-time work. Popular with her colleagues and her clients. I've got lists of both. That's about it so far.'

'What about the door to door?'

'Just going over to catch up with the team,' said Jim.

'I'll meet you there,' replied Greg. 'We need to add questions about who might have given her a curry meal. And if you find anyone with a penchant for boating on the Broads, you might ask some pointed questions about hemlock.'

'Hemlock,' exclaimed Jim. 'Wasn't that what killed Socrates?'

'It was,' replied Greg. 'And it's also what probably killed Marie Leakey.'

7

Same day: in Wymondham

Over in Norfolk Police HQ, Wymondham, Jill was catching up with paperwork. The incident involving Leonard Ware had been put to bed with a report. Concentrated scrutiny of inner Norwich CCTV had identified umpteen dark cars fitting the non-description of Mr Ware's hit and run. Interviews with fellow cast members had failed to uncover any witnesses, other than Mr Ware himself, so pending further developments the case was parked. She turned with more enthusiasm to the reports from North Walsham. She was just reading the account of the post-mortem on Marie Leakey when the door to the shared office was pushed open by DCI Ram Trent. Jill was immediately reminded of the Chancellor of the Exchequer Rishi Sunak, as seen on TV the previous night. *Only taller*, she amended the thought in her head as she craned her neck to bring his face into focus.

'Morning, sir,' she said, standing up from her desk. 'Can I help you?'

'Sit, please' said Ram with an easy smile. 'I was looking for DCI Geldard but he's not at his desk.'

'He's on his way to North Walsham, sir,' she replied, half sitting down again, then straightening up. Sitting didn't feel right somehow. 'We had a suspicious death last night and the doc thinks it's poison. DCI Geldard is meeting DI Henning over there to catch up with the results of the house to house.'

'Ah, I see,' responded Trent. 'Pity. I'd hoped to have a word with him. I'll leave a note on his desk. I'll be back in the morning, so perhaps I can catch up with him then.'

Jill hesitated over congratulating the DCI on his new posting, decided it might not be tactful and settled for, 'We've been told you're joining us here. Can I be the first to welcome you, Boss?'

'Thank you, Jill, isn't it?' he replied. 'That's kind of you. I'll see you again tomorrow.'

In North Walsham, Greg and Jim had caught up with Bill.

'Not much to report, I'm afraid,' was the disappointing response. 'The neighbour on the right works nights, which is why we couldn't get an answer before. She says she got back this morning around half seven, which is confirmed by the notes of the constable keeping an eye on Leakey's place. Her name's Caroline French, forty-two, and she's a nurse at the hospital in Cromer. Her shift is currently seven in the evening to seven in the morning, so she didn't see anything of Leakey yesterday. She swops to day shifts after three days off, starting now, and says she would normally expect to see Marie for a coffee when their respective hours permit. She described them as good neighbours but fairly casual friends. They only met

42

when she moved next door just before Covid, so she hasn't known Leakey long.'

'Does she know of anyone who might have a grudge against Leakey?' asked Greg.

'No. Says she didn't really know her that well. But, as far as she knows, she was popular at work and seemed to have a lot of happy clients, judging from comments on her Facebook page.'

'Has anyone checked her social media accounts?' asked Greg.

'Not as far as I know, although Ned's team probably have it on their list of things to do,' remarked Jim.

'Ask Jill if she can follow it up,' responded Greg. 'We'd better check the spa and the hotel social media while we're at it. There may be comments or feedback about Marie Leakey on there.'

'Will do,' said Jim.

'Sorry, Bill,' added Greg. 'We interrupted you. What about the other neighbours?'

'The one on the left is shielding; hasn't seen Marie to talk to any closer than a shouted conversation from garden to garden for the last year or so and says she seems a pleasant woman but they didn't know her very well. I had a chat with the two across the road last night, and one of them has a camera doorbell, so I'm about to go back now and see if they've got any footage of interest. When I asked about it last night, they went pale and said their son was the only one who knew how to "work it" and they'd ask him to call in today.'

Jim grinned at the quotation marks provided by Bill's crooked fingers. 'It amazes me how many people seem to have this sort of gadget yet don't know how to use it,' he remarked.

'Often provided by their children, for reasons of security,' said Bill. 'We have the same issue in my family. I have vivid memories of family Zooms where the whole screen was covered by little images of people holding up hastily written signs designed to tell my mother how to turn her sound on!' He went off across the road, still shaking his head.

Thankfully the twenty-something son had indeed turned up to download the camera footage from the day before.

'It's perfectly simple,' he was saying, 'I've shown you before.'

His mother, standing behind him, cast her eyes to heaven and responded, 'Yes, dear, I'm sure it is. But every time we try it ends in a row, with your father saying do it this way, and me trying to follow your instructions.'

'I can hear you, you know,' came a shout from the kitchen.

The son had clearly been on his way to work when he received the *cri de coeur* from his parents. Wearing a bright white shirt and dark trousers, with a security pass slung round his neck bearing the name Guy Weston, he looked up from tapping on his phone.

'Want to see it now?' he asked Bill, then, receiving an affirmative, handed over the iPhone.

Bill watched in silence. The short snippets of video recorded people and cars passing up and down the street. He discovered he could adjust the focus of the image to improve his view of Marie Leakey's bungalow opposite, and wound the time back to around 5pm to watch again.

'I'd like a copy of the recordings taken between sixteen-thirty and shortly after Marie arrives home. Say, up to twenty hundred hours,' he said, digging around in his pocket. 'Can you put them on this memory stick?'

'Not without my laptop,' said the son. 'But I can email them to your phone, if that's OK.'

'That'll do, thanks,' said Bill. He turned to see Greg and Jim getting back into their respective cars and rushed over to catch them before they departed.

'Got an image of a car pulling up outside Leakey's place at around five-fifteen. The driver seems to get out and leave a package on top of one of her wheelie bins. At least, when the car drives away there's a parcel there that wasn't there before.'

'And the driver?' asked Greg.

'Nothing much. They're mostly hidden from the camera by the car. All that's visible is the back of a dark head, possibly wearing a hoodie or a cap. And I can't see the car number plate either. The angle's wrong.'

8

Handovers

'What's puzzling me... well, one of the things puzzling me is how I decide between what Ram should be doing and what I should be doing,' said Greg to Margaret. 'It would be easier in some ways if I was simply taking over the role that you filled.'

Margaret laughed. 'I had a wonderful mental picture then, of you as a cast sheep, lying upside down, buried in paperwork.'

'Thanks very much,' exclaimed Greg in mock indignation, reflecting that their relationship was so much more relaxed now she was on the verge of retirement and he on the verge of promotion.

'I think you have an amazing opportunity to design the system the way you want it,' she replied. 'You're going to have responsibility for Serious Crime across the whole of Norfolk. You'll have two DCIs, two and a bit DIs, plus detective sergeants and constables. It's the first time the whole area has been pulled together under one controlling mind.'

'Yes. I don't really know the North Norfolk team very well,' mused Greg. 'I've met them, obviously, but only in passing.

I need to make getting to know them a priority. They've functioned separately from those of us based in Wymondham for as long as I've been here.'

'Yes, and I always thought that was a mistake,' said Margaret. 'I've said so on numerous occasions. Basing them in King's Lynn did give them the scope to work closely with their counterparts in Lincolnshire, but they ended up as a separate fiefdom. Sorting that out is going to be one of your challenges. The other problem, as you've already noted, is how do you divide up the work. You could stick with a geographical division of labour, but that will perpetuate the existing divide.'

'Or I could divide the workload by type of crime,' replied Greg. 'To be honest, that's the way my mind's been heading, but that too has the potential to be messy. For example, what do we do with crimes that start off as GBH, and then the victim dies and they turn into murder? Or the murders that arise out of drug dealing. All the intelligence would lie with those tackling the drug angle, but the solving the murder would fall elsewhere.'

'You're thinking in terms of a murder squad?' asked Margaret.

'I had been thinking about it, but whatever way you cut the cake, you end up with crumbs,' answered Greg.

'Another option is a version of what happens in Citizens Advice offices,' remarked Margaret. 'Whoever's free picks up the next case through the door.'

'Even messier, in our circumstances.' Greg dismissed the suggestion out of hand. 'I need to give it more thought, after I've met our colleagues in King's Lynn. I'll go over there this afternoon.'

'What's on at this end?' asked Margaret cautiously.

'Still waiting on analytical chem for the determination of what killed the masseuse in North Walsham,' replied Greg. 'Plus, the ongoing investigation of the county lines, which have woken up as the lockdown restrictions have eased. And, of course, the pending court case of the murderer who killed DC Steve Hall, amongst others.'

'Ah, yes. Have they confirmed the date?'

'End of the month,' said Greg. 'We're ready for them, don't worry.'

Around an hour after leaving Margaret, Greg was approaching the suburb of King's Lynn that housed the impressively large police station.

He was greeted in reception by a clearly forewarned uniformed sergeant who introduced himself as Jonas Hackman and wasted no time in hurrying him through to the inner corridor.

'The lift's there,' he said, pointing. 'It's the third floor and DCI Bell is waiting for you.'

Greg vaguely recognised the impressively fit woman in the third-floor corridor but couldn't remember where from. She was leaning her smoothly coiffured dark head against the wall opposite as he emerged from the lift.

'DCI Helena Bell?' he asked, holding out his hand.

She took it in a firm grip and gave it one brisk shake before letting go, her small eyes taking in every facet of the man opposite her. Greg was aware he was under scrutiny, so took the time, in his turn, to assimilate the details of his new officer. He added to the immediate impression of overall fitness and neatness, the details of the severe bun pinned firmly to the back of her head, white shirt and dark trousers, single slim gold chain round her neck, plain gold stud earrings and sharp features.

She saw a strong man around six feet tall. *Bit thicker around the middle than he'd probably like,* she estimated, with regular features and close-cropped, dark brown hair. Clad in slightly crumpled chinos and a short-sleeved blue shirt as he was, she thought he'd blend in with most crowds, which was perhaps his intention – until she caught a flash of his keen grey eyes. Suddenly she wondered if perhaps she was at risk of underestimating him.

'I think you'd be able to produce a reasonable photofit of me,' he said with a grin that went some way to softening the eyes.

'Snap,' she replied. Then said, 'Sorry, sir. I take it you're Detective Superintendent Geldard.'

'Not quite, but soon will be,' replied Greg. 'I know we must have met before, but I can't remember where, and I don't think I've met any of your team, so this is a get-to-know-you visit.'

'There's only four of us full-time,' she explained, leading the way down the corridor and pushing open the door to a big, shared office well-lit by large windows and filled with cluttered desks. 'We're in here. This is DI Roberts, and DC Challinor is over there.' She waved in the direction of the second man standing behind a desk. 'DC Waterton is on leave today. We're short a sergeant, as you probably know.'

Faced with the team, or most of it, in person, Greg was struck again by the thought that had come to mind when he checked their details in preparation for this visit. Apart from the DCI, they were all male and all under forty. The other thing he noticed was that they had all stood up the second Bell entered the room. It seemed she ran a tight ship, and possibly a formal one. The gender disparity he might look into later. It could be just accident, but it wouldn't be the first time he'd come across senior women who were more comfortable with male than with female subordinates.

'Pleased to meet you all in person,' he said generally. 'I think you probably know the position. When Chief Superintendent Tayler retires in a week or so, responsibilities are being reorganised and I will be taking over as head of Serious Crime for the whole county of Norfolk. In resource terms, that means your team, currently based here in King's Lynn, and my old team, which has been working out of Wymondham. DCI Ram Trent will take over from me in Wymondham, and we will have an intelligence resource in the shape of DI Mathews, working part-time.' He paused to await the predictable question. He'd noted the quick interchange of glances around the room, and it came from DI Roberts.

'Glyn Roberts,' he introduced himself. 'You said, "*currently* based here in King's Lynn," ' he said. 'Do you have plans to relocate us?' It was apparent that wherever he lived now, DI Roberts had originally hailed from the Welsh valleys.

'I have no firm plans as yet,' responded Greg honestly. 'But I do have some aspirations. One is to create a single team working together across Norfolk. That doesn't necessarily mean relocation, but I would like to see more cross-county working and more efficient use of what are scarce and valuable resources – ie us. We all got used to virtual team working during the lockdown,' he added. 'That might be an option we can explore.'

'You mentioned aspirations, plural,' remarked Bell in what Greg felt was a studiedly neutral tone. 'What are your other priorities?'

'I have a few,' admitted Greg cheerfully. 'But I suppose I'd list the top two as improving our clear-up rate and ensuring rapid response to reported crimes. As I'm sure you realise, they're all interlinked. More efficient use of resource will speed up response times, and both will contribute to our clear-up rate.' He was looking round as he spoke, noting reactions. Roberts, a slim man with an ill-considered beard, and Challinor, clean-shaven university graduate, looked interested, maybe even excited, but Bell's face remained inscrutable.

'But I'm here to listen to your ideas,' he added. 'What do you think? What would you like to change if you could? What do you think you do best, maybe better than other teams? What would you like to do more of and less of. Now's your chance.'

When he got back into his car for the journey home, his main thought was how to free Bell's team from her rod of iron without upsetting what was clearly an intelligent and committed officer. But it had rapidly become clear that no one was encouraged to think for themselves while she was around, and challenge wasn't encouraged, except from her. He acknowledged with a wry smile, that challenge to his plans was highly likely to come from DI Helena Bell.

At home, after sneaking his good night peek at his son, he was keen to pick Chris's brains on the subject.

'DCI Bell,' he said over their nightcap before bed, 'what do you know about her?'

'Smart, committed, ruthless, doesn't take prisoners,' replied Chris. 'I wondered when you'd ask.'

'Needed to make my own mind up first,' he remarked. 'Now I've met her in person, and most of her team, I wondered what you thought.'

'I think, if you can get her on side, she'll be an asset,' replied Chris instantly. 'But I don't think you'll find it easy. She doesn't like being put straight on anything.'

'Do I gather you've tried in the past?' asked Greg with a grin, thinking that must indeed have been a clash of the Titans.

'Once or twice. I think the honours are more or less even,' admitted Chris. 'The one thing I don't like about her, if I'm honest, is the way she puts down her juniors. Some of those lads might really blossom if they had the chance to innovate, rather than just do everything her way.'

'Hmmm.' Greg thought that he'd need to consider that issue at greater leisure. Meanwhile, bed beckoned.

9

Acting up

The Northfolk were unwinding at the pub. A second rehearsal had gone as well as could be expected, given all the cast were out of practice and the producer was struggling to adapt to the new reality.

'But, Louise, my darling,' he was still complaining, 'those songs are well within your range. Why the bum notes at the top?'

'Because, Barry,' said Louise through clenched teeth, 'I had over a year without singing. Or at least without singing anywhere other than in my shower, and my top notes have gone. My singing teacher says I'll get them back with time and work, but it's not going to happen overnight. So, either you transpose those songs, rearrange them, or I speak the affected words à la Rex Harrison in *My Fair Lady*.'

'Just so long as it's not Stanley Holloway,' remarked Dean aka 'Bill', a somewhat ageing Lothario of the boards. Luckily his comment went unnoticed as it was drowned in the 'Aubrey, please!' correction from the producer.

'Aubrey, sorry,' said Louise. Myrtle 'Hattie', sitting beside her, rolled her eyes and intervened hurriedly.

'Anyone heard how Leonard's getting on?' she asked.

'Coming to the next rehearsal, he says,' replied Louise. 'He's home now and getting on pretty well, considering.'

'I heard he was mainly suffering from histrionics,' said Dean. 'Highly infectious amongst the luvvies but not generally life-threatening.'

'Just shows what you know about it,' replied Louise briskly. 'He had some bad bruising, and they were checking his heart over when I left the hospital.'

'Panic attack,' said Dean sotto voce, then louder, 'Well you'd know all about his heart, wouldn't you, Louise. I thought it was another you'd got hanging on your bedpost.'

'Another drink anyone?' asked Louise, ignoring the comment, with a slightly heightened colour, then went to the bar, accompanied by Myrtle.

'You should take no notice,' counselled Myrtle. 'He's only jealous.'

'He's peevish as a toddler,' snapped Louise.' I get tired of the sarky comments, Myrtle, and so would you if they were aimed in your direction.'

Myrtle opened her mouth to point out that, at twenty years older and a lot plainer, she'd never had the opportunity to put herself about the way Louise had, but shut it again without making the comment. It wouldn't help, much as she enjoyed plain speaking.

'How is Leo really?' she asked.

'Getting there,' replied Louise. 'He genuinely has got some nasty bruises, and he hurt his back when he threw himself between the parked cars. I've been trying to get him an appointment with my masseuse in North Walsham, but I can't get hold of her. Odd, because I thought she was back at work now.'

A row broke out behind them, apparently consisting of loud excuses from Dean 'Bill' and a lot of fuss from Josie that was not part of her 'Lois' script.

'What now?' demanded Myrtle.

'He's probably tried to grope her,' replied Louise carelessly. 'They don't call him the muffled titter for nothing, you know.'

'I thought that was a reference to his endless unfunny jokes,' muttered Myrtle, trying to pick up four full beer glasses at once.

'It is, partly,' said Louise. 'But it's also a reference to his wandering-hands syndrome.'

'The poor girl doesn't have to put up with that,' exclaimed Myrtle, outraged. 'I'll soon sort him.' She gave up her fruitless struggle with the beer glasses and marched over to the corner where Dean was holding court.

'Aubrey won't thank you,' said Louise to her departing back. 'You know we're chronically short of men.'

Myrtle's intervention did not quieten things down. Her loud expostulations about bad manners and worse behaviour were met with equally loud complaints about no sense of humour and 'for God's sake get a life'. Aubrey woke up to what was happening when Dean threatened to walk out, and intervened in a hurry.

'Now, now, girls and boys,' he said. 'No need to get overexcited with the new freedoms. I'm sure Dean is sorry.' He bent a minatory eye in Dean's direction, and after a mutter that could have been a 'sorry', added, 'And Josie is bighearted and will accept his apology.'

Josie flushed to her roots and said something like 'Oh yes. Sure.'

'OK, boys and girls, I think it's time for a nightcap, and it's my round. Then we'd all better get ourselves home hangover free.' Aubrey beckoned to the barman. 'Whatever everyone's having,' he said, and added more quietly, 'Put it on my tab, darling, and I'll settle up at the end.' *That way I can put it on my expenses.*

Josie followed Myrtle away from the bar and over to Louise. 'You OK?' asked Louise. 'He's a bit of a louse at times. But he can act. Just don't let him back you into a corner.'

'Met his type before,' replied Josie with an assumption of cool. 'When it's someone my own age, it's less of a shock somehow. And I'd have kneed him in the balls. But a man his age! You'd think he'd have grown out of it by now,' she exclaimed.

'Darling, they never grow out of it,' said Myrtle. 'If they're a gentleman at fifty, you can guarantee they were a gentleman at fifteen. On the other hand, if they were a bum-grabbing louse at twenty, they'll still be the same until they can't get it up any more.'

Josie looked at her in shock for a moment, then giggled. 'How do you tell one from the other before they get to the grabbing stage?' she asked.

'Listen to how they talk when they think you can't hear,' recommended Myrtle. 'In fact, I suggest you practise lip-reading. If they tell or laugh at jokes putting women down, they're bad or weak. Steer clear.' She wandered off, leaving Josie looking at Louise.

'Do you agree?' she asked.

'God, don't ask me,' said Louise with feeling. 'I'm a rubbish picker. I've had more dodgy men than you've had hot dinners.'

'Including Dean?'

'Was that a shot in the dark, or have you been listening to rumour?' asked Louise, then sighed. 'Yes, including Dean. Briefly and not happily.'

10

22 July: Wroxham garage

Nick wiped his hands on an already oily rag, making little difference to either rag or fingers.

'I won't get round to it until tomorrow at the earliest,' he said, nodding at the small van parked across the entrance to his garage.

'I thought you'd be quiet,' complained the van owner, 'what with lockdown and all.'

'That's what everyone thought, including me,' said Nick, tossing the rag onto a pile of similar rubbish by the door. 'Unfortunately for everyone *except* me, sitting without being used for the best part of a year has not done internal combustion engines much good. And also, everyone wants their MOTs done in a hurry.'

'But I need the van for work,' complained its owner. 'And it's not the engine. It's just the wheel bearings.'

'That's still the best part of a day, on my own,' replied Nick. 'Especially on a van like that. It's never as straightforward as you might hope, getting the old ones out. Do you want to leave it with me or not?'

'I'll bring it back in the morning,' replied the grumpy owner.

'OK. Get it here for seven, please. I like to make an early start. Or if that's a problem, you can park it over there this evening' – he indicated the space by his office door – 'and post the keys through the letterbox.'

'OK. Will do,' was his reply, leaving it vague as to which option he would take.

***

Over in Wymondham, Greg had arrived to make an early start on paperwork and plans for his handover, in both directions. The first thing he noticed was a piece of paper propped against his laptop, and the second, the half-familiar handwriting.

'Ah,' he said as he read the brief note from Ram Trent, saying he hoped to catch up with him that morning. 'Right. OK.'

After much thought and discussion with Chris, he still wasn't sure how to play the first, awkward, meeting. Apologising for having won in the race to promotion didn't seem very sincere. Pretending he didn't know Ram had been a contender wasn't realistic. He was well aware the rumour mill had discussed the situation ad nauseam and knew Ram would have heard it too.

Chris, unsurprisingly, had advocated the blunt approach. 'Acknowledge you know, then forget about it,' she had said. 'Treat him like anyone else.' Greg felt the advice had much to recommend it, but wasn't sure how well Ram would react.

'Soon know,' he said aloud, and had barely sat down at his desk when the man himself was in front of him.

'Superintendent Geldard,' he said, holding out his hand. 'Congratulations. Or perhaps I should call you Boss.'

He sounded sincere, thought Greg as he stood and shook the hand offered. 'Greg will do fine,' he replied. 'Take a seat. How long are you here for? Today, I mean,' he added.

'Till this afternoon,' answered Ram. 'I have a meeting with HR to sort out the formalities, then I was hoping to spend a little time with the team, catching up on current business. If that's OK with you. After that, I have some leave to take before I start here next week.'

'No problem at all,' replied Greg. 'If you like, I'll get us a couple of coffees and I'll talk you through the cases we have on hand, from my perspective. Jim could join us shortly, if you'd like that.'

'Sounds good,' said Ram. 'Only tea for me, please. No milk, no sugar.'

'Got it.' Greg rose from his desk, then paused. 'There's something I want to say,' he added. 'I don't intend to make a big song and dance about it, but I should acknowledge that I know you applied for the superintendent job. I hope that won't get in the way of us working well together. I have a great respect for you, and I think we're lucky to have you.'

'I won't pretend I wasn't disappointed,' replied Ram. 'Of course I was. But they made a fair point about my lack of leadership experience. It's one reason I accepted this job when it was offered.'

'Good. We understand each other,' answered Greg, and went off to fetch the drinks. As he leaned against the table while he waited for the kettle to boil, he hoped it was true. He had an opportunity to test out his working philosophy immediately on his return with the brimming mugs.

'Do you always get your own, rather than asking a junior officer or a civilian?' asked Ram.

'Depends on circumstances,' replied Greg, thinking *That didn't take long*. 'If we're all together in a group then, yes, it's probably one of the juniors who'll fetch drinks for everyone. On our own like this, then I'll do it myself.

'When I was working in York,' he said, setting the mugs down on the desk, 'I met a man, the director of the Rowntree research lab, who refused to employ lab assistants on the grounds that his scientists could do their own clearing up. He said he paid them to think, and they could think just as well washing test tubes as they could sitting at a desk. Well, I'm paid to think too, and walking up and down the corridor is a help not a hindrance. Plus,' he said, 'it pays off in goodwill from the team.'

'I'll try it,' said Ram, with only the faintest trace of scepticism.

11

---

23 July: in the office

A ping from his inbox heralded the message from Ned he'd been waiting for. Greg read it eagerly, then picked up the phone to Jim.

'Seen the analytical results on Marie Leakey?' he asked without preamble.

'Yes. Hemlock in her gastric tract, the remains of the curry in her bowl and in the scrapings from the plastic box Ned's folk found in the bin. Pretty conclusive that the toxin was in her supper, and probably that the meal was what she picked up outside her house, donated by the mysterious "C".'

'We can't prove the last bit, but yes, I agree with you,' replied Greg. 'Didn't one of her neighbours have a name beginning with C?'

'Yes. Caroline French, nurse at Cromer Hospital. She'd know about hemlock, I imagine.'

'Well, probably,' agreed Greg. 'Although I doubt being a nurse automatically makes you an expert on botany.'

'And that ignores the person who got out of a dark car and delivered something to Leakey's front door,' agreed Jim. 'French was still at work then.'

'True. To be thorough, we'd better have someone asking French about hemlock and checking through her larder, bin, etc. But I think our priority needs to be the dark car. Let's see if we can spot anything on any other CCTV in the area. Not just the traffic cameras, but commercial premises and even other people's doorbells. The ones with video are getting very popular.'

'I'll get uniform to do a sweep round,' said Jim. 'See what we can find. Funny it's another dark car,' he added, 'on top of the one that tried to run down the amateur actor in Norwich, if his account is to be believed.'

'I don't suppose there's any connection?' asked Greg, turning back to his overflowing inbox.

'Not as far as we know,' said Jim. 'And there's a lot of dark cars about.'

Greg sighed as he turned to his emails and scanned his new messages using a methodology not a million miles from Jim's 'throw them down the stairs and see what sticks on the top landing' approach. He was just jotting down some thoughts on a new team structure when he was interrupted by Jill at his door and the simultaneous ringing of his phone.

'New shout, Boss,' she announced.

Greg held up his hand to mute Jill as he tried to listen to the voice on the phone: 'Attempted murder reported in Wroxham.

He looked up at Jill. 'You have the details?' he asked.

'Yes, Boss.'

'In that case, let's get underway and you can brief me en route. Have Forensic Science been informed?' he asked of the phone. Getting an affirmative, he replied, 'We're responding. ETA around' – he checked his watch – 'ten forty.'

Slightly breathless from the rush to the car, Jill fastened her seat belt and checked she had everything she needed.

'OK, what's the story?' asked Greg, pulling out of the car park.

'Seems someone calling at Wroxham Car Services to collect their car was irritated to find the garage closed. All the doors were locked, including the big one to the main service area. When they peered in to see if their vehicle was still on the ramp, they spotted two legs sticking out from under a car. They shouted and banged on the door, got no response, so raised the alarm. The nearest station is Hoveton. Two officers from there attended and, also getting no response, broke the door down. The ambulance arrived soon after they got access and has taken their patient to the N&N. He had a serious head trauma, was unconscious but breathing. The attending officer has identified the victim as the garage owner. He knows him, apparently, from the local darts club. He reckons he'd been hit on the head by a spanner or similar, but has had the good sense not to go looking for the weapon and has secured the scene. That's it so far.'

'OK. Thanks, Jill. I'll just give Jim a ring, then I'd like you to check in with Ned.' A couple of taps on the screen behind the steering wheel, and the phone connected to Jim.

'On your way to Wroxham?' was his greeting.

'Yes. Jim, I'll have to leave the follow-up on Marie Leakey to you.'

'Already on it,' he replied. 'The North Walsham locals are walking the streets near the hospital, checking for other CCTV possibilities. I'll update you when we have anything.'

'Thanks, Jim.' He would have said more, but the screen signalled another incoming call. 'Have to go. Speak later,' he said, and accepted the second call.

'DCI Bell,' an incisive female voice announced. 'I wanted a word following up from your visit yesterday.'

'I'm in the car on hands-free,' interrupted Greg. 'DS Jill Hayes is with me.'

'Ah.' The voice ground to a sudden stop, obviously taken by surprise. 'Right. OK. Perhaps we could speak later.'

'Of course,' said Greg. 'I'm on my way to a suspected attempted murder at present. I'll ring you later.'

'Thank you, sir,' she replied and rang off.

Jill looked sideways at Greg. 'I'll ring Ned now, shall I?' she asked.

'Yes. Thanks, Jill.'

When they arrived outside the garage, crime scene tape was protecting the small forecourt and parking area, while two police cars and the Forensic Services van were lined up down the road. A police officer stepped forwards to wave them on, but stepped back when he recognised the warrant card Jill was holding up to the side window.

'Morning, ma'am, sir,' he said, bending down to peer into the car. 'Best you park behind the van. There's not a lot of room here.' Greg nodded and, looking at the feed from his rear camera, reversed back down the narrow road and pulled in behind the row of official vehicles. He and Jill pulled on overalls, shoe covers and gloves before ducking under the tape and approaching the main up-and-over garage door, now open to reveal a couple of similarly clad anonymous figures working around the half-raised ramp.

One of them turned and came towards them, stopping them at the entrance. Pulling his hood back, Ned said, 'Probably best I brief you out here first, then I can show you the main exhibits.' He turned to point above the door. 'The first thing you need to note is the CCTV camera. It's broken. Judging from the fact that the last thing it recorded was at five o'clock this morning, just before it went black, I'd say it was put out of action on purpose.'

'Which makes this a premeditated attack,' commented Greg.

'Exactly. There's still a functioning camera in the office, and that recorded the arrival of the owner, Nick Atkinson, just before six thirty this morning. He was found supine, half under this car.' Ned pointed at a red Mini. 'The officer now out front was the first on the scene. He checked for signs of life, found a pulse and put him in the recovery position. Shortly after that the paramedics arrived, did all their checks, applied a heart monitor and so on, and scooped him up to take to the N&N. So, as you can imagine, there's been quite a lot of disturbance around where the victim was found.

'However, there's enough in the way of blood spatter and other marks to suggest that he was attacked just inside the garage door. Not the big one, the pedestrian one to the side there.' He pointed. 'And we found this.' He changed the orientation of his hand and indicated a large tool of some kind already secured in an evidence bag and placed on a bench near the wall. Greg looked at Ned with one eyebrow raised interrogatively and, receiving a nod, walked over to the bench.

'A spanner?' he asked.

'A wrench,' said Ned, 'and a big one. The doc will say whether the shape fits the wound, but the blood on it would suggest it was the weapon.'

'So not brought here? Just picked up?' asked Greg.

'Probably,' agreed Ned. 'There is a range of wrenches over there.' He indicated a wall with various tools hanging on it. 'The one missing is the right size for the one we found with blood and tissue on it.'

'Fingerprints?' asked Greg without much hope. *Even the least criminal mind knows about fingerprints!*

'Not so far, not on the wrench, anyway. Just smudges suggesting gloves. Obviously, we'll keep looking. But gloves mean there's not much hope of DNA either. At least, not from the perp. Plenty there from the victim,' he added.

Greg glanced round again. 'Which way was the victim – Atkinson, did you say? Which way was he facing when he was attacked?'

'Indications are he was facing the door, and his attacker was behind him. As far as I can see, the attacker threw the wrench down and left through the door.'

'Leaving his victim for dead?' asked Greg.

'Looks like it. But the smears on the floor suggest Atkinson came to at least partially and dragged himself towards the office, before collapsing near that car.' Ned pointed.

Greg looked at the marks on the floor, flagged by the forensic team's markers, and back at the door. 'Any signs of a break-in?'

'None,' replied Ned. 'I know where you're going…'

'Yes. If he let his attacker in then turned his back on him to go out through the side door, he probably knew him. At least as a customer, if no better than that. Jill, once Ned gives you the OK, go through the office and see what you can find, particularly about anyone due to leave or collect a vehicle from here today. In addition to all the usual family and friends contacts of course. Incidentally, has anyone contacted next of kin?' he asked.

'No idea,' responded Ned. 'I suppose the hospital may have done by now.'

'True. I'll get over to the hospital now and get Bill to join you here.'

'Any sign of replacements for Steve and Jenny?' asked Jill. 'We're under a lot of pressure already, Boss, and temps seconded in from uniform are a bit variable.'

Greg knew she was understating the case. The last secondee had spilled his coffee into his laptop and reversed a squad car into a bollard which he swore 'hadn't been there when he arrived!'

'I'm interviewing with HR the day after tomorrow,' he promised. 'In the meantime...' An idea struck him. 'I'll see if we can borrow some resource from King's Lynn.'

Out in the street again, he looked up and down to see if he could spot any other CCTV. Nothing obvious met his eye, and he turned to make the call. 'DCI Bell?' he asked. 'We can have that chat now, if it's convenient.'

'Thank you,' she replied. 'I just wanted to say...' She hesitated slightly then went on in a firm tone. 'I just wanted to express my concern about you encouraging my team to be critical. I felt that it undermined me, especially as you didn't discuss it with me first.'

Greg perched himself on the wing of his car while he considered how to respond. 'I'm sorry you felt like that,' he said at last. 'It wasn't intended that way. Inviting suggestions for things we can do better was about seeking ideas not criticising the status quo. I'm sure none of us would ever claim that we were perfect. We all have room for improvement, and new ideas are always worth considering even if we don't take them all up. But you have a point,' he added. 'I should have told you beforehand what I intended to do. Just be aware, I'm always interested in the suggestions of all of my team. Sometimes the best ideas come from the unlikeliest places!

'Now we've got that straight,' he went on, 'it's fortuitous we're having this conversation, because I wanted to ask you for a favour. You probably know that we're a couple of officers down in Wymondham, and we have a new case reported this morning. We're a bit stretched, and I would like to borrow one or two of your chaps. It would be a good way of starting to get to know each other, so we'd kill two birds with one stone. I know it's over a week before I take over formally, but I wanted to check with you first before I sought clearance up the line.' *That was a flash of inspiration,* he thought. *I may be getting more diplomatic after all!*

There was a short silence, then Helena Bell replied, 'I can let you have one of my DCs. I'll send Challinor to you. Where do you want him?'

'Wroxham,' replied Greg. 'If you give me his number, I'll get my sergeant to give him a ring.'

12

Personal note

Two survivors, one dead. So far at least. The local newspaper reporting the attack on the 'much loved' garage owner described him as 'in an induced coma'. I suppose you could call it that.. A bloody big wrench applied behind the ear is a pretty good inducement.

Thought it would do for him. He must have a head as hard as rock. Or no brains to addle. Three down. The halfway point. Wonder how long it will take before she notices all her lovers and supporters are dropping like flies?

13

Acting out

With The Garage temporarily unavailable, 'Refurbishment gone wrong, darlings,' Aubrey had said to his core cast. 'Wouldn't you have thought they could have got on with the painting and decorating during lockdown instead of waiting until now? Most irritating. As it is, we'll have to do the trek over to Sharrington and use their village hall.'

At least it's got a stage, Louise had contributed to their *WhatsApp* group.

Bit small, but yes, it's not so bad, Aubrey had conceded.

Now here they were, trying to adapt to the more limited space. After Leo, warmly welcomed back to rehearsals after his hospital stay, nearly fell off twice, Aubrey gave up on choreography and decided to revert to dialogue.

'OK, girls and boys, everyone offstage who's not in Act One, Scene Three. Let's take it from the end of "Wunderbar". Boys, run through the dialogue about the IOU, and then we'll go straight in to "So in Love". After that,' he said, looking round at who was available, 'we'll try a run through "Tom, Dick or Harry." '

Under cover of the onstage drama while Louise, as Lilli, accepted an imaginary bouquet of flowers from Leo, Dean was hissing his complaints and excuses.

'So, I get to the garage, only half an hour late, and what do I find?' he asked. 'The whole road's blocked with ambulances, police cars and vans; there're uniforms everywhere and when I try to park, some jumped-up bitch in blue threatens me with a parking ticket and/or arrest if I don't make myself scarce. Well, I wasn't going to have that, not from some c—' He amended himself, noticing Josie seemed to be taking an inordinate interest in his conversation. '...some character in a skirt with more boobs than brains. So I took no notice and drove on. Next thing I know there's a panda car across my bow and I have to put the brakes on in a hurry. "Get out of the car, sir," I'm told. The "sir" I take to be ironic. And—'

'Cut the long story short,' recommended Tom, 'we're going to be onstage in a tick.'

'Well anyway, turns out someone's clobbered my mechanic with a wrench and I can't get my van fixed. Which is why I'm late. Had to drive like a slug to avoid the wheel falling off.'

'Why didn't you come in your car?' asked Dick.

'Because—'

Dean was interrupted by an irritated Aubrey. 'If you've got so much to say, you lot, you can come and say it onstage. Let's go through "Tom, Dick and Harry". Thanks, Louise. Those top notes are improving. You must have been working hard.'

Louise smiled an acknowledgement as she and Leo took seats at the back near Josie.

'Sounded great,' said Josie to Louise. 'By the way, I applied Myrtle's test to Dean, and he's still a louse, judging by his conversation. It's definitely a knee in the balls the next time his hands wander in my direction. Good to see you back, Leo,' she added. Leo was fidgeting in his seat.

'Still got backache?' asked Louise. 'Did you manage to get hold of Marie yet?'

'No. Haven't you heard?' whispered back Leo. 'I did get through to the hotel, and they told me she died very suddenly. Suspected food poisoning they said.'

14

24 July: near the Bure

Greg and Chris were having a quiet morning by the river. Jamie was rolling around on a blanket on the rough lawn, watched sharply by mother, father and a still-suspicious cat.

'Bobby's still not sure, is she?' remarked Chris.

'Keeping her tail out of reach, I should think,' responded Greg. 'He can't half move around now! I think I'd better get those fencing people in sooner rather than later.'

'It's such a pity to fence off this view,' exclaimed Chris, looking to where their garden ran down to the river. 'Still, I suppose we could take it out again, once he's sensible enough to be trusted, and can swim.'

'About thirty years then,' answered Greg. 'The sensible bit, I mean. I'll ring them in a minute.' He was pre-empted by his phone ringing with the tone he'd allotted to Jim: the bleat of a sheep followed by a scream.

'Why a homicidal sheep makes you think of Jim, I'll never know,' said Chris. 'Still, I suppose it's better than the someone-throwing-up ringtone that you use for Ben.' She picked up Jamie and headed for the cottage.

Greg's attention was on his phone. 'Hi, Jim. What've you got? Any progress?'

'A little,' was the response. 'We found three more sources of CCTV. One's at a large vets practice down the road a little. Possibly too far off, but it is on one of the possible routes back to the main road from Leakey's property. The other two are camera doorbells. Limited field of view but on the same road. We've collected all the footage for the relevant period, and I'll get the civilian team to go through it on Monday, since we can't spare any officers.'

'What about Marie Leakey's friends and family? Anything there?' asked Greg.

'Not much. She doesn't seem to have been in a significant relationship since before lockdown. We've got a name for an ex-boyfriend, but he lives near Cambridge, so he's well off the scene. I'll follow it up, but I doubt it's promising. The neighbours agree that they haven't seen anyone calling on Marie for a long time. As for family, her parents are dead, and her sister moved to New Zealand three years ago. I've spoken to her on the phone, but given the rigidity of New Zealand's Covid rules, there's no likelihood she's been over here.'

'Clients?' asked Greg, clutching at straws.

'I've got a list from the hotel. There are a couple of names beginning with C: a Colin and a Christine. But I think the C on the note was just a red herring. Still, we'll follow them all up.'

'Thanks, Jim. I'm having a catch-up with Jill shortly, about our battered mechanic.'

'Has he come round yet?' asked Jim.

'No. I'm hoping for an update from the hospital too. But it's not looking too good.' As he put the phone down again on the grass by his deckchair, Chris reappeared carrying a newly cleaned up small boy sucking vigorously on a bottle of juice.

'I've been thinking,' she said, putting Jamie back on the rug and sitting down next to Greg. 'I know you're desperately shorthanded. You must be if you're asking favours of Helena Bell! So, how about if I start back to work sooner rather than later? I mean working from home,' she added, 'obviously. But if we could get someone to come in and keep an eye on Jamie for two or three hours a day, I could use that time to pick up the intelligence portfolio.'

'You'll need the time to sleep,' forecast Greg. 'You'll be knackered, coping with Jamie and work, even if we do get someone to come in.'

'Let's give it a try,' she urged. 'I'm bored stiff doing nothing, and—'

'You're not doing nothing,' exclaimed Greg. 'You have Jamie.'

'That's not what I meant, and you know it,' she replied. 'You promised, Greg. You know you did. I *can* be mother and DI. In fact, I have to be, or I'm not me.'

'OK, we can give it a go,' Greg capitulated. 'Do you have anyone in mind?'

'In the first instance, my mother,' she answered. 'She offered. And I think she knows of someone that might be interested in a longer-term role too. We're agreed then. I'll talk to my mother about coming in on Monday, and I'll start catching up with what's going on.'

'Just pace yourself,' urged Greg, knowing as he did so that it was a fruitless instruction. As long as he'd known her, Chris had only one pace. Flat out.

15

Sunday 25 July

Having taken Saturday off, Greg was back at work with a vengeance on Sunday. He smiled to himself as he recalled Chris's reaction to that description of their Saturday. He'd certainly spent most of the day enjoying the sun in their riverside garden and the antics of passing boats steered by unpractised tourists. But, as Chris had pointed out, she didn't think the term 'off' was an accurate summary of a whole day spent either on the phone to colleagues or catching up with paperwork. No matter. At least he'd clarified his ideas on how to run his new department, and he'd had a brainwave with regard to their current staffing issues. But first, the ITU at the Norfolk and Norwich Hospital and a chat with doctors.

It was no surprise to find the hospital car park was as busy as ever. Rummaging in his glove compartment, he extracted a regulation clinical mask and walked briskly over to the In-patients East and Centre Block entrance. From past visits he knew the critical care centre, which housed both the intensive therapy and high dependency units, was on the third floor and headed for the lift. There was a sign limiting passenger numbers, which he assumed was Covid-related, but luckily, he didn't have to wait for the next.

At critical care reception he identified himself, asked for Nick Atkinson and was surprised to find he had been transferred to the high dependency unit.

'I thought he was still in the ITU,' he said.

'So he was until this morning. Then the consultant said he'd improved to the point he could be cared for in the HDU,' replied the receptionist. 'To be honest,' she added, 'I think there was an element of *there are patients worse off than him.* We had a stabbing come in late last night, and she's critical. She was in theatre overnight and the vascular team had a tricky time with her.'

Greg guessed that 'tricky time' was hospital-speak for *she nearly died on the table.* A bit like 'comfortable' was used for anyone not actually screaming in agony. 'Have the police been involved?' he asked, wondering why he didn't know anything about this case.

'I believe there was an officer with her when she was brought in, but it was before I came on duty,' she said.

'I'll do some checking after I've seen Mr Atkinson,' replied Greg. 'I'd like to speak to his doctor too, if possible.'

'You're in luck,' answered the chatty receptionist. 'Ward round is just starting.'

Nick Atkinson was in a bay containing two beds. A nurse was clearly dividing her time between both patients but looked up as Greg approached.

'Can I help you?' she asked quietly.

'DCI Geldard,' replied Greg, holding out his warrant card. 'I need a chat with Mr Atkinson's doctor when he's available. I don't suppose Mr Atkinson is up to talking to me?'

'Not yet,' replied the nurse. 'He's heavily sedated still, but he has shown some signs of consciousness, which is why he was transferred across from the ITU. He's breathing for himself now.'

'I gather you want to speak to me,' interrupted a voice behind them. Greg turned to see a short man of around forty to fifty, with not a trace of grey in his shining black hair and a sallow complexion. 'I'm Mr Kwok,' he said, 'neurosurgeon. I've been treating Mr Atkinson.'

'Thank you, Doctor,' said Greg. 'I have a few questions, but I'll try not to take up too much of your time. The main one is, will Mr Atkinson be able to answer questions anytime soon?'

'Unlikely but not impossible,' replied Mr Kwok. 'I performed a craniotomy around thirty-six hours ago, removed a blood clot and tied off a bleeding vein. With that pressure removed, he improved markedly, regaining some consciousness and breathing for himself, as you see. But he was very confused and rather distressed. We sedated him and it will be an hour or two before we reduce that again. Even then, I wouldn't expect him to be able to help you with your enquiries. He's unlikely to remember much of the time immediately before the trauma, and he may indeed have permanent disabilities. More than half of patients with a traumatic brain injury do, you know.'

Greg did know. That depressing statistic had been at the forefront of his mind when Chris had suffered a head injury the year before. He still thanked God every morning he woke up to find her snoring alongside him.

'Thank you for telling me,' he replied. 'Our understanding is that he was struck a severe blow on the side of his head with a wrench, wielded from behind him by a right-handed assailant. Does anything you have observed contradict this assessment?'

'I'm not a forensic expert, you understand,' answered Mr Kwok with care. 'But by the nature of my work I do see quite a lot of deliberate head traumas. Mr Atkinson's injury is consistent with the scenario you have outlined. The only thing I'd add is that it was a very hard blow, and death would not have been a surprising outcome. Mr Atkinson has only done as well as he has because he has an exceptionally hard head! Now, if you will excuse me, I should get on.' He bowed very slightly, nodded to the nurse and moved away down the ward.

Greg turned to the nurse. 'Thank you too,' he said. 'If anything should change, I take it you know how to get hold of us?'

'We do,' she confirmed, and turned back to moisten the lips of her other charge.

Back in the reception area between the ITU and HDU, Greg moved as far from the ward entrances as he could and rang headquarters. The duty officer in the incident room turned out to be Bill, on overtime yet again.

'What do we know about a stabbing victim taken to the N&N last night?' demanded Greg.

'Not reported here, Boss,' replied Bill. 'I checked the overnight log when I came on duty this morning. Let me check the database. Ahh,' he said.

'Ahh what?' asked Greg, guessing that he knew the answer.

'The database has been updated since this morning, and a suspected attempted murder has been logged by King's Lynn. DCI Bell's team dealing.'

'OK, thanks, Bill. I'll check with her.'

His fingers hesitated over his phone, then he returned it decisively to his pocket and headed for the reception desk again.

'The stabbing, brought in last night,' he said. 'Can you give me a name? And I'd like to go through and see her doctor. I don't imagine she'll be up to questions.'

The receptionist checked the screen in front of her. 'Sharon Jones. Her husband is with her at the moment.'

'Perfect. I'll have a chat with him too. I just need to make a call first.'

He was short and to the point in his exchanges with DCI Bell. Just the right side of civil. 'I'm at the N&N, about to go and have a chat with staff and the husband of last night's stabbing victim,' he announced. 'Bring me up to speed on the case, please.'

DCI Bell responded in kind. 'Stabbed outside her hair salon after a late-night opening. Found by a passerby, who called an ambulance. Should have gone to the Queen Elizabeth Hospital in King's Lynn, but they're still overwhelmed by Covid cases and she was sent to the N&N. DC Waterton is with her. Looks like a mugging gone wrong.'

Greg took a breath to complain about the delayed entry on the incident database, then let it go again without voicing his complaint. *Better to tackle that when I'm properly in charge.*

'As I'm here, I'll have that chat with the husband. We can catch up later,' he said, and rang off. He waved to the receptionist, beginning to feel like an old friend by now, and she pressed the button that released the lock on the door to the ITU.

He was, as ever, startled by the degree of noise and bustle within the specialist ward. Nurses and doctors rushed hither and yon, performing incomprehensible tasks apparently at the whim of equally mystifying signals from the buzzing and clacking machinery that surrounded every patient. He wondered how long it took someone to learn how to interpret all the alerts, let alone what to do in response.

'Mrs Sharon Jones?' he asked a passing nurse, who paused long enough to point to a bed halfway along. As Greg approached, he saw an unshaven man in his sixties sitting by the bed, clinging to the one hand that seemed to be free of lines and cables. A nurse was standing opposite, apparently engaged in trying to persuade him to take a break and go for some refreshment.

'If there's any change, we'll be sure to get hold of you,' she assured him. 'But it's not likely now. She's still very ill, of course, but the surgery went well, and we'll take good care of her, I promise.'

Greg stepped forwards, noting the absence of any DC Waterton. 'I'm DCI Geldard. Am I right in thinking you're Mr Jones?'

The man looked up. 'About time too,' he said. 'Does this mean you're taking it seriously?'

'You mean the attack on your wife?' asked Greg. 'Yes, of course. Look, if I heard the nurse correctly, you're OK to leave your wife for a short while. How about I get you a coffee and something to eat, and I can ask you some questions at the same time?'

The man looked uncertain for a moment, then agreed. 'OK,' he said. 'Just for a few minutes. Then I need to get back.' The nurse nodded her approval to Greg as the two men made their way towards the exit.

Greg rejected out of hand the vending machine option and led the way down to the ground floor and the charity cafe. As he sat Mr Jones down at a quiet table in the corner, with a coffee and an egg sandwich, he was startled by the sudden appearance of a young man in jeans and neatly pressed shirt at his elbow.

'What are you doing here, Mr Jones?' he demanded abruptly. 'I thought I said to wait for me upstairs.'

Greg held up a hand to stop the flow. 'He's having a much-needed coffee and answering a few questions for me,' he said.

'And who the hell are you?' demanded the young man.

'I'm Geldard, your new boss,' replied Greg, stretching a point. 'I assume you're the missing Detective Constable Waterton. Sit there.' He pointed to the opposite side of the table. 'You can take notes.' *And shut up*, he might well have said, as the words hung clearly in the air between them. Waterton dithered from foot to foot for a moment, then sat, pulling out his phone as he did so.

'You can put that away,' said Greg. 'All you need is your notebook and pen. I assume you have both.' Waterton flushed an ugly red but complied.

'Mr Jones,' said Greg. 'Sorry for the interruption. Can we just have your full name, for the record.'

'Sam Jones,' said the man. 'Samuel if we're being formal, but everyone calls me Sam.'

'Thank you,' said Greg. 'You can call me Greg. Is the coffee OK?'

'Yes, thanks,' said Sam, reminded that it was in front of him and taking a gulp.

'Now, I gather that your wife was stabbed outside her hair salon last night and found by a passerby. When did you learn what had happened?'

'When the ambulance got to her,' replied Sam. 'I was on her phone as her ICE.'

'Good to know that works,' said Greg. 'What time was that?'

'After half ten,' answered Sam. 'She'd decided to do a late-night opening as a favour to clients who're rushing to get their hair done, after all the lockdown stuff. And to be honest, she needed the extra takings for the same reason. She intended to work until ten, but she rang me around then to say that her last client had been held up, and she'd be late. The next thing I heard was the call from the paramedic. First they said they were taking her to the Queen Elizabeth. Then after I was already on my way there, they said they'd been diverted here. I got here shortly after them. Sometime after midnight.'

'And you've been here ever since?' asked Greg. 'You must be shattered. How are you getting home?'

'My car's outside,' replied Sam. 'But I won't be driving, don't worry. Our daughter's on her way here with her husband, and one of them will drive me home. But I don't want to go until I'm sure Sharon's going to make it. It's a long way to come back, and I couldn't get here very quickly if anything ... if anything, happened.'

'I'm glad to hear you've family coming,' said Greg. 'Where does your daughter live?'

'Cambridge. Well, just outside really, in Longstanton. I didn't let her know until half an hour ago. I didn't want to disturb her last night. Not till I knew what was happening.'

'How did you spend your evening, while your wife was working?' asked Greg.

For a moment the man looked guilty, then, 'Down the pub,' he confessed. 'I was playing darts with friends. Haven't played for months, and crap we were. But we were having a good time until I got that call.'

'Can we have the name of the pub?' asked Greg. 'And some contact details for your friends. It's just routine,' he reassured Sam. 'We always ask these questions when there's been an incident involving violence.'

'Always check the husband?' asked Sam with a wry grin. 'I get it. Lucky I was playing darts then, no matter how often I missed the target. At least you don't have to waste time suspecting me.'

Sam drank his coffee and ate his sandwich with the speed of a man who wanted to get back to his critically ill wife. 'Will you let me know what's happening?' he asked Greg.

'We will,' promised Greg. 'And I'll see you're allocated a family liaison officer. We'll speak again soon, and someone will be round to take a formal statement from you.

'You mentioned her last client was late,' he added. 'Where would we find a list of her appointments for that evening?'

'At the salon,' replied Sam Jones as he headed for the door.

Waterton stood up to follow, but Greg shook his head. 'You stay here a moment,' he said. Once Sam was well on his way, he added, 'Not the ideal way for us to meet. I'll assume you thought I was press or something, but if I ever hear you being rude to members of the public like that again, you'll wish I hadn't. Where were you?'

The flush reappeared on the young man's face. 'I'd gone to the gents,' he muttered.

'Do you have a medical problem?' asked Greg.

'No,' he replied, startled.

'The gents available for use by visitors opens off the reception area. I was there for some minutes before I went into the ITU. If you were in the gents all that time, you must have a problem.'

Waterton opened his mouth, thought the better of what he was about to say, and shut it again. Greg let the silence get uncomfortable, before he broke it.

'Good decision. Don't ever lie to me, DC Waterton. Now, get yourself over to that pub Mr Jones mentioned and check out his alibi. Can you do that?'

'Yes, sir,' muttered Waterton.

'Good. Report to me later, by phone, and update the online record before the end of the day. I'll brief DCI Bell.'

16

Monday 26 July: acting tough

Arriving early for the first day in his new job, Greg near as dammit headed for his old office near the incident room. He only realised his mistake when he saw the rear view of Ram Trent disappearing through what was now *his* office door.

'Whoops,' he said, and, spinning on his heel, headed for the stairs to the floor above and the slightly more spacious accommodation afforded a detective superintendent. He was relieved to find that he was there before that new acquisition: a secretary, and had all of ten minutes to enjoy settling in before she arrived.

'Sorry I'm late, sir,' she said, flustered at finding him already sitting behind the, bigger, desk and enjoying the improved view of the car park.

'You're not, Sue,' he said. 'I'm early. You'll find I often am, so don't be worried by finding me here first.' He looked at the smart middle-aged lady in white shirt topping black trousers and reflected that, if she did but know it, he was probably as nervous about having a secretary as she was about her new boss. *What am I supposed to do with her?*

'Coffee, sir?' she asked, slightly wary of Greg in his new incarnation even though she'd known him for months as a DCI. 'I know you like it black, no sugar.'

'That would be great,' replied Greg as a further thought occurred to him. *I don't have to make my own arrangements any more!* 'Then can you arrange a meeting for me, please? I'd like to see both DCIs and both DIs asap. Either in person or by Zoom, if that's more efficient. Shall we say...' He checked his watch. 'At eight thirty? You can tell them I don't expect it to be a long meeting. And I'd like you to sit in, not to record the discussion but to make a note of any action points. Is that OK?'

'Yes,' she said with a smile. 'It would be a pleasure. And do you want coffee for those attending in person?'

'That would be...' He nearly said *great*, again, but amended it to, '...very kind. Thank you.'

He spent the next thirty minutes marshalling his notes and his thoughts, sipping his excellent mug of black coffee as he did so, then looked up as Ram, Jim and, somewhat to his surprise, Glyn Roberts filed in and took seats round his small conference table.

'I was over here this morning,' said Glyn in his slight Welsh intonation, 'but DCI Bell will be joining us by Zoom.'

'So I understand,' replied Greg. At that moment Sue reappeared, pointed a remote control at the screen taking up the far end of the conference table, and DCI Bell appeared. Sue took a seat at the corner, slightly behind the screen, and took out a notepad. Greg took the seat they'd left for him, by tacit agreement, at the head of the table, and looked round.

'Welcome, everyone, and thank you for showing up so promptly with little notice. I don't intend to keep you for long, as I'm only too aware we have a lot to do.

'First of all, I want to welcome DCI Ram Trent, who has also started his new role here today. Welcome, Ram.' There were murmurs around the table and from the virtual DCI on screen.

'Second, I want to explain how I plan to manage this new, integrated, Serious Crime team. The key principle, I want us to apply is shared intelligence. If we operate in silos, the only people who benefit are the criminals. That makes no sense at all. But nor do I want to create a whole load of new bureaucracy. The policies and processes we already have should be sufficient, provided we do actually apply them. With one addition, but I'll come on to that in a moment.

'The first point I want to make is, therefore, that intelligence on the police national database needs to be updated promptly. And the local Norfolk Police database, ditto. I want to be able to get up-to-date intelligence on all our activity on demand. And I want DI Mathews to be able to collate and integrate different items of data in real time, to inform our investigations.'

Ram cleared his throat to indicate he had a question, and Greg nodded to him to go ahead.

'Is DI Mathews coming back to work soon?' he asked. 'It's already clear to me we miss her intelligence function.'

'Next week,' replied Greg. 'At least that's the formal date for her return, but don't be surprised if you start to see her around before then.' There were grins from most of those who knew Chris, which, as Greg noted, amounted to four fifths of those at the meeting. DCI Bell was looking down at something off screen. 'My second point relates to the one additional process I want to introduce. I want to trial meeting like this, maybe weekly.' He held a hand up to stem what appeared likely to be more than a few objections. 'Let me explain first how it will work and what I want it to achieve, and then I'll take comments.

'This will be run as though it's a bird-table meeting, and, by that, I mean the very short impactful meetings the military use to share intelligence when managing an emergency. We won't go so far as to hold the meetings standing up, as they do, but the other terms of engagement will apply. Everyone will provide a very short situation report, or sitrep, on the cases they have in hand. Short questions or comments, directly relating to the reports, are allowed. Anything more detailed is taken up outside the meeting. Any decisions arising out of the meeting will be recorded by Sue here and shared by email immediately after the meeting.

'The purpose of the meeting is to make sure we all know what is going on across the whole county, and to identify synergies or links. I stress the emphasis on short. These meetings *have* to be short and snappy or they're a waste of time and resource. OK. Any comments or questions?'

There was a silence, then Ram said, 'Sounds like it could work.'

And DCI Bell said from the screen, 'We can suck it and see, sir.'

'Fine,' said Greg. 'That's OK by me. As this has come out of the blue for all of you, and Ram has only just started, I'll kick off with the first sitrep today and you others can chip in as appropriate. In the future I will expect sitreps from Ram, Helena, Jim, Glyn and Chris in that order, and I will go last. OK.' He looked round the room and at the screen, took silence to mean consent, and started.

'The Norwich-based team currently has five open investigations. One, an alleged attempted murder of Mr Leonard Ware by hit and run outside the Norwich Theatre Royal, is going cold for lack of any evidence that it was indeed more than a hit and run. The car involved has not so far been traced.

'Two, we have a suspected murder by hemlock poisoning of Marie Leakey, masseuse at the Walsham Hotel and Spa. No key suspect identified so far. Leads being explored include the source of the hemlock, and a person caught on CCTV delivering a curry meal to Leakey's door that was almost certainly the source of the poison.

'Three, a case of attempted murder of a Wroxham garage owner, Nick Atkinson, by blunt instrument. Again, no hot leads but links to a range of possibilities, including customers, family and friends, are being pursued.

'The final case I will mention is a stabbing of a King's Lynn hairdresser, Sharon Jones, working late on Saturday night. The first response to this incident was by DCI Bell's team from King's Lynn. The casualty was brought into the N&N, where I was visiting Nick Atkinson, and I had an opportunity to speak to her husband about the circumstances of the attack and his whereabouts that evening. I'll let Helena update us on anything since then. Helena?'

On screen, DCI Bell looked up from her notes. 'The short version, as requested, is that the husband's alibi checks out. We're currently checking up on clients, and especially the no-show on Saturday evening, but nothing so far. I still think it's a mugging gone wrong. We're checking CCTV as well.' She put her notes down with a finality that suggested a certain level of dissatisfaction.

'Ram, I'm skipping over you on this occasion, as you've been in post less than an hour, unless you have anything you want to say?' Greg went on.

Ram shook his head and added for good measure, 'I'm happy to be a silent witness on this occasion, thank you.' He sipped from his cup of tea as Greg turned to Jim.

'Anything to add Jim?'

'Just on the county lines investigation. Signs are that they're coming out of cover since the lockdown lifted. The Great Yarmouth team intercepted two kids carrying deliveries in the last week. Both were using electric scooters. The first was caught because they were using an illegal scooter, but there've been others that have been chased and not caught owing to their speed and manoeuvrability. I think it's possible this is a new tactic on the part of the drug gangs, with the scooter being part of the pay-off. The carrot, if you like, alongside the stick.'

Glyn, sitting alongside Ram, stirred in his seat, and Greg turned to him. 'Anything to add, Glyn?'

The Welshman coughed, looked uneasily at the silent DCI Bell on screen, then said with some diffidence, 'We've seen a sudden increase in scooters too. In King's Lynn.'

'Then I suggest you put your heads together, Jim and Glyn, and discuss a shared strategy,' said Greg briskly. 'Thank you, everyone.'

The screen went blank instantly. Ram, Jim and Glyn all rose from their seats, thanking Sue for the coffee and tea.

'Ram, I'll be down in fifteen minutes for my handover to you,' said Greg. 'If that's OK?'

'Suits me,' said Ram. 'Thank you. But I can come back here, if you prefer?'

'Better down with the team,' said Greg. 'See you in fifteen.' As the door closed behind the departing men, he looked at Sue. 'What do you have in your notes?' he asked.

'Jim and Glyn to discuss scooter use in county lines. Arrange next bird table for eight thirty next and every subsequent Monday,' she replied concisely.

'Exactly right, thanks, Sue.'

She smiled at him, and got up to go to her desk. 'Don't forget the Chief Constable wanted to see you this afternoon,' she said.

'He did?' Greg was aghast. 'I was planning to spend some time with Ram! Is this a regular thing?'

'It's in your diary.' She pointed to the iPad on his desk. 'Have you checked the calendar I manage for you?'

'No, I haven't,' he admitted. 'And I'd better share my calendar with you, hadn't I. Then you'll be aware of any clashes.'

'I will, if you keep it updated,' she answered, with the cynicism born of a long career.

***

After a long session crawling over all the work being undertaken by Ram's team, Greg was satisfied on two counts. Both that Ram already had an excellent grip on the details, and that he shared Greg's priorities. Ram's next words increased his feelings of satisfaction, that here he had a jewel among DCIs.

'I'm very impressed by the team,' was Ram's remark. 'DI Henning has a wealth of local knowledge and an impressive grasp of the cases he's dealing with. DS Hayes has an almost equally thorough understanding and seems to have a real talent for analysing video footage. The DCs I've yet to get to know very well, but I've seen nothing to cause me any worry. You've handed me a good team, Greg.'

'I know, but thank you for saying that,' replied Greg. 'What do you think about my little innovation?'

'The bird table?' Ram arched an expressive eyebrow. 'I think if you had a well-integrated team, or less geographical spread, it would probably be unnecessary, because the discussions would happen organically, in and around the incident room. As it is, and subject to how the next one goes when we all have a say, I think it's a practical solution to the problem.'

Greg smiled, noting how quickly Ram had assessed the situation. 'And your colleague Helena Bell?' he asked.

'I don't think she was quite so keen,' replied Ram with caution.

'No. I think you're right. Probably because she doesn't agree there's a problem.'

'There is one thing that's bothering me,' added Ram. 'And that's resource. We're busy now, as you know. If anything else happens, we're going to be stretched too thin. And I don't think we're making best use of intelligence either. We really do need Chris back.'

'The good news on that front, from your perspective at least, is that she can't wait to be back.'

It was Helena Bell's misfortune that when she did eventually get through to Greg on the phone, it was at the end of a long and busy day and after his stressful session with the Chief Constable during which the subject of the King's Lynn team had come up.

'What do you think about the King's Lynn situation?' had been the question put to Greg.

He'd been anticipating the issue arising and had a response prepared. 'I think DCI Bell seems very competent and runs a tight ship. But there's room for improvement on how the whole Serious Crime team works together, both in terms of cooperation and shared intelligence.' Then he'd succumbed to the temptation to add, 'But the issues seem a little obvious, which makes me wonder why they weren't addressed before.' It had been bugging him that so experienced an operator as Margaret Tayler hadn't sorted things out long ago.

'Politics,' was the reply he got. 'The last MP in northwest Norfolk had strong views about King's Lynn as an important centre of population and the need for a local policing team. He had pretty similar views about the local hospital,' the Chief added.

'Surely King's Lynn always had a local station,' said Greg. 'Why did that extend to serious crimes?'

'You tell me.' The Chief Constable spread his hands. 'Margaret had a go at changing the arrangements a couple of times and was firmly put in her place. I think her support for your new post was part of her cunning plan to get her own way in the end. The change in MP didn't hurt. But you need to make it work, Detective Superintendent Geldard. Or the pressure will be back to recreate independence for King's Lynn.'

'No pressure then,' Greg muttered as he went back to his office.

And then his phone rang with the call from Helena Bell. 'I wanted to follow up on the meeting this morning,' she announced without preamble. 'Could you not have given me more notice, so I had chance to prepare?'

'You had exactly the same notice as everyone else,' responded Greg with a degree of irritation that was exacerbated by his recent conversation with the Chief. 'And I didn't expect *anyone* to prepare. The meeting itself was, in effect, preparation for future bird tables.'

'I'm sorry, sir, but I do feel that you are bouncing me into things without warning,' complained Bell. 'First you pay me a visit and invite my team to criticise how I do things, then I get called to perform at a meeting with my peers without any notice. And in between, at the weekend, you involve yourself in one of my investigations.'

Greg took a deep breath, feeling that this risked becoming outright war unless he defused the situation.

'I think it's a question of perspective,' he said, in as mild a tone as he could manage. 'I didn't invite criticism, I invited suggestions for doing things better. None of your peers were given any more notice of the meeting this morning than you, and your "performance", as you term it, was fine. As for the Sharon Jones case, yes, I was concerned that the incident hadn't been recorded on the database, and that the family hadn't been allotted a liaison officer – just a DC who was notable by his absence when I met them. No doubt you've got to the bottom of what he was up to when he should have been at the victim's bedside?'

'I, er, I'm talking to him later today, when he's back on duty,' replied Bell. Her voice sounded stiff, and Greg was left with the impression that she hadn't expected him to bring that subject up.

'I realise your team was probably thin on the ground on Sunday,' added Greg in a more conciliatory tone. 'But you know as well as I that the first few hours after an incident are crucial to a successful investigation. I'm still concerned that the assumption of a mugging has meant some evidence and lines of inquiry being neglected. I'd like to see exactly what led to that conclusion, and to the other possibilities being dismissed.

'You can email me a summary report,' he finished. 'By tonight, please.' And he rang off. When he looked up, Sue was hovering with another mug of coffee.

'Thank you,' he said. 'Sue, I'd like a chat with the call-handling coordinator. Can you arrange it, please?'

'And HR want a word about the possible new DCs you interviewed,' said Sue. 'It's in your calendar.' There was just the faintest hint of disappointment in her voice.

17

Personal note 2

Monday evening. My plans are almost in place. I've pondered this one long and hard. I've debated blades, poisons, ropes, accidents, and I keep coming back to the cleansing power of fire. The tricky bit will be making it look like an accident. But I've got some ideas about that too. At least the letterbox looks practicable. And if they survive, well, so be it. It's in the hands of God, which at least seems appropriate. The question I still have to solve is, where do I get the battery from? Halfords seems like a possibility.

18

Monday 26 July: late afternoon

Monday 26 July: late afternoon

By four, Greg felt his feet hadn't touched the ground. He was losing his voice from incessant talking, in danger of twitching from caffeine overload and he still hadn't spoken to HR about his new DCs or the missing sergeant at King's Lynn. The looks of reproach from Sue were also beginning to get him down. He sighed heavily, hoped that not every day would be like this first one and leaned over to peer through the open door into the outer office.

'I'll speak to HR now,' he said.

Sue picked up her extension with an air of triumph, and they were on the line to Greg in what felt like seconds.

'I have mixed news,' said Jack from HR, a no-nonsense team leader Greg had always respected. 'One of our front runners has accepted a job with the Met.'

'More fool them,' grunted Greg unsympathetically.

'Yes. Well, I won't be surprised if we hear from them again,' said Jack. 'But the other has accepted. They can start in a week.'

'So soon,' exclaimed Greg. 'Which one?'

'Graham Clarke. I did a deal,' said Jack with well-justified pride. 'He's coming from Cornwall, and they are desperate to recruit uniformed PCs. I let them have one of ours from the Thetford team who wants to move closer to family in Truro, in exchange for Clarke.'

'So I'm in trouble with Thetford?' asked Greg.

'Don't worry about that. I'll do another deal,' said Jack with confidence. 'I've got some ideas up my sleeve. Anyway, I'm sorry you're still a man down, but at least you've got DC Clarke.'

'Yes, I liked him,' replied Greg, recollecting the fresh-faced constable with little experience of detection but bags of enthusiasm and common sense. *Good sense*, he amended to himself, remembering Chris's mantra. 'I'll let Ram have the good news.'

With a strong feeling that he and the desk were already becoming too well acquainted, he headed for the door and the stairs. A vague twittering following him down the corridor suggested that Sue was less than satisfied with his approach.

He found Ram, Jim and Jill all in the incident room: Jim entering something on a whiteboard at the far end, Ram and Jill peering at one of the big screens on Jill's desk.

'It's a pity we can't see more of the number plate,' Ram was saying as Greg entered. 'But very well spotted, Jill.'

'Developments?' asked Greg, going over to stand behind them. The image frozen on the screen was of a dark car with a number plate partially visible. 'AO20DE-something,' he read aloud. 'Or could be DL, I suppose. What's the significance?'

'Jill's run AO20DE? and DL? through the DVLA database, and one of the possibilities is a Dean Mason. And the reason that's significant is that he's a customer of Nick Atkinson's. That image is taken from CCTV at a shop just down the road from the garage in the early hours of the twenty-second of July.'

'And Dean Mason was the chap with the small van that was on the current list of jobs for the garage. In fact, he was intercepted trying to drive around the crime scene tape that morning,' added Jill. 'So if his van was booked in for a service, why was he driving around there in a different vehicle a few hours earlier?'

'Worth a few questions,' agreed Greg. 'Where does he live and work?'

'In Great Yarmouth,' answered Ram. 'He's a plumber, hence the van. We're just about to get him in for questioning.'

'Excellent,' said Greg.

'Jim has some news too,' said Ram, picking up his loose-fitting jacket and heading for the door. 'I'll let him bring you up to date.'

Jim turned round from the whiteboard. 'I'm looking at the poisoning case. No arrests here yet, but we have found a couple of accessible locations on the Broads where hemlock is growing. I had a word with a friend who works for the Broads Authority,' he explained.

Greg went over to the whiteboard and studied Jim's latest additions. 'Barton Broad and Hickling,' he read. 'When you say accessible, do you mean by boat or by road?'

'On foot,' replied Jim. 'The Barton Broad boardwalk goes past a stand of hemlock. It would involve a bit of scrambling about and plodging through wet ground, but it's doable if you're reasonably fit. The Hickling plants are within the Norfolk Wildlife Trust nature reserve. You pay to go into the reserve, so I've sent Bill to see if he can find a visitor with links to Marie Leakey. I need someone to check out CCTV near Barton Broad and Neatishead to see if we can identify anyone of interest heading for the boardwalk, but as we don't have anyone to spare at present, I thought of asking Broads Beat if they can help. We really could do with some more hands,' he added in what was a major moan by Jim's standards.

'I've some good news on that front,' said Greg. 'Damn, I meant to tell Ram, but he's already left. I'll give him a ring. We've got a new DC starting next week from Cornwall. A DC Graham Clarke.'

'How did you get that organised so quickly?' asked Jim.

'HR did it, and don't enquire too closely,' replied Greg with a grin. 'I suspect use of the dark arts myself.'

A phone call to Ram later, and Greg was ready to call it a day. It was horribly tempting to hang around for the arrival and subsequent interview of Dean Mason, but he was all too aware that to do that would undermine Ram and tread heavily on his toes. *If it's possible to undermine someone and tread on them at the same time*, he thought.

'Sue, I'm off now. I'm heading over to King's Lynn in the morning to catch up with DCI Bell and find out exactly what's happening on the stabbed hairdresser case, so I won't see you until later in the day.'

'Noted, sir,' she said. 'Oh, before you go, there was a callback from the call-centre team. They said, "OK, can do."'

'Good,' said Greg, and left without enlightening her as to the meaning of the cryptic message.

He was more than happy to get home at a reasonable hour. Not least because he had a strong presentiment that such opportunities would be few and far between.

'But it doesn't feel right, leaving other people to get on with it,' he complained to Chris as she cleared the kitchen table of the mess left by Jamie's rusk-and-milk supper. Bobby was doing her best to help by licking the tabletop, undeterred by the vigorously wielded damp cloth.

'I don't think Ram would thank you for breathing down the back of his neck,' remarked Chris.

'No. I know. That's why I'm here, not there. But it's not easy.' He took the top off a bottle of red wine and poured a couple of glasses.

'Not too much for me,' said Chris. 'It wakes me in the night, and I get enough of that from Jamie.'

Greg tipped a little from one glass into the other. 'OK,' he said. 'But I don't want to drink too much either. I'm going to get fat, sitting at a desk all day, and this won't help.'

'Never mind,' said Chris with little sympathy. 'You can go and bother Helena Bell tomorrow. That should keep you on your toes.'

'How did you know I was going to do that?' asked Greg.

'You've already told me she was making a fuss about your new bird-table meetings, and that you weren't happy about how she's handling the Sharon Jones case, so it wasn't a difficult deduction,' replied Chris. 'Not for someone who knows you.'

'She's obviously got used to running her own show with little interference,' remarked Greg. 'That wouldn't be so bad if I thought she was faultless, but I don't know... There's something not sitting right with me. When I met them in King's Lynn, I thought she was a good officer but a bit of a martinet. Now I do have some worries about competence. She seems to be jumping to conclusions on the Sharon Jones case, and the DC she sent to the hospital seems sloppy.'

'I gathered he hadn't impressed you, from what you said last night,' said Chris. 'Who was it?'

'A DC Waterton,' answered Greg, sitting down on the battered old sofa and instantly being joined by Bobby purring and butting his hand. 'Steady on, Bobby! You nearly made me throw wine all over the place.'

'Waterton,' said Chris, stirring a pot on the stove. Something in her tone caught his attention.

'What? What do you know about Waterton?' asked Greg. 'Don't tell me he's another ex-Met misogynist!'

'No, nothing like that.' Chris put the spoon down on the counter and turned to face Greg. 'This is only rumour,' she said. 'I have no proof. But rumour has it she's sleeping with him.'

'Helena Bell's sleeping with Waterton?' Greg clarified. 'Ah. If true, that explains a few things.' He took another swig of his wine. 'Of course, if I tackle her on it, you know what she's going to say.'

'You think she'll bring up our relationship?' asked Chris.

'Well, wouldn't you?'

'Probably,' she conceded. 'But there are a few differences. You were open with Margaret from the very start. And you made sure you were never my direct line manager. And Waterton is a married man.'

'Is he indeed?' responded Greg. 'Well now...'

19

26 July: evening

Jill had pointed out to her new boss that they could save a lot of time if they met Dean Mason in Great Yarmouth, and the local force had their interviewee lined up before they got there. As Ram was currently renting a house in a village near the seaside resort, it made a lot of sense to him too. It was, therefore, two officers from Great Yarmouth who intercepted a furiously protesting Dean Mason on his way out of the door.

'I've got an important rehearsal tonight,' he repeated for the umpteenth time. 'I've told you, I'm needed. Why can't I pop in tomorrow, or even after the rehearsal if it's really that critical you talk to me today?'

'Sorry, sir, our instructions are to take you to the station now,' stated the imperturbable close-to-retirement constable. 'Please come with us now. If you don't come willingly, I may have to arrest you.'

'Arrest me. For what?' exclaimed Dean. 'Oh for God's sake, if you're going to be like that I'll come now. Just let me make a phone call. It won't take long,' he added, seeing the two officers exchange glances.

He hit speed dial for Aubrey on his phone and sighed irritably when it went to voicemail. 'Aubrey, sorry but I'm not going to make the rehearsal tonight. Something's come up. If I can get along later, I will. It's Dean,' he added belatedly, just in case Aubrey didn't recognise the number or his voice. 'OK. Let's get going and get this over with,' he said.

Ram and Jill arrived at Great Yarmouth police station barely minutes before Dean was brought in. They were still chatting to the desk sergeant in reception when the sulky face of the plumber cum would-be rama star appeared through the street door.

'That was quick,' complimented Ram. 'Thank you. I believe we have an interview room waiting for us. Sorry, I should have introduced myself. I'm DCI Ram Trent. I don't think we've met before.'

'We have,' said Jill, also holding out her hand. 'When you helped rescue DI Sarah Laurence from her abductors. Good to see you again, Henry.'

'Won't be around much longer,' said Henry, taking his cap off and mopping his head with a large handkerchief. 'I retire in a few weeks.'

'We'll miss you,' replied Jill, then taking her cue from Ram's glance towards the door, added, 'See you before then, hopefully,' and followed her new boss towards the interview rooms. Dean followed reluctantly, ushered along by Henry and his sidekick, the youthful Constable Shaw, who was still finding his feet and showed it.

Ram stood aside at the door to the interview room, to allow Shaw to place Dean at the far side of the table. He noticed, absently, that the skinny young constable had dandruff on his collar and pimples on the back of his neck that were being rubbed by his collar. Shaw went to stand in the corner of the room by the door as Ram and Jill took their seats opposite Dean.

While Jill checked the recording equipment, Ram took the opportunity to survey his interviewee, who despite his earlier objections had now gone quiet. What Ram saw was a good-looking man in his forties with slightly too long dark hair and the sort of beard that's only a fraction up from failed-to-shave. He was shifting uneasily in his seat.

'Has anyone asked you if you would like a solicitor present?' asked Ram.

'Er, no,' replied Dean. 'I thought this was just a chat. Why would I need a solicitor?'

'Well, I think we'll do this as an interview under caution, just to be on the safe side,' answered Ram. 'So, you have the right to have a solicitor present if you wish. We can supply a duty solicitor, or you can have one of your own choosing. It's up to you.'

Dean hesitated, looked at his watch, then seemed to come to a decision. 'Let's just get on with it,' he said. 'I've somewhere else I need to be, so let's get going and not waste any more time. What do you want to know?'

'First things first,' said Ram, and administered the caution before introducing himself and Jill. 'Right, now that's sorted, please be aware this interview is being recorded. How well do you know Nick Atkinson?'

'Atkinson? Fairly well, I suppose. I've used his garage for some years now. Both for my work van and for my car.'

'Why not use a garage closer to home?' asked Jill. 'It's a bit of a trek from Yarmouth to Wroxham, isn't it? There's no shortage of garages in Yarmouth.'

'True,' said Dean. 'But I used Nick when I lived near Wroxham, and he's a good chap, so I kept on going there after I moved here. It seemed only fair. He'd always given me a good price, and he's an old friend of a friend, so one way and another...' He shrugged.

'Even so, isn't it inconvenient to leave your work vehicle in a garage so far from home? What do you do while the van is in the garage?' Jill pursued her point.

'Usually, the man I work with picks me up and runs me home, or we do a job together.'

'You have an employee?' asked Ram. 'We'll need his name and contact details.'

'Not an employee as such,' answered Dean. 'He's an independent trader too, but we cover for each other, and if it's a big job we work together and split the bill between us. It's an informal arrangement, but it's worked well for years. We trained together as apprentices. Here!' He dug around in a trouser pocket and came up with a dog-eared business card. Here are his details.' He handed the card over.

Ram put it down between himself and Jill. 'Let's turn to the twenty-second of July,' he said. 'What were you doing in the early hours of that day?'

'Well, I got up fairly early to take my van into Atkinson's, as arranged,' responded Dean. 'You should know that. You folk were already there when I arrived.'

'According to our records, you arrived in a small white van at around nine thirty when, according to the garage appointments book, you were expected to have left your van the previous night, or to arrive in time for an eight thirty start on the service. Why so late?' asked Ram.

'Was it really half nine?' asked Dean. 'I thought it was nearer nine. Either way, the morning got away from me a bit. Had a bit of a heavy night,' he added with an attempt at a conspiratorial grin. 'You know how it is.' He looked at Ram's unmoving features and added, 'Well maybe you don't.'

'Perhaps you can explain why you were driving near the garage just before five am that morning,' went on Ram. 'In your car, that is.'

'What? I wasn't. I was in bed, asleep. In fact, I overslept, as I said. I didn't get up until after eight.'

'We have your car on CCTV just down the road from the garage at four fifty that morning,' said Ram, unmoved. 'DS Hayes is showing Mr Mason a video of his car,' he added for the tape.

Jill turned her laptop round and played a short recording to Mason, who screwed his eyes up to see the images better.

'Again?' she asked.

'Yes.' He nodded. 'But I can tell you now, that's not my car.'

'It's got your number plate,' pointed out Ram, not mentioning that only the first five digits were visible.

'It seems to have,' conceded Dean. 'But I know it's definitely not my car. And I'll tell you for why – there's no dent in the passenger door. Mine's waiting for a visit to the body shop since some prat at the supermarket dinged it with a bag or trolley or some such.'

'It's not a very clear image,' argued Jill. 'This could be a dent, here.' She pointed at the screen.

'It's not in the right place, if it is a dent not just a shadow,' argued Dean in return. 'And anyway, I told you I was in bed, sleeping it off.'

'Anyone with you?' asked Ram.

'Unfortunately not,' said Dean. 'Now can I go? I have a rehearsal to get to, and the director will be hopping mad if I miss it.'

After a little more to-ing and fro-ing, Ram was forced to the realisation that he just didn't have enough to hold Dean and let him leave. But, as he said to Greg on the phone, 'I'm still not happy. It's unlucky we didn't get the whole number plate, but I think we need to keep an eye on Mr Mason.'

***

By the time Dean reached Norwich, the rehearsal was all but over. He'd known full well he would be too late but wanted the opportunity to make a song and dance of his latest tribulations. Hence his noisy arrival just as the rest of the cast were packing up to go home.

'Sorry, Aubrey, sorry. Hope you got my message, but those flatfoots kept me even longer than I feared. They interviewed me under caution, would you believe. Absolutely outrageous. All because they thought they had my car on CCTV by the garage. And me in bed asleep at the time. If they try that again,' he carried on in full cry, 'I'll get solicitored up, believe me. Absolutely outrageous.'

Louise turned round in surprise. 'Was that about poor Nick?' she asked. 'Were you there when he was attacked?'

'No, I bloody well was not!' exploded Dean. 'That's what I've been saying. And what I told the Old Bill. I was in bed, asleep. Well, hungover actually,' he admitted. 'Which was why I was late taking my van in to the garage. By the time I got there the place was crawling with cops.'

'In that case, why are they asking you questions?' asked Myrtle.

'Because they have part of a number plate that looks like mine on a camera shot at five in the morning. Five in the morning, I ask you! As far as I'm concerned, there's only one five o'clock in any day and it doesn't happen in the bloody morning. And how many cars have numbers that start with "AO" in Norwich? That's the area code for Norwich, isn't it?'

'Well, East Anglia, at least,' said a new voice from the corner. 'But you're right, there's lots of them around. My car has them.'

Dean glanced over. 'Oh God, you're back, are you?' he exclaimed rudely. Louise flushed, but the suited man in the corner smiled, unmoved.

'Good to see you too, Dean,' he said. 'I'll be off, Louise, if you're sure there's nothing you need.'

'No, I'm fine,' she said. 'Don't let me keep you.'

'Time for you all to go home,' announced Aubrey. 'See you at the weekend, principals. And I hope that means you this time, Dean.'

'Flatfoots permitting,' he snarled. 'Anyone for a drink?'

There was a general rush to decline. Dean didn't look like good company for anyone. Myrtle, Josie and Louise exchanged meaningful looks and headed for the door together in a small, tight group.

'How about you ladies?' persisted Dean.

'Not this time, Dean,' said Louise. 'We're heading home. You look like you need your bed too,' she added. 'You look like something the cat brought in and didn't want.'

Myrtle snorted, then tugged Josie's elbow. 'I'll give you a lift to the wine bar,' she muttered. And the three of them headed off.

20

Late evening, 26 July: The Last Wine Bar

Louise was already settled at a corner table when Myrtle and Josie arrived.

'As it's getting late, I got us a bottle of red. Hope that's OK,' she said, waving them to the seats opposite.

'Lovely,' said Myrtle, already reaching for her full glass before she'd settled into her seat.

'I can't stop long,' said Josie. 'I'm on an early shift in the morning.'

'Busy are you?' asked Myrtle.

'Not so bad.' Josie worked as deputy manager in a supermarket outside Norwich. 'We still haven't got back to normal. Lots more orders and deliveries than there were before the virus.'

'I guess a lot of people found it was more convenient than they realised,' commented Louise. 'I know I did.'

'What do you think about Dean getting interviewed by the police?' asked Myrtle, bursting to get to the main topic of interest. 'Think there's anything in it?'

'Nooo,' replied Louise on a long sceptical note. 'He's a bit of a toerag, and his hands wander like a blindfolded octopus at a piano recital, but I've never known him to be violent.'

Josie choked on her wine as she tried to swig and giggle at the same time. 'Sorry,' she said, mopping at herself with a hankie. 'But that was such a very good description!'

Myrtle joined in the laughter, but Louise's face had darkened. 'God, I really hope not,' she added. 'I introduced him to Nick when Dean and I were an item. Years ago. I'd feel terrible if it was Dean.'

'I'm sure you were right the first time,' said Myrtle briskly. 'I've never known him be aggressive either. Tell Josie how you met.'

A smile spread across Louise's face. 'It was in *The Beggar's Opera*,' she explained. 'I was Lucy Lockit, and Dean was one of the highwaymen but also the understudy for the lead, Macheath. We were doing a four-night run, and the bloke playing Macheath had a meeting in Brussels that week. He swore blind he'd be back in good time, but his plane to London City got held up, and Dean had to go on for the first night. All credit where it's due, he did a good job, but it was a modern-dress version and he had a problem with Macheath's costume, which was a tight white-denim suit. Dean was a bit on the porky side even then, but he squeezed into the costume, and everything went fine until the scene where Macheath's in handcuffs, surrounded by the chorus of tarts, who in this version were all wearing satin halternecks split to the thigh.

'I'm in the wings at this point, and suddenly there's a lot of whispering and fussing going on among the tarts. The zip had gone on Dean's white jeans. His paisley pants were on display to the audience, and the tarts were arguing about which of them was going to safety pin him together. Their exchange of 'you do it, you're married' and 'no, you do it, I'm not going near his groin!' was studded by pleas from Dean regarding the safety of his wedding tackle. It was a lot more interesting than the dialogue front of stage and the audience was getting distracted.'

Myrtle and Josie were both giggling helplessly, even though Myrtle had heard the story before.

'How did it end?' asked Josie.

'Dean did the rest of the scene with his back to the audience, bellowing his lines to the backcloth, and came off swearing.'

'Time, ladies, please,' said a voice from the bar.

'Gosh, that's gone quickly,' said Josie as they gathered up their things and headed for the door. 'By the way, who was your new chap tonight?' she asked Louise, emboldened by drink and shared laughter.

The smile left Louise's face as though someone had hit Undo. 'That wasn't a new man, it was an old one,' she said. 'My ex.'

21

Wednesday 28 July: across Norfolk

When Greg left home that morning, his soon-to-be mother-in-law was already ensconced on the old sofa in the kitchen, spoiling his son rotten, while Chris, with an unmistakable sigh of satisfaction, was booting up her laptop at the kitchen table.

'See you later,' he said, kissing the top of first Chris's then Jamie's head. 'Thank you,' he said to Jane Mathews.

'No problem,' she said. 'I'm happy to get to know my first grandson. On a part-time basis, anyway,' she added with a smile. 'I'm working on finding a longer-term solution.'

He waved a goodbye, picked up his bag and stood aside to let Bobby out of the door, before heading for his car and the road to King's Lynn. His phone rang before he had even joined the A47.

'Hi, Ram,' he said. 'Any news?'

'Not good, I'm afraid,' replied Ram. 'Which do you want first? The bad or the worse?'

'Like that, is it?' asked Greg. 'Go on, hit me with it.'

'First, the hearing on your homicidal tree surgeon, Warren Thorne. It's been brought forward to next week. Apparently, they had an issue with another scheduled case. Something about the defendant being taken ill. So they had an unexpected gap and decided to fill it with Thorne.'

'Inconvenient, but not the end of the world,' remarked Greg. 'We've had all our ducks in a row for months. I'm afraid it'll take up a good bit of my time though. Which means more load on you.'

'Which brings me to the worse,' said Ram drily. 'We've had a report of an arson attack on a vicarage in Martham. Two casualties, both with serious injuries, and clear signs of an accelerant being involved as well as an e-bike battery.'

'Dear God!' exclaimed Greg as he signalled to overtake a slow-moving truck on an incline. 'What's got into people? That's four murders, or attempted murders, within a few weeks.'

'Five if you count Leonard Ware's hit and run,' said Ram. 'When I accepted this job, I had no idea Norfolk folk were so savage.'

'Maybe it's all been stored up during the lockdown,' suggested Greg. 'I don't know. Ram, are you OK to manage the preliminaries? I'm on my way to King's Lynn and would like to sort things out with DCI Bell before I turn my mind to the Crown Court and so on.'

'Sure,' said Ram. 'But it will mean I park the Ware case for the foreseeable future. We're stretched too thin as it is.'

'Understood,' responded Greg. 'Roll on Monday and our new pair of hands.'

DCI Bell was ready and waiting when he arrived at King's Lynn, sitting behind her desk in the glass-walled corner of the main office. Greg took a quick glance round and noted that the room was empty except for two civilian staff tapping away at laptops. He stopped in his tracks, and diverted to say hello.

'I don't think we've met,' he said, holding out his hand to each in turn. 'I'm Detective Superintendent Geldard. Perhaps you could introduce yourselves and outline your roles here.'

A chubby girl with vivid blue eyes held out her name badge for inspection. 'Geraldine Dennis,' she said, 'known as Gerry. I do clerical work. Data inputting mainly.'

Her colleague, a skinny young man in jeans and open-necked shirt, shook long hair back from his face and followed suit. 'Chas Young,' he said. 'Data analysis.'

'Good to meet you,' said Greg, and turned to see he was being observed by Helena Bell, now standing at her desk. He went over to the corner and closed her office door behind him.

'Useful resource, I imagine,' he commented. 'Especially data analysis. We should put him in touch with DI Mathews when she's back at work.'

'Back from maternity leave,' said Helena pointedly.

'That's right,' said Greg, not rising to the bait. 'Do you have an update on the Sharon Jones case? I saw your report last night, but I'm still of the view that we shouldn't rule out other possibilities to a mugging.'

'I beg to differ, sir,' she responded. 'But I will of course follow your instructions if you are happy we have sufficient resource.'

'It shouldn't take too much effort to check out the customers who had appointments with Sharon that evening,' answered Greg. 'Why not put one or other of those two on the task.' He nodded to the two civilians. 'They seem bright enough. On the subject of resource, I'm afraid I need to do a spot of rebalancing between your team and Ram Trent's. You currently have one assault and the county lines case on your hands. He has four plus county lines. That's plainly not a sensible allocation of tasks, so I have two changes in mind. First, I'd like DC Waterton to work with DI Henning on the Marie Leakey murder. He didn't exactly impress me at our first meeting, but anyone can make a mistake, and this gives him a chance to show me what he can do.

'Second, I've discussed with the call-handling team a change in their protocols. At present, they call you only when there are cases firmly located in the northwest of the county. The rest of the time they call Ram Trent. That's going to change. You will still get first call on cases occurring west of a line drawn south from Hunstanton. Similarly, Ram will pick up any cases east of a line running south from Cromer. All cases occurring in mid-Norfolk will be allocated to one or other of you according to the cab-rank rule – in other words, in strict turn. With, of course, the option for either of you to appeal to me if the workloads become unbalanced.'

There was a silence. Greg watched the thoughts cross the face opposite, which was trying to remain impassive. He guessed that she was torn between excitement at the possibility of a greater range of activity, irritation at a change instigated by someone else and some emotion relating to DC Waterton that he couldn't quite identify.

'When do you propose to introduce this change?' she asked.

'Immediately.'

Another silence. Then, 'I can see some benefits. But I can't say I'm happy about a simultaneous increase in workload and loss of resource.'

'Nor am I,' agreed Greg. 'But it is what it is. Like any demand-led service, the troubles that come over the horizon are outside of our control. The best we can do is deal with them as efficiently as we can.'

'Keep calm and carry on?' she asked.

'Something like that. And I will see what I can do about finding you a sergeant.'

Back on the road and on his way to Wymondham, he rang Chris.

'How'd it go?' she asked.

'About as I expected. Perhaps a little better. I think I may have found you an assistant.'

'Who?'

'One of Bell's civilians. Chas Young. He says he spends most of his time on data analysis. Seems a bright lad, although obviously I haven't seen him work. Worth a try anyway, and it will help the integration process if you work with someone from King's Lynn.'

'I'll have a chat with him,' promised Chris. 'How did you tackle the Waterton issue?'

'I didn't discuss it. I just transferred him temporarily to Jim, to deal with the Leakey case.'

'Good move.' Chris approved.

Over in Martham, Ram was deep in conversation with the fire service incident commander. Fisher had perched himself on a convenient wall as he pulled his helmet off and wiped a weary hand over his face and head. An ambulance crew behind them were tidying away equipment, and two fire crews were still damping down the blaze that had destroyed the entrance to the mid-twentieth century vicarage.

'We're lucky it was no worse,' said Ram. 'Two cases of smoke inhalation—'

'Plus two of my crew, hurt when the hall ceiling came down,' added Fisher. 'But those are minor injuries, thank God. Their protective suits did a good job. The occupants now... they can thank their working fire detectors for their lives. They just about gave them enough warning that they were able to raise the alarm before it was too late.'

'And you must have got here like bats out of hell. Don't devalue your speed of response,' replied Ram. 'That played a huge part too.'

'Still wouldn't have helped if they hadn't heard the alarms,' responded Fisher. 'In my opinion, the fire was set in a way and at a time that trapped them upstairs. If we hadn't been able to rescue them through the bedroom window, they'd have died for sure. I think this was attempted murder, not just arson.

'Sorry. That's a judgement for you, I know,' he added. 'But that's my opinion.'

'How did the fire start?' asked Ram. 'An accelerant, I heard?'

'Yes. But it was what the accelerant kicked off that caused the major problem. Obviously, our fire investigator and your forensic folk will be crawling all over the place, but I can tell you now that the speed and intensity of the fire was down to an electric-bike battery and thermal runaway.'

'Meaning?' asked Ram.

'Subject to more detailed investigation, I think what happened was that an accelerant was propelled through the letterbox into the hall and set alight. There was a bike battery in the hall, and the heat damage from the accelerant triggered an unstoppable chain reaction in the lithium ion battery.'

'Couldn't it have been the bike battery that was the problem?' asked Ram. 'I've read about other cases.'

'If we hadn't found evidence of an accelerant, then yes, that's right. It could have been the explanation,' replied Fisher. 'But the burn patterns don't support that. The way the flames flared across the hall and towards the stairs is strongly indicative of an accelerant.'

Greg had joined the pair unnoticed and heard the last couple of sentences. 'Morning, Bob,' he said. 'Any sign of an electric bike on the premises?'

'Haven't noticed one so far,' responded Commander Fisher.

Ram had been making notes. 'As soon as we can talk to the occupiers, we can ask about a bike and the bike battery,' he said. 'Jill has gone to the hospital and I'm going over there now. When can the forensic team get in?' he asked.

Bob Fisher turned to look at the ravaged house. 'A couple of hours, I'd think,' he said. 'The fire's out now, but there are some hotspots and the structure will need assessment before anyone can go in safely.'

'You've obviously got things under control here,' Greg said to Ram as the fire commander donned his helmet again and hurried over to a crew busy rolling up hoses. 'I'll check in with Jim on the Leakey case, then, with luck, I'll be heading over to Wymondham to blow the dust off my Warren Thorne notes, ready for next week. Which leaves the garage owner assault?'

'The Nick Atkinson case?' asked Ram. 'I've asked Great Yarmouth for help checking out Dean Mason's story about the morning of twenty-second of July, and civilian staff are checking the ANPR between Yarmouth and Wroxham that morning to see if they can pick up his car prior to five am. Apart from that...' He shrugged.

'And Bill?' asked Greg. 'Sorry, I realise I'm treading on your toes. What your team does is up to you. But I'm trying to do a fairer job of balancing resource and workload across the county.'

'No problem. Bill's still checking out the garage customers, to find anyone who might have reason for a grudge and, or, was around that morning.'

'Ram, I'm sorry you're having such a torrid introduction to Norfolk,' responded Greg.

'It can only get better,' said Ram with a tired smile. 'But on the bright side, there's no better way to get to know the team, and so far they've been faultless. But I am looking forward to the new DC starting on Monday.'

'I've swopped DC Waterton over to you this morning, as well,' said Greg. 'I've sent him over to help Jim with the Leakey investigation, as we discussed. And I've identified some possible analytical assistance from the King's Lynn team, for Chris.'

'Thank you,' said Ram. 'But how is Helena Bell feeling about that?'

'Resigned, I think,' said Greg. 'Now for North Walsham and Jim.'

***

Final stop on my tour of Norfolk, thought Greg as he parked his car by the police station in the town centre. He found Jim sharing a tea break with the inspector in charge of the station.

'Thank you for your help and for accommodating this chap,' he said to Inspector Coles.

'No problem,' she replied, picking up her mug and levering herself off the desk where she was perched. 'We're old friends. But I'd better get on, so I'll leave you in peace.'

'DC Waterton arrived yet?' he asked Jim.

'Half an hour ago. I've asked him to run a check on Marie Leakey's clientele, as Bill didn't get much further than the neighbours before he was snatched away for the Atkinson case.'

'Good. Any progress with the hemlock?'

'I've got the records of cars entering the Hickling reserve car park. Literally just finished checking through them, and one may be of interest. I've reported it to Ram.'

'And?' asked Greg.

'It's a partial number. Part of the plate is obscured, perhaps by mud, but the bit we can see starts "AO20".'

22

Personal note 3

The lunchtime news was disappointing. I made a point of watching Look East, but the announcement of a fire in Martham was anticlimactic. Evidently the two occupants of the house are suffering no more than smoke inhalation, and it's being treated as suspected arson.

So much for an accidental battery fire. Must do better.

23

Change of focus

'I know, I know.' Greg held up his hands, part apology, part plea for understanding. 'I'm here now. And sorry I hadn't warned you about how long I'd be gone. Fact is, I wasn't expecting an arson case to pop over the horizon! And on the positive side, I did get your message about the change of date for the Thorne case.'

His secretary's ruffled feathers smoothed, visibly. 'Is that the man who killed DC Steve Hall?' she asked. 'I was working at home then, but we all heard about it.'

'Steve Hall *and* four cyclists,' said Greg with a grim note in his voice that made her look up sharply. 'I'll need the files...'

'Already on your desk, sir. Frank from the CPS is lined up too.'

'Amazing,' said Greg. 'Just one thing then...'

'And your coffee machine is on,' she announced with an air of triumph.

It didn't take long for Greg to re-familiarise himself with the detail in the files. Indeed, some elements of the case would, he feared, never leave him. The images of Steve's last hours were particularly searing: the sinking feeling he'd had when Steve had chased after the fleeing tree surgeon; the way Thorne had turned and thrown a hatchet; the police dogs at first recoiling from pepper spray, then bringing Thorne down as Greg had run to Steve's side; and that moment he'd relived a thousand times in his dreams, when the blood from Steve's carotid artery had spurted across his hands and run away into the peaty soil of the forest floor.

He shook himself, realising his coffee was going cold and that he'd spent several minutes staring out of the window. A cough from the open door suggested that his attention was being sought. Frank was poised uncertainly on the threshold.

'Didn't like to interrupt,' he said. 'You were deep in thought.'

Greg gave himself another mental shake. 'Sorry. Come in, Frank. Don't stand on ceremony. Let's compare notes on strategy – we don't want this one getting away. Who's prosecuting?'

'Luckily the QC I booked originally is OK with the change of date: Sir Frederick Seymour.'

'That's good, isn't it? Wasn't he the prosecutor in the Gabrys case a couple of years ago?'

'Yes. And it *is* good,' affirmed Frank. 'A, he's all across the detail. B, he's had a lot of experience of diminished responsibility pleas.'

'Is that what they're going with?'

'We believe so. Technically, acting while suffering an abnormality of mind", such that he didn't know what he was doing. And Greg, I think you'll need to be ready for criticism of heavy-handed tactics. They're likely to argue that you already knew he was paranoid and that he was pushed, by police action, to the extreme measures he took.'

'Oh, are they?' Greg's voice was cold. 'In that case, let's go over all the arguments to the contrary. On the side of premeditation, we have the mantrap he set in the woods, the fact he was armed with pepper spray and hatchet—'

'And the escape route he'd prepared into the tree canopy. They all argue logical forethought rather than impulse, I agree,' responded Frank. 'And when it comes to the four cyclists he ran over then left for dead, we have the fact of the cloned number plates he was using. That too argues premeditation.'

'Not to mention he concealed the bodies,' added Greg. 'Surely they don't have a leg to stand on.'

'Doesn't mean they won't give it their best shot,' said Frank. 'And we need to be ready for that. You know as well as I that juries can be unpredictable.'

There was a silence while Greg ruminated, yet again, on the implications of a diminished responsibility plea. 'In short, you're warning me he may well get away with a verdict of manslaughter by way of diminished responsibility and a sentence of no more than twenty-four years, of which he might serve only half, rather than the whole-life term he deserves as a serial killer.' His tone was heavy.

'Or he spends the rest of his life in a secure hospital.'

'But that depends on a medical opinion. And we all know how that can play out. No, Frank. The only way we can be sure to protect the public is a murder verdict. Anything less is failure.'

***

'Hi, Ram.'

'Chris! I hadn't realised you were back at work!' Ram fumbled with his phone as he simultaneously tried to open a door and hang on to a file of papers.

'I'm easing myself in,' she said. 'Welcome! I haven't had chance to say hello since you arrived back in Norfolk. I'm looking forward to meeting up properly.'

'And I'm really looking forward to having your support,' replied Ram with considerable feeling.

'How can I help?' asked Chris practically.

'To be blunt, I'm swamped with cases and associated data,' replied Ram. 'Can I get the DCs and the civilian staff to send you everything they've got? I'm sure I'm missing something.'

'Send away,' responded Chris, feeling the old excitement flooding through her veins. 'Which are the cases that are bothering you?'

'All of them,' said Ram. 'The hit and run on the amateur actor in Norwich, the poisoning in North Walsham, assault in Wroxham, the stabbing in King's Lynn and now we have a case of arson in Martham. I'm just on my way to interview the survivors.'

'And the names? Of the victims, I mean, so I can relate the data to the right cases...'

'In the same order: Ware, Leakey, Atkinson, Jones – Sharon Jones, that is – and Newell.'

'My God, what's got into people?' exclaimed Chris, echoing, had she known it, Greg's comments earlier.

'Tell me about it,' said Ram wearily. 'I hope it's not too much for you!'

'I gather I've got a bit of help from some chap in King's Lynn. Chas somebody. I'll get him on to it too.'

It wasn't the first time Ram had been to the Norfolk and Norwich Hospital, but it was the first time since Covid. He navigated the new instructions and rules with some care, eventually arriving at the entrance to the non-Covid A&E. Flourishing his warrant card, he asked for Mr and Mrs Newell, the victims of the fire at the Martham vicarage.

'Mrs Newell is in Cubicles,' said the harassed lady on the reception desk. 'I'm not sure about Mr Newell. I think they sent him to Resus.'

'The smoke inhalation was bad then?' asked Ram. 'Can I speak to them?'

'I don't know,' she replied, her attention already turning to the slightly reeling and distinctly battered figure behind him in the queue.

'I've been here hoursh,' the man declaimed. 'Hoursh and hoursh.'

'They'll see you as soon as possible,' she assured him, catching Ram's eye and raising an eyebrow just slightly. The tiny gesture said *self-inflicted!* as clearly as words. 'You need to talk to the doctor,' she said to Ram. 'Here...' She pointed to a man in green scrubs dashing through the department. 'He might be able to help.'

He was moving so fast, Ram had to run to catch him up. He waved his warrant card again and said, gasping slightly, 'DCI Trent. I'm hoping to speak to Mr and Mrs Newell?'

'Mrs Newell is in Cubicles. You can have a few words with her. But that was Mr Newell.' He pointed to the trolley he was chasing down the department. 'He's on his way to intensive care. Heart attack.'

'Does his wife know?' asked Ram.

'Yes.' The busy doctor had no time for more and ran to the already closing lift door.

Ram hesitated a moment, then turned back to the desk. The receptionist was still arguing with the slightly battered drunk and looked up at Ram with an expression of relief.

'Sorry to bother you again,' he said, then as the inebriated protestor grabbed him by the elbow, he turned sharply and produced his warrant card.

'Grab me again and I'll arrest you for assaulting a police officer,' he snapped, his voice low but his determination evident. 'And stop bothering this lady. Sit down over there' – he pointed at an empty chair – 'and wait your turn. She's got enough to do and there's a lot of people who are much worse off than you.'

The man reeled back a step or two, shock twisting his features, his mouth opening and closing but no sound coming out. Then he shambled away and did as he was told.

'Thank you,' the receptionist said quietly. 'I should be used to it, but it does get you down after a bit. The lady you're looking for is in there. Cubicle three.' She pointed.

Ram smiled his thanks, noticing that although she looked tired, her expression had lightened. She blushed a little under his gaze and swept some loose brown hairs from her face.

'She'll be going up to the ward soon,' she prompted, and Ram realised he was still staring.

'Sorry, yes, thank you,' he said and followed the line of her finger.

Mrs Newell had a nurse with her when he entered the cubicle, apparently engaged in recording details from the monitoring machines that buzzed and clicked around her. He looked at Ram with an interrogative twist of an eyebrow.

Ram introduced himself. 'DCI Trent. I just need to ask Mrs Newell a few questions.'

'Keep it short,' said the nurse, then to his patient, 'I'll be back soon. Try not to worry. Your husband's in the best hands.'

Mrs Newell was flushed an unhealthy pink and still had an oxygen mask over her nose and mouth. She lay propped high on multiple pillows, and her hands moved ceaselessly on the counterpane, twisting and picking at the covers.

Ram introduced himself again and placed a reassuring hand on hers. 'I'm sorry to bother you, Mrs Newell,' he said. 'I realise this is a terrible time for you. But the sooner we have some answers to a few questions, the sooner we can catch the people who did this.'

She pulled her mask away from her face for a moment to ask, 'Do you have any news of my husband?'

'No, I'm sorry. He was being taken up to ITU when I arrived, but I believe you know that.'

She replaced the mask and nodded.

Taking in her state of mind and health, Ram decided to prioritise. There was lots he wanted to ask, but some of it could wait for later. 'Just a couple of questions for now,' he said. 'First, and this might seem an odd question, but were you charging an electric-bike battery last night? In the hall?'

She shook her head negatively.

'And do you even own an electric bike?' he asked.

Another head shake.

'When your husband raised the alarm last night, did you see or hear anyone in or near your house? For example, outside in the garden?'

This time she pulled her mask away and replied, 'No. When the smoke alarm woke us, he went to the door, opened it and then slammed it shut.' She paused for another breath from the mask and added, 'He told me to pull some clothes on while he rang for the fire brigade. I didn't see anything but the smoke that came into our room.'

'Last question, for now,' said Ram. 'Do you know of anyone who might want to hurt you or your husband? Any enemies?'

This time she just shook her head again and lay back listlessly on the pillows, apparently worn out by the effort of talking.

'I'll leave it there for now,' said Ram, and squeezed her hand again. 'Thank you for your help. I'll come back when you're feeling a little stronger.'

Back in the reception area, he waved to his new friend on the desk and headed towards the exit, then changed his mind and turned back. 'Is there a cafe?'

'Several,' she said with a smile. 'The best is the one in the entrance to Block 3.' She pointed to indicate the direction he should go, then hesitated and added, 'I'm taking a break now. I could show you, if you like?'

'Thank you. That would be kind,' he said. 'I'll wait for you outside.' As he stepped through the automatic doors, he took his phone out and turned it back on. Multiple messages but nothing that needed his immediate attention. A cough at his elbow alerted him to the fact that he had been joined by the receptionist. As he followed her towards Block 3, he noticed both that she came up to his ear and that she was wearing flat shoes. *Perfect*, he thought, then almost blushed.

'I don't know your name,' he said. 'Call me Ram.'

'Oh dear, I'm known as Sam,' she said, laughing. 'Sam and Ram! That's not great, is it?'

'Oh I don't know,' he said, 'could be worse. Is it short for Samantha?'

'It is,' she said with a grimace. 'Stick with Sam, please!'

By the time they'd settled down with sandwiches and coffee, they were chatting like old friends. Ram, who was usually on the shy side with women, surprised himself. And by the time the coffees were drunk, he had her phone number safely tucked away in his mobile. That was when he noticed the text from Jim.

'Sorry, work,' he said and read:

R U still @ hospital? Just notified Mr N died of heart attack few mins ago.

Ram sighed, turned the phone off again and looked at Sam. 'I need to go back and talk to the doctor who was treating Mr Newell.'

'Was?' said Sam.

'Yes. It seems he's died.' Ram was clearing up the plates and mugs as he spoke.

'Leave that to me,' said Sam, standing herself. 'I'll clear up.'

'Thank you.' Ram took a moment to look at her. 'I'll ring you, if that's OK?'

'Very OK,' said Sam.

Even as Ram hurried back into the A&E reception, he heard a choking wail of anguish from Cubicle 3. Sam's substitute, a young man of around twenty-five, Ram guessed, was similarly beleaguered by waiting patients.

'I need to speak to the doctor,' said Ram.

'He's just having a word with Mrs Newell first,' replied the lad.

'There's only one question I need to ask him now,' responded Ram.

'Which is?' The voice behind him was both tired and distinctly depressed. Ram spun round to see the doctor who had chased the trolley into the lift a little while earlier.

'I've been told Mr Newell has died of a heart attack. Is that correct?'

'Not quite,' said the doctor. 'Come into my office for a moment.'

He led the way into a corner office, and sat down with a sigh on the desk, removing his stethoscope from round his neck and stretching back.

'At first we did think he was having a heart attack, but it was an aortic dissection. It's easy to confuse the two, as they present with similar symptoms. We thought for a while that we'd be able to save him, but he died very rapidly as he was rushed into the theatre.

'Was it the result of the arson attack?' asked Ram. 'I mean, can the two be linked? Was the dissection caused by the trauma of the smoke inhalation?'

'I'm sure you'll be asking your pathologist that question when she does the post-mortem. Dr Paisley, isn't it? But, for what it's worth, in my opinion the aortic dissection and therefore his death is directly attributable to the raised blood pressure caused by the trauma and the smoke inhalation.'

'Thank you, Doctor,' said Ram. 'That's all I need for now.'

Outside again and on the phone to Greg, Ram made his point forcibly. 'If he hadn't been subjected to the arson attack, he wouldn't have suffered the aortic dissection. That makes it murder,' he said.

'We'll see if Dr Paisley agrees with you,' replied Greg. 'But it sounds convincing to me.'

24

29 July: Wymondham

Greg managed to escape his secretary's clutches and the siren call of the morning's paperwork with the excuse that he had to catch up with Ram. Then shot down the corridor with a heartfelt sigh of relief.

He found Ram and Jim in the former's office, both on the phone with one finger in the free ear to avoid having to listen to two conversations at once. Ram was the first to ring off, and he looked at Greg with a welcoming smile.

'You've saved me another phone call,' he said. 'We're about to do a general roundup of where we've got to on all the current cases, and I thought you might like to join us. I'd appreciate your insights.'

'Happy to,' replied Greg. 'I was just about to suggest something similar.'

Jim put his phone in his pocket and looked up. 'Chris will join us by Zoom, and that lad Waterton is on his way here. Should arrive in a minute or two. The only person missing is Helena Bell. But I think she's on leave this morning, so we'll have to carry on without her. Roberts is here. Challinor will also join by Zoom.'

'OK, let's at it,' said Ram, and led the way down the corridor to the incident room.

Greg took his accustomed place in front of the whiteboards and looked round the room. Ram was perched on a table to his left, in what he felt was a nicely judged compromise between joining the group sitting round the central table and standing beside Greg.

'Morning, everyone,' said Greg. 'And especially to those of you joining on screens.' He nodded to the big screen at the other end of the room. The display was a montage of two scenes: one containing Chris against the backdrop of their kitchen; the second bearing the head of DC Challinor. 'I'm going to hand over to Ram in a second, but I just wanted to thank you for all you're dealing with at the moment. But let's not waste time – we have precious little to spare. The purpose of this meeting is to review where we've got to on each current case, identify common threads, if any, and ensure we all know what has to happen next. Ram...'

'I suggest we deal with each case in chronological order,' said Ram. 'Which makes first up, Jill and the hit and run in Norwich.'

'Mr Leonard Ware,' said Jill. 'Accountant and keen amateur actor. Aged fifty-four. Hit by a dark car that seemed to drive at him deliberately in the road between the Theatre Royal and the rehearsal space known as the Garage. CCTV in the immediate vicinity had been put out of action, which may or may not be a coincidence. I've checked the footage leading up to the damage inflicted on the camera, and you can see a shadowy figure in a dark hoodie taking aim with what looks like a stone. But that's all I can see. The car is still unidentified. There are a number of dark cars showing on CCTV in the town centre that evening, but nothing with a number plate that is already known to us. And sorry, Boss, but that's where we're at on that.'

'What's your gut feel?' asked Greg.

Jill started to speak but stopped when the door was flung open and DC Waterton entered noisily. He stopped dead when he saw the assembled company then, affecting an air of nonchalance, he came in and sat down at the end of the table.

'Sorry I missed the start,' he said.

Greg gave him a cold stare and went to close the door properly.

'In answer to your question, Boss,' said Jill, 'I know Mr Ware genuinely thinks he was targeted, and I think he's probably right, but we have nothing much to go on. We've interviewed the *Kiss Me, Kate* cast. You know, the folk he was due to be rehearsing with that evening, and we've also chatted to friends and neighbours, but turned up nothing of interest so far. And I was told to switch to the Leakey case. All the interview reports have been logged and sent to DI Mathews,' she added. Greg's eyes flicked to the screen at the end of the table, and he saw Chris nod agreement.

'We'll come back to Chris at the end,' said Ram. 'For now, let's go on to the Leakey case. Jim?'

Jim stood up and Greg grinned to himself. He knew Jim always spoke better on his feet.

'A couple of facts which I think you're all familiar with, plus a lot of speculation,' he began. 'Marie Leakey, well-regarded masseuse with a regular job at the Walsham Hotel and Spa, lived alone in a quiet back street in North Walsham. Cause of death confirmed as hemlock poisoning. The source of the toxin is confirmed as a pre-prepared curry meal. Evidence from a doorbell cam over the road suggests the curry was delivered to her door by someone driving a dark car, but don't get too excited about that – there's a lot of dark cars about! Like the Ware case, Bill and I, and latterly Jill, have interviewed a lot of family, friends and colleagues. No likely suspects identified. In fact, she seems to have been generally well liked both at work and by her neighbours.'

'What about her clients?' asked DC Waterton. 'Can be a dodgy lot, folk going for a massage. It's often a cover for prostitution.'

'Not in this case,' said Jim firmly. 'It's a properly run spa business, and most of Marie Leakey's clients were middle-aged or elderly ladies with bad backs.'

'The interview reports have been logged and passed to Chris as before,' Jill chipped in. 'But I haven't found anything to suggest an obvious suspect.'

'One more thing,' added Jim. 'We've been looking into two known locations where hemlock grows on the Broads. Bill has been checking visitors to the nature reserve at Hickling, and Broads Beat took on Neatishead and the boardwalk. No sightings of people gathering hemlock material so far, and we're still checking car details. What data we have has been sent to Chris.'

Greg looked at the image of Chris out of the corner of his eye, and thought he detected a grimace.

'OK, let's turn to Sharon Jones. DI Roberts, please tell me you've made some progress,' said Ram.

'Not much, I'm afraid, Boss,' replied Roberts with his slight Welsh lilt. 'Although I think Superintendent Geldard might be pleased with where we *have* got to.'

Greg looked up. 'And why's that?' he asked.

'We haven't found a smoking gun,' said Roberts. 'But it is looking likely that you were right, sir. It probably wasn't a mugging.'

'Ah,' said Greg. 'In that case, I'm glad you took a second look. What've you found?'

'We've been through her client appointments for that evening. All of them but one were regulars, and all but one showed up on schedule, according to her desk diary and her bank account. She seems to have ticked off each appointment as the client arrived, and payments into her bank account that evening support this. The only one not ticked off is the last client, and the last payment was for the penultimate client, so it looks like the last was a no-show.'

'Which was what her husband said,' added Greg. 'Have you spoken to that missing client?'

'Haven't been able to contact them,' replied Roberts. 'The only contact details are a mobile number and an address. The mobile number seems to be a burner phone, and the address is for a corner shop run by two very camp, and very bald, lads. They deny any knowledge of Sharon Jones and her hairdressing establishment, and I believe them. In fact, they laughed out loud when I raised the question.'

'Now let's look at Nick Atkinson,' said Ram. 'Bludgeoned with one of his own wrenches in the early morning of the twenty-third of July and left for dead. At the moment he's in the high dependency unit at the N&N. Expected to survive but there's still a question mark over how much brain damage he may have incurred. Here we have a partial number plate on CCTV that is consistent with the registration details of a car owned by a plumber named Dean Mason. Mason is a client of Atkinson's who was due to bring his work van in on the morning Atkinson was attacked. We've interviewed Mason, and he claims to have overslept that morning owing to a heavy evening's drinking the night before. He insists that the only journey he made to the Wroxham garage was in his van, arriving around nine thirty. The Yarmouth team have checked his alibi, such as it is, and it seems to hold up. He was drinking heavily in the Swan that evening, although the barman can't swear to the time he left, as they were busy.'

'The ANPR cameras picked up a couple of cars corresponding to the partial number we have,' chipped in Jill. 'But, as they were all behaving themselves, we don't have any images. I also had a quick word with the chap Mason says was going to pick him up from the garage after he dropped his van off, and he confirmed the arrangement. Said he was waiting for Mason to tell him when he was ready to be collected but, in the circs, just got a message saying not to bother, the service was off.'

'Nothing that moves us forward. Pity,' commented Greg. 'What's your feeling about Dean Mason?' He turned to Ram with a raised eyebrow.

'I'm still not one hundred per cent happy,' admitted Ram. 'I agree, we're no further forward, but the alibi has holes. And

I'm always a bit suspicious about someone with a convenient alibi, if that doesn't sound daft.'

'Still a person of interest,' agreed Greg. 'Which takes us to...'

'The arson in Martham and the Newells,' said Ram. 'Mr Newell was the local vicar and Mrs Newell is a retired catch-up reading teacher. The residence attacked is the local vicarage near the church, and the fire service are satisfied it was arson. An accelerant was used to set light to the hall, and the fire was greatly intensified by the presence of an electric-bike battery. According to Bob Fisher, the initial fire triggered a thermal runaway in the lithium battery.

'I've spoken to Mrs Newell and not only were they not charging a lithium battery in the hall, but they don't even possess one. So I agree with the fire service conclusion that this was attempted murder. And, as Mr Newell has since died directly as a result of smoke inhalation, in my view it's now a murder case.'

'Have we had Dr Paisley's report? And what is Ned's view?' asked Greg.

'No to the first. Due any moment. What I reported just now was the opinion of the doctor who treated Mr Newell. And Ned agrees with the fire service. Unfortunately, the fire was so intense it destroyed any chance of DNA or prints on the battery. They did lift some prints from the letterbox, but they are probably the postman's, as they also found smudges that looked like gloved fingers. On the other hand, they did find some prints on the garden gate. But those are a bit of a forlorn hope. If the arsonist had the sense to wear gloves at the door, he'd surely be wearing them at the gate.

'We're just beginning interviews of the couple's relatives and friends, so nothing much yet from that process.

'Chris, over to you,' added Ram.

'Sorry to say, nothing much to contribute yet,' said Chris from the screen. 'I've a mass of reports still to trawl through, and I'm very grateful for the help I've just started getting from Chas in King's Lynn. To be blunt, we're a bit swamped by all the reading and collating we need to do.'

Greg thought he detected a slight smirk on the face of DC Waterton, which may or may not have been reflected in the on-screen image of Challinor, but decided with a shrug that he was being oversensitive.

'Next steps then, Ram?' he asked.

'Subject to your comments, sir,' said Ram formally. 'In my view we should park the hit and run for the time being. Not ideal I know, but I think we have higher priorities for our scarce resource.

'On the Leakey case, the main potential lead is the source of the hemlock. DI Henning and Waterton to deal. We need a minute-by-minute scrutiny of any CCTV footage near the two locations identified. We also need to identify the owners of all cars visiting adjacent car parks in the run-up to the poisoning.

'Sharon Jones – well, this is DCI Bell's case, but I assume your team will be following up on the missing final client?'

'That's so, sir,' confirmed DI Roberts. 'Given we can't get an answer on the burner phone, assuming it is one, we're trying to triangulate its location both then and now. We're also still checking CCTV footage in the area as well as interviewing clients. Finding it wasn't a mugging has put a whole new complexion on this investigation.'

Greg nodded as Ram went on. 'Regarding Atkinson, I think we take a closer look at Mason's so-called alibi. Jill will lead on interviewing folk who were in the bar that evening, and we need another look for possible CCTV footage around where Mason lives. I know the ANPR didn't turn anything up, but we haven't yet looked at commercial CCTV or doorbell cameras. Also, have we checked the movement and location of Mason's mobile phone that morning?'

'Not yet, Boss,' said Jill, scribbling.

'Finally, the Newells. We've barely started on door-to-door interviews. Bill will coordinate some help from the Yarmouth station on that while I catch up with Dr Paisley at the Newell post-mortem. Do you have anything to add, sir?' he asked Greg.

'No, I don't think so...' was what Greg started to say. Then he had a second thought. 'There is just one thing,' he said, 'and it's a bit random, so don't spend too much time on it. But it might be worth checking if there's any link to the am-dram lot. It occurs to me that Dean Mason and Leonard Ware are both in the cast of *Kiss Me, Kate*, and the dark-car theme shows up in the hit and run and the Leakey poisoning case. And Mason has a dark car.'

Jill was scribbling busily again. 'I'll take a look at that,' she offered.

'And so will I,' said Chris from the screen.

25

30 July: locations near Norwich

Dean was irritated. He'd had two jobs in quick succession that involved replacing toilet macerators – always his least favourite job. Then a blocked drain that, it turned out, serviced both a kitchen sink and the bathroom above. The size of the grease block had to be seen to be believed, and the quantity of grey water backed up above the blockage didn't help matters. Normally, while not his favourite sort of day, he would have taken the discomforts and smells in his stride. But today he couldn't even listen to music while he worked. When he came to take his earbuds out of their case, one was missing. So an uncomfortable day became a boring one, and by the end of the afternoon he was in a thoroughly bad temper.

Sitting in his van, wheel bearings still not replaced thanks to Atkinson being *hors de combat*, he went over his memories of when he had last used them.

'I'm sure I had them before the last rehearsal,' he muttered to himself. 'Maybe I dropped them there.' He reached for his phone and flicked through his contacts. Then rang a familiar number.

'Hi Louise,' he said when the phone was answered. 'I wondered if you might have seen one of my earbuds. White with a black soft bit on the end. The last time I had them was at our last rehearsal and now one's missing.'

'No, I haven't,' replied Louise in a harassed tone. 'And I've got too much on at the moment to be worrying about them, sorry, Dean. But if you were wearing them the other day, that might explain why you kept missing your cues.'

'I did not,' exclaimed Dean indignantly. 'I took them out for the actual rehearsing, of course I did. That's how one might have gone missing. And I did *not* miss my cues. Those were dramatic pauses.'

'Well if you keep inserting dramatic pauses before you speak, you're going to keep the prompt busy,' responded Louise. 'I was always taught to pick up a cue quickly, then pause, if a pause is needed.'

Dean grunted, was tempted to retort then thought the better of it. 'Either way,' he said. 'Can you ask around and see if anyone else picked it up? I need it for work.'

'I will if I'm talking to anyone, but, frankly, I'm a bit busy and a bit upset right now,' she said. 'So don't count on it.'

'Upset? Why?' asked Dean.

'I've just heard that the lady who does my massages has died unexpectedly. What with Leonard nearly getting run over and now Marie dying, I'm looking round me for the third piece of bad luck.'

Reflecting that it had been worse luck for Leonard and the poor cow of a masseuse, Dean said, 'That must be Nick Atkinson.'

'What must be Nick Atkinson?' asked Louise, confused.

'Your number three. Nick was attacked in his garage the other morning. It's why I'm still driving round in my van with a wheel threatening to drop off. And it's why I was late to the last rehearsal – the police wanted to talk to me.'

'The police wanted to talk to you about Nick!' exclaimed Louise. 'I heard you say something about police, but I didn't know it was about Nick. How is he? And why were they talking to you? What've you been up to now, Dean?'

'Nothing!' Dean was indignant again. 'It was just that I was due to take my van in that morning to get the bearings fixed. And to answer your other question, I think Nick's in the N&N. That's all I know.'

'I must go and see him. That's terrible,' responded Louise, and rang off while Dean was still waffling on about his missing earbud.

***

Over in Wymondham, leaving Ram marshalling his troops, Greg had returned to his office and his preparation for the Warren Thorne trial the following week. He was deep in files and notes when Sue placed yet another full mug of coffee at his elbow and murmured, 'Frank Parker wants to see you.'

'Thanks, Sue,' he said. 'Send him in, and ask if he'd like a coffee, would you? And you'd better stop making me any. If I drink more caffeine today, I'm going to be twitching.'

'Will do,' she said, and held the door open for Frank, who was clutching a similar pile of files to that cluttering Greg's desk.

'How's it going?' asked Frank, sitting down at the conference table opposite Greg.

'OK, I think,' responded Greg, leaning back in his chair and stretching. 'But these chairs are damn uncomfortable to sit in for very long.'

'Why don't you work at your desk then?' asked Frank in a tone that implied he was talking to an idiot.

'Because I needed more space to spread this lot out,' replied Greg with a wave at the multiple piles of paper. 'With four different deaths in this case, even before he took it into his head to take a hatchet to Steve when we were trying to arrest him, that makes for a lot of paper.'

'Are you all across the details?' asked Frank.

'I think so. And especially Steve. Thank God it's not often one of your team gets cut down in front of you by a nutter throwing a hatchet. It's certainly not something you forget in a hurry.'

'Ah. That raises my point exactly,' said Frank. 'That's why I wanted to see you. You need to be careful how you use the term "nutter".'

'Not politically correct enough?' Greg snorted. 'Obviously I wouldn't use it in public, but personally I don't find murder politically correct, and—'

'No.' Frank interrupted his flow. 'Just that "nutter", or to use the language the opposition will employ, "a person labouring under such a defect of mind as to render him incapable of distinguishing reality from fantasy" is the defence they are planning. Don't make it easy for them by making it clear you too think he was disordered of mind.'

Greg slapped both hands down on the table in front of him, paused for a moment then leaned back in the uncomfortable chair.

'Problem is, who in their right mind leaves random cyclists dead or dying all over Norfolk?' went on Frank. 'You can see we have a hill to climb.'

'Maybe,' said Greg carefully, 'someone who knew full well what he was doing when he failed to take his medication. Someone who was medicated when he took that decision and therefore was competent and aware of what not taking the medication would involve. Someone, moreover, who can be proven to have set lethal traps all around his property, including an antique mantrap, and who threw a hatchet at a police officer in front of several more. And that's before I mention pepper spraying the poor dogs.'

'I'm just saying,' went on Frank, 'that they have a powerful argument, and they will use it. Be prepared for a verdict of manslaughter and a hospital order.'

Greg breathed heavily for a moment then asked, 'What's the risk of manslaughter and *no* hospital order? That would be the nightmare scenario from the point of view of public safety.'

'It's possible, but unlikely,' admitted Frank. 'It's up to us to ensure there is a full understanding of the risks he poses.'

***

In Hoveton, by the marina, Jim Henning was enjoying a coffee and a cheese-and-ham bap with his Broads Beat colleagues. The likelihood of refreshment was one reason he'd opted to send DC Waterton to check the car park at Hickling. The other was his burgeoning conclusion that Waterton was a prat and if he had to upset anyone, better it was the Hickling car park attendant than fellow officers in Hoveton. The following thought, that if Waterton upset Broads Beat he might find himself accidentally on purpose going for a swim, nearly persuaded him to the opposite conclusion. But the ham had swung it.

'So, what've you got?' demanded Jim through a tasty mouthful.

A burly Sergeant Heath leaned over his desk to pick up a sheaf of reports, swallowed hastily himself and responded, 'Two sightings of a car that matches the partial you told me you were already investigating – AO20D-something – close to the parking area for the Barton Broad boardwalk. One was as the car approached the parking. The other was as it drove away.'

'Interesting,' said Jim. 'And unlucky. You'd think at least one of the cameras would have got the whole plate.'

'I've got a theory about that,' replied Hathaway. 'Are you familiar with stealth sprays?'

'I've heard of them. I haven't come across them on the job yet,' responded Jim. 'But don't they hide the whole plate?'

'Deployed properly, or improperly depending on your point of view, yes,' said Hathaway, leaning back in his chair and scratching in a way that made Jim glad Chris wasn't present. *She'd have had something to say!*

'Normally, the perp sprays the whole number plate, and while it looks OK at a glance from the naked eye, the spray reflects light, including infra-red, back from flashes and makes the plate hard to read by an enforcement camera. In this case, it looks to me as though only the last two or three digits on the plate have been sprayed. Either he didn't do a very good job, or he ran out of spray.'

'Is there any other explanation for these images?' asked Jim, picking up one of the two partially blurred photos from the table.

'Not that I can think of,' said Hathaway. 'Obviously we've got other cars paying a visit to the parking area. Lots, in fact. I'll email you the full list. But this was the only number that looked interesting to me.'

'Thanks,' said Jim. 'And what about the hemlock itself? Any sign of it being disturbed?'

'Difficult to tell,' was the response. 'Could be. And it's not far from the boardwalk, so quite accessible to walkers.'

Heading for his car, Jim decided to ring DC Waterton for a catch-up. 'Got anything from Hickling reserve?' he asked.

'Just a long list of car numbers,' was the reply. 'But the visitor centre manager did say that some people park over by the Pleasure Boat Inn. I thought I'd check that out next.'

Jim was pleasantly surprised at him taking the initiative. 'Good idea,' he said. 'Send Chris your data so far, and report back to me after the inn.'

***

Back at the hospital, Ram was reflecting that a post-mortem was far more upsetting when it dealt with someone he'd met as a living, breathing person. Even though his prior contact with the Revd Newell had only been as he was wheeled into an ambulance, coughing and spluttering, seeing him laid out in the mortuary was still disturbing. He took a deep breath, heavily tainted by the Vicks on his upper lip, and tried to focus on what Dr Paisley was saying.

'I believe you want a judgement from me on whether this death was due to the fire, and to the smoke inhalation specifically, or was a disaster waiting to happen,' she was saying. 'It's a tricky one. I can tell you that I've found some indications of long-standing hypertension, but it was relatively mild. For example, the left ventricular heart muscle is slightly thickened, but not excessively so for a man of his age, and I didn't find any evidence of damage to the kidneys. On the other hand, there were clear signs of pulmonary oedema in addition to the obvious split in the aortic wall and the pooling of blood in the pericardial sac.

'In short, I concur with the emergency registrar's judgement. I agree that, on balance, this was a death caused by smoke inhalation. I've asked for analysis of the blood for epinephrine levels. Adrenaline,' she translated for him. 'But I'm pretty confident this will support my conclusion.'

'Thank you, Doctor,' said Ram.

'My report will be on your desk by the morning,' she said.

By the time Ram reached his car, his phone was buzzing. Hoping this wasn't yet another suspicious death, he was mildly relieved to see it was Ned.

'Got some good news – possibly,' said Ned. 'We've got DNA and fingerprints on the garden gate at the Newells', and the prints don't match those we found in the house or on the letterbox. So, it's just possible our arsonist made a mistake. We've also found an earbud in the garden.'

'A what?' asked Ram. 'Sorry, an ambulance went past just as you spoke and I missed it.'

'An earbud. You know, one of those things people listen to music on,' elaborated Ned. 'We haven't checked it yet, but there's a good chance that will have DNA on too.'

'Could belong to the Newells,' remarked Ram, not wanting to get too excited about a possible music-loving arsonist.

'Could do,' said Ned. 'But we haven't found any others in the house. And we found this one near the garden gate.'

**

When Greg got home at the end of a long day, he was met by a young girl making her farewells at the back door to the tune of persistent wailing from inside the house. Chris looked both harassed and relieved to see him. With a sinking feeling, Greg realised that a quiet evening in the garden was looking unlikely.

The girl with long dark hair in a ponytail, wearing a coverall over jeans and a light top, turned to greet him. 'You must be Dad,' she said brightly. 'Hi. I'm Carole.'

'I'll be back at nine thirty on Monday,' she said to Chris, 'if you want me.'

'Yes, please,' said Chris fervently. 'And thank you for today. See you Monday.'

As the girl drove off in her slightly battered Mini, Chris said to Greg, 'That's my mother's discovery. Carole Ives. Seems OK, and she has all the certificates. Worth a trial anyway. Can you see to Jamie for half an hour while I finish what I was doing. I need to give Chas a quick ring.'

Greg dropped his armful of papers on the hall table and his keys into the fruit bowl. 'Will do,' he said. 'Then let's order a takeaway. I don't feel like cooking this evening and I don't imagine you do.'

'Sound idea. Jamie's milk is in the fridge.'

Greg picked up his indignant son, and by a sniff to his bottom, a practice well known to all parents, established that his nappy appeared to be clean.

'Although no doubt that's temporary,' he said to the calming baby now distracted by movement and the promise of a bottle being removed from the fridge. 'Just let me warm this up a bit, and then we'll sort out that terrible hunger you seem to have. Then with a bit of luck, I can hand you back to your mum before it all leaks out at the other end.'

'I heard that,' said Chris through the open door. 'I'm sure it's your turn for the nappy.'

Flipping a kitchen towel over his shoulder to protect his shirt from random throwings-up, Greg sat down on the battered kitchen sofa and was instantly joined by Bobby, rubbing her head on his thigh.

'I expect you're waiting to be fed as well,' he said to the cat as they all enjoyed the temporary peace. 'And no doubt Tally too.'

Chris came into the kitchen, took in the scene and reached into the fridge for a couple of cans.

'Beer?' she asked.

'Please,' he said, propping the baby over his shoulder and patting.

'What do you fancy tonight? Chinese or Indian?'

'Don't really mind,' he said. 'Indian?'

'Sure.' Chris plucked a folded menu from the pinboard on the back of the kitchen door and held it out. 'You can give him to me now,' she said. 'With luck I can settle him down before the food arrives. Pick what you want. I'll have one of their mixed tandoori grills and a naan.'

Greg handed over the now quiet baby with slight reluctance and picked up the menu. 'Shall I telephone the order through?' he asked. 'And how's your day been?'

'Yes, please, and not bad,' she said. 'I'd say Chas and I are just about getting our heads above water on the data inputting. We can start the analysis now.'

'Was there so much?' asked Greg.

'Was there! It's like a data haystack! I'm sure there'll be something useful, but finding the needle in that heap of detail is going to take some time. How about you?'

'How about me what?' asked Greg.

'Your day?'

'Partly spent catching up with what's happening on the four suspect deaths, and mainly on going over my notes on Warren

Thorne. Frank thinks they're going to run with an insanity defence.'

'Unfit to plead?' asked Chris.

'No. Not that. It's too difficult to prove. Rather, that he was temporarily insane when he killed the cyclists and Steve.'

'It was rather a long temporary, wasn't it?' asked Chris. 'The deaths were spread over several weeks.'

'So they were, and my point exactly. My argument is he was fully in possession of his faculties when he stopped taking his medication. And it's not just that he left his victims to die. He actively chose to run over them in the first place. Oh, don't get me started on that, Chris, or we'll ruin our day off. I'll order our takeaway, then let's plan what we're going to do tomorrow. I'll need to spend Sunday doing my homework for the Crown Court on Monday.'

26

2 August: in court

Monday morning saw two of Norfolk Police's finest pacing nervously. Greg was marching up and down outside the combined courts in Norwich, repeatedly consulting his watch and wondering where the hell Frank was. DC Graham Clarke, newest recruit to the Major Crimes team, was performing similar manoeuvres outside HQ in Wymondham. Both were relieved almost simultaneously. Graham, by his watch telling him that, at last, it was time for him to report to DCI Trent. Greg, by the emergence of Frank's head from the entrance behind him.

'You must have got here early,' was Greg's greeting. 'I thought you hadn't arrived.'

'Sir Frederick likes an early start,' said Frank. 'I've been here for an hour at least. He wants to call you as first witness, so you shouldn't have too long to wait.'

'When is the case scheduled to begin?'

'Ten. Then, what with swearing in the jury and so on, it'll be a bit later before we call you. So if you want to get a coffee and go to the witness room...'

'Will do,' said Greg. 'Is Thorne here?'

'Arrived about ten minutes ago. I'm surprised you didn't see the Serco truck.'

'I've seen a couple,' admitted Greg, 'and didn't think about it, to be honest. I'm glad they took his security seriously, on the run from the hospital I mean. Where's he staying during the trial?'

'As far as I know, back at Bure prison,' replied Frank. 'Where he has additional supervision by doctors from the mental health trust, as necessary.'

Greg grunted, which Frank chose to interpret as qualified approval, and the two men parted: Greg to the police witness waiting room and Frank into court.

It was over an hour later before an usher came to fetch Greg.

'All ready for you now,' she said cheerily. 'This way. Good luck!' She opened the door and stood aside to let Greg enter the courtroom. Apart from the very few people in the public gallery, the social distancing of the jury members and the extra screens protecting against random virus transmission, it looked much the same as usual.

Greg glanced at the dock as he took his place on the witness stand. *Thank God. This time the defendant is both seated quietly and not displaying his personal equipment to the court as he did during his allocation hearing at the magistrates' court.* Of all the elements of this case that Greg felt were indelibly imprinted on his memory, Warren Thorne's loose trousers sliding down to his ankles during his attempted climb out of the dock was not the least!

'Do you wish to swear or affirm?' asked the clerk to the court, bringing Greg's attention back to the present.

'Swear,' replied Greg, and placed his hand on the Bible before him. The oath administered, Greg looked over at Sir Frederick Seymour rising to his feet.

'Detective Superintendent Geldard,' he began, 'could you please outline your role in the investigation into the deaths, between the eighteenth of August and tenth of September 2020, of Carol Hodds, Anne Cooper, Phil Saunders and Kain Smith?'

'I was the senior investigating officer in the unexplained deaths of Anne Cooper and Phil Saunders, whose bodies had been discovered in St Michael's Broad Road and the River Thurne, near Martham, respectively. As such I was in overall control of the investigation. Part of our enquiries included an assessment of data regarding missing persons in Norfolk, and particularly those who had last been seen cycling. This revealed some other cases of concern. Two other probable victims were identified and, subsequently, their bodies located. These were Carol Hodds and Kain Smith.'

Sir Frederick took Greg through each case, question by question, until the full details of each death had been expounded. It took a surprisingly long time, and Greg was beginning to wilt slightly by the time the indefatigable prosecution barrister paused and turned to the jury.

'You will hear expert evidence from specialist witnesses on the results of the post-mortems and other forensic detail,' he said. 'While we have Superintendent Geldard on the stand, I'm now going to focus on—'

The judge stirred in his seat and interrupted. 'The jury and indeed Superintendent Geldard might benefit from a brief break,' he said. 'I suggest we adjourn for some lunch.'

'All rise,' said the clerk as the judge left the bench and headed for the back room.

Frank joined Greg outside the courtroom. 'I've organised sandwiches in my room,' he said. 'So far, so good.'

They were joined by Sir Frederick, looking rather less imposing without his wig. 'Lead me to them,' he remarked jovially to Frank. 'My stomach thinks my throat's been cut.'

'Didn't you get breakfast at the Maids Head?' asked Frank, surprised.

'God no,' said Sir Frederick. 'Hotel breakfasts are the devil if you're trying to lose weight. And Lady Seymour is convinced I'll die of Covid if I don't lose some avoirdupois. At least, that's the excuse she's using.'

They'd reached the room Frank was using as an office at the court, and all of them were pleased to see several clingfilm-covered plates of sandwiches and sausage rolls. Sir Frederick didn't wait to be asked. He ripped the film off the nearest plate and seized a handful of sandwiches. One was already in his mouth before Frank had managed to ask if he wanted coffee. The reply was somewhat masked by mastication, and Frank had to take a guess at its import.

Greg joined Frank at the side table with the insulated jugs of coffee and gave him a sideways glance, eyebrow raised. *This is a changed Sir Frederick.*

'New wife,' muttered Frank in an undertone. 'Much younger.' And gave Greg a knowing look.

They rejoined Sir Frederick at the table and handed round the mugs of coffee.

'I was about to ask about the night DC Hall was killed,' said the barrister. 'Perhaps it's as well you have a little while to prepare yourself. It must have been a gruelling experience.'

'Not good,' agreed Greg. 'I'm mainly concerned now to make sure justice is done for Steve and Thorne's other victims.'

'That's what we're all here for,' said Sir Frederick. 'I believe Frank has warned you that the cross-examination's likely to focus on police tactics and specifically whether Thorne's reaction was reasonable in all the circumstances of the case.'

'He has,' said Greg.

The barrister looked at him over his glasses. 'If you keep your replies in court similarly short and to the point, as indeed you have so far, we should do well,' he remarked. 'Don't forget – surplus words turn septic.'

***

Refreshed and renewed, Greg was back on the stand facing more questions.

'So, Detective Superintendent Geldard,' began Sir Frederick. 'We reach the evening of the sixteenth of September 2020. You have already outlined the evidence that led to you seeking a search warrant for the home of the defendant. Tell me in your own words, what happened when you arrived there?'

Wondering, as many a witness had before him, whose words he would use if not his own, Greg embarked on the story of that evening. 'We arrived at the property at around 7pm,' he began and was almost immediately interrupted.

'Perhaps you could describe the environment for the benefit of the jury?' prompted Sir Frederick.

'Of course,' responded Greg. 'The defendant, Warren Thorne, lives in a cottage on the edge of the woods near Ormesby Broad. The cottage is fronted by a rough yard and there are several outbuildings housing equipment for his timber and firewood business. At that time there was also a large pile of cut firewood. The yard backs directly on to the woodland with no fence or hedge in between.'

'We have a diagram which you might find useful. The usher is bringing you copies,' Sir Frederick said to the jury, adding, 'It's Number Seven in your bundle, My Lord.' The judge nodded his thanks, and the jury studied their maps earnestly. 'Now, Superintendent Geldard,' said Sir Frederick, inviting him to continue.

'Thank you, sir,' said Greg. 'Given the area we had to cover, we had two search teams of three men each, backed up by our scenes of crime experts. We began by knocking on the door of the cottage and announcing our intention to execute our search warrant, but got no answer. While two officers searched the cottage for Mr Thorne, others searched the grounds. We did not find him, but we did spot someone running into the wood who did not stop when challenged. DC Hall followed but was brought down by a prepared tripwire, and the runner got away. At almost the same moment, one of the other officers uncovered from the woodpile several cloned vehicle-registration plates that were relevant to our enquiry. A further search uncovered two bicycles, which on examination proved to belong to two of the cycle-killer's victims.'

'I think we're getting ahead of ourselves a bit,' remarked counsel. 'What did you do after the mysterious runner disappeared into the woods?'

'Given the terrain and the time of night, I sent for dog search teams and the police helicopter. The helicopter arrived first, but the warmth of the night made it difficult for the crew to distinguish between heat signatures. The dogs, however, got on to a trail quickly.'

Even with the barrister's interruptions and prompts, it seemed to Greg that he reached the difficult part of his evidence remarkably quickly.

'Now we come to the final part of the chase,' prompted Sir Frederick.

'The helicopter identified a heat signature in the trees near the Broad,' reported Greg. 'They advised that he was unlikely to be able to move further in that direction and that we were spread across his line of retreat. The first of the police dogs was released and found his target, but was pepper-sprayed by the defendant. As the dog fell back, and before the second dog could be released, PC Hall ran towards the defendant. I saw the defendant throw something which hit PC Hall, who fell to the ground.

'The second dog brought down the defendant just as I reached PC Hall.' Greg paused to steady himself, then continued as unemotionally as he could manage. 'I found that the projectile I had seen was a hand axe. It hit PC Hall in the joint between his neck and shoulder and severed his carotid artery. He bled out under my hands.'

The barrister left the court silent for a moment, while the jury took in the enormity of what Greg was saying, then he continued, 'and you clearly saw the defendant throw the axe.'

'I did,' affirmed Greg.

***

It was mid-afternoon by the time Sir Frederick had finished with Greg and it was the opposition's turn. With the comforting thought that it could only be for a few hours, then the court would rise for the evening, Greg faced the defence barrister.

'Good afternoon, Superintendent Geldard,' he began. 'I suppose I should first congratulate you on your promotion.'

Greg inclined his head but said nothing.

'Was it as a result of you arresting my client?' asked the weasel-faced, middle-aged man in the slightly tatty wig and black gown turning green with age. Greg took his time replying and, as he'd hoped, the judge intervened.

'Is this relevant, Mr Fordyce?' asked His Lordship. 'If not, perhaps you could move on. It's already getting late.'

'As Your Lordship pleases,' muttered Fordyce. 'Let's abandon the civilities and get on then, Superintendent Geldard.

'You have explained that you were accompanied by two teams of officers plus forensic science experts when you executed your search warrant. So, you turn up mob-handed and unexpectedly at my client's home, and you're surprised he is startled and runs away.'

'We clearly announced ourselves as police,' asserted Greg without waiting for the question.

Fordyce disregarded the response and went on. 'What about the dogs and the helicopter? I suggest you went in mob-handed and were still surprised that my client ran away.'

'The additional search teams were only called in after Mr Thorne ran,' responded Greg.

'And do you consider that was a proportionate response to a single man running away on foot? A man, moreover, whom you knew to suffer mental health challenges. A man who could be described as vulnerable.'

'I thought it a proportionate response to the need to track and apprehend a suspected murderer through dark woods at night,' replied Greg. 'The safest and the most effective response.'

'Safe for whom?' asked Fordyce. 'Not for the vulnerable man running away in a panic. Nor for the officer who died as a result.'

Greg was silent while he considered and discarded several possible replies.

'Don't you have an answer for me, Superintendent Geldard?'

'I'm not sure what the question was,' said Greg. 'Perhaps you'd like to repeat it?'

'All right,' responded Fordyce. 'Here's a clear question. What justification did you have for sending dogs after my client?'

'Trained police dogs are demonstrably the safest means of tracking and detaining a fleeing person under many circumstances, and definitely so in a dark wood at night when the person fleeing is an experienced woodsman and suspected killer. By then, following the preliminary search of his house, we also had good reason to believe that he had been diagnosed with a psychosis and to suspect he had not been taking his prescribed medication. This increased the risks he posed, both to himself and others, rather than lessened them.'

'So you did know he had mental health difficulties,' announced Fordyce in a tone of triumph.

Greg caught Frank's eye for a moment, but his expression was unreadable.

'We knew that he had medication in his home that suggested both a mental health condition and that he had not been taking it,' responded Greg cautiously. 'And we were already aware that he had been a patient of the mental health trust.'

'Yet you still went in mob-handed to arrest a vulnerable mental health patient,' declared Fordyce. 'What about your duty of care to my client? That's a question, Superintendent Geldard, in case it's not clear to you.'

'I have a duty of care to public safety as well as to your client,' replied Greg. 'In this case, use of the dog teams meant that we were able to apprehend your client without further attacks on the general public and with only minor injuries to himself.'

'But incurred the death of a serving police officer,' remarked Fordyce. 'Whose failure was that?'

Greg paused, unable to find the right reply.

'We're waiting,' said Fordyce.

'It was Mr Thorne who threw the hatchet which delivered the fatal injury,' said Greg at last. 'I witnessed him do it and so did several other officers.'

'As we have already heard,' agreed Fordyce. 'But who was responsible for the hatchet being thrown? The man who threw it, or the man who terrified a vulnerable patient with a dog-chase across a wood at night?'

Greg opened his mouth but was rescued by Sir Frederick. 'My Lord,' he complained. 'I object to that question. My learned friend is asking the witness to speculate about the defendant's state of mind.'

'I agree,' said the judge. 'Move on, Mr Fordyce.'

'As you wish, My Lord,' responded Fordyce. 'You have already stated that the night was dark, as justification for the hunt by dogs,' he said. 'If that was the case, how could you possibly see my client throw anything, least of all a specific hand axe?'

'By that stage of the chase,' responded Greg, 'the defendant had been located by the helicopter and was clearly lit by their searchlight. I had no difficulty whatsoever in seeing him throw something which hit PC Hall, and subsequently in identifying that something as the axe which was embedded in the wound on PC Hall's neck. Moreover,' he added, before Fordyce could interrupt him, 'the axe had the defendant's fingerprints on it.'

'How far away from the defendant were you when you witnessed this event, lit only by a helicopter searchlight?' asked Fordyce, fighting a rearguard action.

Greg paused for a moment. 'Roughly as far as the defendant is from the bench now,' he said.

As though at a tennis match, the jury turned to look at the dock, and then at the judge, clearly assessing the space.

27

Same day: new blood

Over in Wymondham, Ram was getting to know his latest detective constable. 'Paramedic to police isn't a common career route,' he was saying. 'But I do know of a precedent.'

'You do, sir?' responded Graham, looking interested. He was a young man still, notwithstanding his prior career. *Thirty-eight*, Ram noted from the details in front of him. He was tall and well built, with dark hair receding slightly and a dark beard, full but neatly trimmed.

'Yes. An ex-district nurse, ex-police, now first responder,' he said. 'Remind me to introduce you to Ben Asheton. What brings you to Norfolk?' he asked.

'Opportunity and family,' said Graham with an engaging smile. 'It's the first opportunity for a move to detective constable that I've spotted, and also, my old dad lives in Norfolk. Near Gorleston. By the way, please do call me Gray. Everyone does.'

'If you've made it on your first attempt, you have done well,' replied Ram, remembering the three applications he'd had to make before he got on the ladder. 'OK. I'll introduce you to the rest of the team – those that are here. Then you'll need to get stuck in straightaway. We have what you might call a workload crisis at the moment, so you'll have to learn on the job.'

He led the way down the corridor to the incident room.

'Jill, here's our new recruit,' he said as he pushed the door open. 'DS Jill Hayes, meet DC Gray Clarke. Show him around and get him started. We've no time to waste.'

He left Gray smiling slightly nervously under the close scrutiny of DS Hayes and the two men who'd turned round from their computer screens to look at him.

'Welcome, Gray,' said Jill. 'Sling your stuff here, and meet DC Bill Street. He'll show you the ropes.'

28

Analyses

Chris came off her call to Chas fired up and raring to go. It was, therefore, doubly frustrating to be unable to contact either Greg or Ram. Greg's silence wasn't surprising. He was, after all, probably in court. She left a message and tried Ram. When he failed to pick up too, she tutted loudly enough to startle Carol, currently entertaining Jamie on his play mat, and tried Jim. All she got there was an Ansaphone message to say he was on leave that day and to text him if urgent. She briefly considered a text but decided that would be unfair. Even more briefly considered Helena Bell. Then rang Jill.

'I've got an update for you,' she said.

'Go ahead,' said Jill. 'I'm just showing our new DC his way around and introducing him to folk. DI Chris Mathews, meet DC Gray Clarke.' She held the phone out towards Graham.

'Delighted you've arrived,' said Chris's disembodied voice. 'We seriously need more people. Welcome.'

'He's another Ben Asheton,' added Jill, recovering the phone. 'Ex paramedic.'

'That's going to come in handy,' said Chris.

'I really must meet this Ben, remarked Gray. 'Everybody mentions him.'

'It's only a matter of time,' said Jill. 'But you said you had an update, Chris?'

'Yes. Chas and I haven't finished analysing all the data you lot have dumped on us recently, but we did notice that a partial number plate recorded visiting a car park near Barton Broad is similar to one you logged as potentially involved in the poisoning incident in North Walsham—'

'The same as Dean Mason's car?' interrupted Jill.

'The same.'

'That's very interesting. We're already looking at him again, but for a different reason.'

'Oh. What?'

'When we had him in the station for his last interview, he agreed to DNA testing. It's come up as a match for a sample on an earbud found near the arson attack in Martham. Ned reported the result only half an hour ago and, as Greg is in court and Ram busy, I thought I'd better follow it up.'

'But what connection does he have with either of those victims?' asked Chris.

'None, as far as I know. That's something we're looking into. But I think we need to interview him again.'

Chris hesitated, not wishing to undermine Jill, then said with some care, 'I think Ram would want to know. Where is he?'

'On his way to King's Lynn to follow up on the Sharon Jones stabbing. I believe he's planning to review the case with DCI Bell.'

'Right,' said Chris. 'I need to have a chat with him too. I'll update him, shall I?'

'Yes, thanks,' said Jill, and rang off.

Chris was on the phone to Ram immediately, and as luck would have it, managed to catch him just as he entered a rare area of decent signal.

'Hi, Boss,' she said. 'There's an update on Dean Mason that I think you'll want to know about. His DNA has been found on an earbud that Ned's team picked up near the rectory gate in Martham. And we've got a partial number plate at Barton Broad that matches the partial from outside the Leakey place.'

'By the rectory, you mean the site of the arson attack?' asked Ram. 'Very interesting.'

'And now two partials that match his car registration,' repeated Chris. 'Jill's planning on another chat with Mason. I gather she tried to contact you about the DNA report but couldn't get through. And Greg, of course, is in court.'

'No signal,' said Ram briefly. 'The fact that they're partials is frustrating, but the evidence is mounting that Mason is tied in to these attacks somehow. If we count him being a customer of Atkinson, that makes at least three: Atkinson, the Newells and Leakey. Thanks for letting me know, Chris. I'll tell Jill to bring him in, and we'll carry out an interview under caution at the station. The Jones case will have to wait for another day.'

Ram rang off, glanced around him and took the opportunity, at the end of a short section of dual carriageway, to perform a U-turn and head back towards Norwich. Then he rang Jill.

'Hi, Jill. Have you reached Mason yet?'

'Not at home, Boss,' she replied. 'His Ansaphone says he's on a callout. I'm about to try ringing him.'

'Don't spook him,' warned Ram. 'We don't want him to make a run for it. I want him brought in for an interview under caution. See if you can narrow down his location from his phone signal and then spot his van.'

'Do we arrest him if he won't come?' asked Jill.

Ram hesitated. 'Not yet,' he said finally. 'I don't think what we have is enough to count as reasonable suspicion. Just do your best to bring him in, and if he flat out refuses, let me know. I'm on my way back.'

Back in the cottage on the banks of the Bure, Chris was on a Zoom call to Chas.

'What's the excitement about?' she asked the young man almost dancing up and down in front of the camera.

'I think I've got something interesting,' he said, took a deep breath to steady himself and sat down at his desk. The wall behind him held untidy bookshelves crammed with an eclectic selection of fantasy, science fiction and WW2 history books. A battered, stuffed koala acted as bookend on one shelf, and what looked like a marble horse's head balanced it at the other. Chris dragged her attention back from the bookcase.

'You already know that we have partials that could fit Mason's car registration at the Leakey property and near Barton Broad. Plus, he's a customer of Nick Atkinson and his DNA is on an earbud found near the arson attack.'

'Yes, I know that,' said Chris patiently. 'But apart from Atkinson, we've found nothing that definitively links Mason to any of the other cases. Nothing to show he even knows them. And the partial we *do* have includes the standard letters for Norfolk, so there must be thousands of cars with those letters. Ram's hoping he'll come in voluntarily for an interview, but if he refuses, we don't have enough for an arrest – even with the DNA.'

'What if we can show a link between all the cases?' demanded Chas.

'A link with Dean?' asked Chris. 'There isn't one. I've looked, believe me.'

'Not Dean as such,' responded Chas. 'But there is a link between the cases. At least, I think so.'

'Go on then,' urged Chris, catching his excitement.

'It's Louise Lacon: the woman in *Kiss Me, Kate*. Marie Leakey was her masseuse, and Nick Atkinson was an old friend. She introduced him to Mason. The Revd Newell was her vicar. And even the possible hit-and-run victim, Leonard Ware, is her co-star. And today, I've just been through the data that's been submitted from the King's Lynn investigation into the Sharon Jones stabbing, and Louise is in her customer database. To be honest, that's what made me go and take a long hard look at all the other reports.'

There was a long pause while Chris thought about it. 'You're right. That is interesting. But, the thing is, Norfolk can feel a small place sometimes. It could be a coincidence. And Louise had an alibi for the hit and run. She was in the rehearsal at the time.'

'Worth asking some questions, surely?' Chas wasn't deflated yet. 'Once or twice might be a coincidence, but five times? And she knows Mason too. Perhaps Mason is an accomplice?'

'It's definitely worth investigation,' said Chris, picking up her phone. 'I'll have another chat with Ram.'

'What about the big boss?' asked Chas.

'He's in court. I'll leave a message and catch up with him later.'

29

Questions and answers

In fact, it proved surprisingly easy to locate Dean Mason and Louise Lacon.

After much scrutiny of phone signals and much driving around the hinterland of Great Yarmouth and Caister – always, it seemed, two streets behind the plumber – all they had to do was locate the evening's rehearsal for *Kiss Me, Kate.*

Ram and his team gathered in the road between the Norwich Theatre Royal and the Garage rehearsal space. He glanced round the assembled company, mentally counting heads. A bus came along behind them and those who had spilled off the pavement hastily moved out of its way.

'Bill, you take Gray and go round to the back. I'm not expecting anyone to do a runner, but better safe than sorry. Jill, you come with me. Challinor – Ian, isn't it? – you find Mason's car and take a look over it. Check the plates for any stealth spray and look for any damage that might be attributable to hitting Leonard Ware. OK. Let's go.'

Ram waited a moment or two to give Bill and Gray time to get round to the back, then led the way into the Garage. For a moment he was puzzled by the number of children moving around, then realised from conversations around him that a children's dance class had just finished.

'I was looking for the Northfolk,' he said to a man pushing a mop-and-bucket combo into the room the children were leaving.

'In the main hall,' he said, pointing, and got back to his mopping.

Ram and Jill followed the pointing finger to a door which, when they pushed it open, they found led into the lower level of a raked auditorium. They incurred a glare from a man sitting halfway up from the stage and a crisp, 'Not in here. We're rehearsing.'

Up on the stage, two men with mops, not dissimilar to the one Ram had asked for directions, paused their manoeuvres and stopped singing. Over at the piano in the corner, a patient-looking woman carried on for a few bars before grinding to a halt.

'I said, no interruptions,' insisted the man with a clipboard. 'You two, take it from the top again, and a bit more energy this time. Thanks, Maggie,' he said to the pianist, who had seized the opportunity to stuff a handful of wine gums into her face.

'OK, Aubrey,' she said indistinctly, and started playing the introduction again.

Ram was looking over the people in the hall. 'He's not here,' he muttered to Jill, under cover of the two men with buckets singing in execrable Brooklyn accents.

Leaving Jill by the door, he walked up the steps to the man he took to be Aubrey and held out his warrant card. 'I need to see Dean Mason,' he said quietly.

Aubrey craned to see the stage past Ram, and muttered, 'He's not here. Please get out of my way. We haven't much time left before first night.'

'I can see he's not here,' persisted Ram rather louder. 'Are you expecting him?'

'He'll be backstage or in the space we're using as a green room. Good God, what was that?' demanded Aubrey.

Ram looked at him, startled, then turned to look at the stage. The pianist stopped again, and the two men with mops were frozen into stillness.

'Just a bit of business,' faltered one of them.

'Well you can cut that for a start,' said Aubrey, getting to his feet. 'I know I said double-entendres, but that was obscene. We don't want an X rating!'

'The words are pretty obscene, if you read them,' the man defended himself.

'I don't care. Don't do that!' said Aubrey firmly.

'Dean Mason?' Ram reminded him, beginning to feel he was trapped in a nightmare farce.

'I told you, in the green room,' snapped Aubrey, and waved them back the way they'd come.

Ram and Jill retreated. The corridor was now devoid of kids, but the man with the mop reappeared. The *real* man with a *real* mop this time, Ram was pleased to note.

'What other room are they—' he started to ask.

'In there,' said Mop Man pointing to a different door, and Jill led the way in.

This space looked much more like a classroom, with tables and chairs. Ram immediately spotted Dean Mason in one corner, lounging as much as was possible in a hard chair and drinking from a can of Pepsi. He was talking to two women with their backs to him. As he moved round the room, Ram realised one might well be Louise Lacon. At least, judging by age and general appearance.

'That's Louise,' Jill confirmed quietly in his ear. He nodded to indicate he'd heard and led the way over.

'Mr Mason,' he said, 'we'd like a word with you, please. Ms Louise Lacon? We'd like a chat with you too. Perhaps you'd both like to come with us to the station.'

'What! Again?' exclaimed Dean before Louise could react. 'Are you arresting me? Because I'm not coming to the station any other way. In case you haven't noticed, I'm at a rehearsal. We're both at a rehearsal' – he indicated Louise – 'and we're needed. So, unless you've got an arrest warrant, shove off.'

Ram was left with a distinct feeling that Dean had moderated his instructions for the sensibilities of present company. His voice, however, had risen, and everyone else in the room was now staring at them.

'Problem, Louise?' asked a resonant voice from behind Ram.

He turned to see that an older, dignified man had come up behind him unnoticed.

'This is Mr Leonard Ware,' said Jill. 'Good evening, Mr Ware. We met at the hospital. I'm DS Jill Hayes.'

'I remember you, yes,' said Leonard. 'But why are you interrupting our rehearsal now?'

'We need a few words with Mr Mason and Ms Lacon,' said Ram firmly. 'At the station would be most convenient, but if that's a problem and there's a quiet room we can use, we can do it here.'

'That would be best,' agreed Leonard. 'That way, you can pursue your, no doubt very important, investigation without completely disrupting our evening.' He nodded at Louise and glared at Dean. 'I'm sure we *all* wish to cooperate,' he said pointedly. 'And I'm sure we can find somewhere suitable.'

'Why not use the office?' suggested Myrtle. By this time, the entire company not currently onstage were hanging on every word. 'It'll be empty at this time of night.'

'Good idea,' approved Leonard. 'Are you happy with that, Chief Inspector?'

'It sounds a very good solution,' responded Ram with some relief. 'Perhaps you'd show me the way. Jill, send Gray to wait here, if the company have no objections. You come with me.' There were a few murmurs that Ram took to be agreement, and he gave Jill a long look. She nodded, indicating she understood that Gray was to keep an eye on things in general and Louise Lacon in particular.

Ram followed Leonard Ware back into the corridor, where he pointed at a small office near the front of the building. After a slightly mutinous hesitation, Dean Mason followed them. A few moments later Jill joined them and the three settled themselves around the cramped desk, Jill and Ram on one side, Dean facing them.

Ram took out his phone and placed it in the centre of the desk, setting it to record. He noticed in passing that it had only thirty per cent battery left and made a mental note that he needed to keep the interview short.

'Mr Mason, thank you for being willing to talk to us—' he began, but was immediately interrupted.

'Do I need a solicitor?' demanded Dean. 'This is the second ... no, *third* time you've wanted to talk to me. Am I under arrest?'

'You're not under arrest at this time, no,' replied Ram. 'And if you want a solicitor, then that is of course your right. But it won't help us to keep this chat short and sweet, which I believe you wanted. It's up to you.'

Dean hesitated, drumming his fingers on the desk between them. 'Ask your questions then,' he said. 'But I reserve the right to stop answering at any time, if I feel I need a solicitor.'

'Of course,' responded Ram. 'But so we can have your replies on the record, I need to caution you that you do not have to say anything. But it may harm your defence if you do not mention when questioned something which you later rely on in court. Anything you do say may be given in evidence.'

There was a pause while Dean clearly reconsidered his options. Then he nodded. 'OK, I've nothing to hide. What do you want to know?' he asked.

'Let's start with some simple questions,' said Ram. 'We'd like to establish where you were on a few dates this month. Let's start with the evening of the nineteenth of July.'

Dean relaxed, visibly, which was of course Ram's intention.

'You know where I was,' he responded, leaning back in his chair. 'I was here, rehearsing.'

'To be more precise, where exactly were you when your fellow thespian Mr Ware was struck by a car outside the theatre?'

'Here,' repeated Dean. 'In fact, I think I was onstage at the time. I was certainly onstage when Pop rushed in to say there'd been an accident. Just ask Josie. She was onstage with me. Or ask Aubrey and Louise. They were watching, to name but two.'

'What about the following evening?' went on Ram. 'Tuesday the twentieth of July. Where were you that day? After, say, 6pm.'

'Well it wouldn't have been a rehearsal day, not two days running,' replied Dean. 'So I guess I was at home or down the local. Probably at home.'

'Would anyone be able to vouch for that?' asked Ram.

'Doubt it,' said Dean. 'I live alone.'

'Friday the twenty-third of July? We know where you were the following morning, because you showed up at Nick Atkinson's garage. Late for your appointment, apparently. But what about the evening before?'

'Same answer. Home or the local,' responded Dean.

'What about Saturday the twenty-fourth of July?' asked Ram.

'Why don't you just ask me what I was doing all week and be done with it?' said Dean.

'Just the Saturday will do for now,' said Ram.

'Down the local, without a doubt,' said Dean. 'The football league hasn't got going yet, so a few pints and a good laugh down the local would have been it.'

'You don't seem to have a very exciting social life,' interjected Jill. 'Except for the Northfolk rehearsals, you seem to be either home alone or down the pub. No girlfriend?'

'Not at the moment – if it's any business of yours,' responded Dean with a scowl. Jill made a note, slightly ostentatiously, and Dean picked up on it. 'Why are you asking about how I spend my evenings?' he demanded. 'I doubt I'm very different from most people. After Covid, it's taken a bit of time to get back to normal. Especially if you spent the lockdowns on your own.'

Ram acknowledged the point was fair. 'So it would be true to say that the theatre and the rehearsals are important to you?' he asked.

'They're a good evening out,' Dean agreed. 'The performances are more fun, of course. Especially for a principal like me. But after lockdowns, even the rehearsals have their moments.'

'How did you get into it?' asked Jill. 'I don't mean to be rude, but I guess you don't see many of your fellow plumbers in the casts of musicals?'

'You mean, it's usually the more intellectual types?' asked Dean with a laugh that sounded genuine. 'You're probably right. You'd *definitely* be right if you were talking plays and such. But musical theatre's a bit different.'

'How did you get into it?' Jill pursued her point. Ram wondered where she was going with this line of questioning but opted to let her run with it.

'A girlfriend got me involved. She heard me singing karaoke in a pub and suggested I come along to a rehearsal and give it a try. I was pretty into her at the time, so I was flattered and said I'd give it a whirl. Of course, I found out later that they were desperate for men. All theatre companies are. But by then I was enjoying myself. I'd made it from the chorus to principal, and I was having fun.'

'Who was it introduced you to musicals?' asked Jill. 'Do you still see her?'

'It was Louise Lacon,' admitted Dean. 'We're not an item any more. Haven't been for ages, but we're still friends.'

Jill shot a covert look at Ram, and subsided, well content.

'One final date,' said Ram. 'Wednesday the twenty-eighth. Where were you then?'

'Definitely at home,' said Dean.

'And still no one to corroborate your whereabouts?'

'No. Sorry. You'll have to take my word for it,' said Dean.

'Thank you, that'll be all for now,' said Ram, noticing that his phone battery was on its last legs. 'Can you send Louise Lacon in next?'

Dean stood up and lounged out of the office with an elaborate farewell wave involving a non-existent peaked cap. As the door closed behind him, Ram looked at Jill.

'Well done establishing the link to Louise Lacon,' he said. 'We'll follow that up now. Have you any phone battery? Mine's run out.'

Jill picked her phone up to check. 'Over seventy per cent,' she reported. 'Should be OK.' And put it on the table in front of her. The door opened to reveal not just Louise but also Leonard Ware.

'I told her she should have a solicitor present,' he said in a pompous tone. 'But as she hasn't got one, I volunteered to accompany her.'

'I'm afraid I can't allow that,' replied Ram, rising in order to look Mr Ware in the face. 'If Ms Lacon wants a solicitor, then that's fine and we'll head off to the station. Otherwise...'

He left the other options dangling.

'There. I told you, Leonard,' said Louise. 'I'll be fine. You go and do your scene with the others. I'll be back asap.' She gave him a little push towards the door, and he went off, still muttering.

'Sorry,' she said. 'He fusses. I realise it's not necessary. I assume this is about Leonard's hit and run? I'm just glad you're taking it seriously. How can I help?' She sat herself down at the table, rearranged her hair and looked up with a smile. 'What was it you wanted to know?'

Ram shuffled the papers on his desk for a moment, hesitating between asking her about her links to the victims and her movements. He decided to keep his powder dry on the former, for the moment, and went through the key dates, one by one. By the end his notes read:

- watching Dean and Josie onstage while waiting for her next scene

- washing her hair

- staying home feeling ill with what she feared might be Covid. 'It wasn't,' she had assured them.

- the same

'Could anyone vouch for your whereabouts on the twentieth, twenty-third and twenty-fourth?' asked Ram.

'Well, I rang a friend to say that I wouldn't be coming to see them on the evening of the twenty-third,' said Louise. 'But no, apart from that I was home alone. That's rather the point isn't it, if you think you've got Covid?'

Ram nodded noncommittally. 'Tell me about Marie Leakey,' he said.

Louise looked surprised. 'Marie? Marie was my masseuse, and a very good one too,' she said. 'I'm really going to miss her. No one has ever looked after my bad back like she did. Admittedly,' she went on chattily, 'it often felt as though she'd unscrewed my arms and was going to hand them to me in a basket at the end. And the way she ground her elbow into your back muscles had to be felt to be believed. For a small woman, she could really get into the knots. As I said, I'm going to miss her. I haven't spoken to the hotel yet about booking anyone else. They said they'd let me know when the funeral was so I could pay my respects, but I haven't heard anything yet. Why are you asking me about Marie?' she said suddenly.

Ram didn't answer. 'Were you on friendly terms with Marie?' he asked. 'I mean, personally. Did you ever visit her at home?'

'No,' replied Louise, looking puzzled. 'I don't even know where she lives. Of course we were friendly, but not bosom pals, if you know what I mean. I'd see her once or twice a month for a massage, but always at the hotel where she worked.'

'Let's turn to Nick Atkinson,' said Ram in a sudden switch of topic that left even Jill with clashing mental gears. 'Tell me about your relationship with Nick Atkinson.'

'We don't have a relationship as such,' responded Louise, slightly indignantly. 'Not if you mean what I think you mean. We've known each other since we were children. We used to live next door when we were at school, and we've been good friends ever since. But never anything like a *relationship*.' She put the word in air quotes. 'I'd as soon have that sort of *relationship*' – she did it again – 'with my brother – if I

189

had one. These days I generally only see him when there's something wrong with my car. Which unfortunately is more often than I'd like. I mean,' she added, suddenly flustered, 'that my car is a bit elderly and keeps breaking down, not that I don't want to see Nick. He's done miracles, keeping it going long past its use-by date.'

'What about Sharon Jones?' asked Ram.

'Sh-Sharon...?' Louise stammered. 'You mean Sharon my hairdresser? What about Sharon? What is this? A tour of all the tradespeople in my life? Are you going to finish up with my plumber, my carpenter, my window cleaner, my—'

'Your vicar?' asked Ram.

'My vicar?' asked Louise, with all the intonation of Lady Bracknell asking about a handbag. 'I know the poor man has had a fire at his house. I read it in the EDP, but...'

'Did you know that Sharon Jones was stabbed to death on the night of the twenty-fourth of July?' asked Ram.

Louise's mouth fell open in a very inelegant gape. 'I, no. No, I didn't. Stabbed? Killed?'

Ram reminded himself that Louise Lacon was an actress. Even so, she was giving a very realistic impression of someone who hadn't known about Sharon Jones's death.

'And Mr Newell died in hospital on the twenty eighth,' he went on. 'Leonard Ware, Marie Leakey, Nick Atkinson, Sharon Jones, the Revd Newell – it seems like being your friend isn't good for anyone's health.'

Louise went white and clutched the edge of the desk in her fingers. 'You mean,' she faltered, 'they're all dead or hurt? And you think it's something to do with me?'

'Well isn't it?' demanded Ram. 'You seem to be the common thread. Have they all upset you, Louise? What did you have against them?'

'Nothing. No, it must be something else. This is mad,' she declared with conviction. 'You're mad. That's it. Leonard was right after all.' She stood up. 'I'm not talking to you any more. Not without a solicitor.' And she stalked out of the room.

Ram and Jill looked at each other.

'She didn't seem to know about Sharon,' said Jill cautiously.

'But she is an actress.' Ram scratched his head. 'I don't know what to think. We don't have enough for an arrest yet. Let's see what we can find out about her movements over the relevant couple of weeks. Get her phone usage details and get someone checking ANPR for her car registration. And let's take another look at any and all CCTV relevant to all four cases. Time for some hard work, Jill.

'Then I think we'll have Ms Lacon back, with her solicitor, for an interview under caution at the station. We never even got as far as her relationship with Mason.'

30

Out of court

Greg was back in the car park by the pub, breathing slightly fresher air with a long sigh of relief, when Chris's message caught up with him.

'Well that *is* very interesting,' he said to himself, and rang her back.

'How'd it go?' demanded Chris. 'Have you done for the day? Do you think the jury are with you? I hope Thorne wasn't waving his willy around again.' She took a breath and Greg seized his chance to get a word in.

'As you'd expect; yes; I don't know, and no he didn't,' replied Greg. 'Was that the lot? Look, before you spout off another twenty questions, I'm interested in your data on Louise Lacon. It's certainly a compelling link. Is Ram following it up?'

'I believe he's trying to get hold of her asap.'

'I'll leave it to him for now,' responded Greg. 'I'm whacked. It takes it out of you, dealing with the inquisition all day.'

'Seriously, how did it go?' asked Chris again.

'Sir F was fine. He asked all the questions I thought he would. In fact, the defence bloke also asked what I thought he would, but not in such a friendly way.'

'Did they ask how much you could see? In the dark, that is. And about bullying the defendant?' asked Chris.

'Yes to both,' said Greg, getting into his car. 'As I said – very predictable. And of course, they've yet to get into the detail about the mantrap we found and so on. There are a lot of other witnesses to hear yet, including the specialists.'

'Did you keep your temper?' asked Chris, metaphorically crossing her fingers.

'Mostly,' said Greg, turning to check the exit from the car park was clear. 'I did say something sarky about *was there a question* but, generally speaking, I didn't get smart with him. Anyway, let's leave that for now. There's nothing more I can do. It's up to Sir Frederick and Frank now. Tell me some more about the Louise link. Is it her? Or is it Dean Mason?'

'Just what Ram's trying to figure out,' responded Chris.

31

Morning of 3 August

Greg was in the office bright and early, and keen to catch up. He found Ram in the incident room as he'd expected.

'Morning, Ram, morning all,' he said generally, to a room that seemed to have more people in it than usual. He glanced round, noting the few absentees were mainly from the King's Lynn contingent, Helena Bell and Colin Waterton among them. And Jim of course, currently taking his turn in front of the firing squad – aka the Norwich Crown Court.

'What progress?' he asked Ram. 'I'm up to date on the Louise Lacon link, but that's it.'

'Not much else to report except a lot of dead ends,' responded Ram.

'We're back to what you call good old-fashioned detection,' added Jill.

Ram nodded. 'And so far, we haven't found anything new. To sum up, all the victims of the recent spate of murders and attempted murders have links to Louise Lacon: her masseuse, her car mechanic, hairdresser and vicar. Even, if we're including Leonard Ware in the sequence, her current onstage – but not offstage – love interest. I'm completely stumped as to motive, unless Louise is a woman who develops a serious grudge against anyone she gets close to. And that just doesn't ring true.'

'Although she is an actress,' Greg reminded him. 'But I agree, it's not a convincing narrative. What about means and opportunity?'

'That's where we're focussing our efforts now, but without much success, as I said. Our prime candidate with opportunity is Dean Mason, what with his car number plate appearing near the Leakey and Atkinson cases and his earbud at the Newell case.'

'What's this about an earbud?' asked Greg. 'I hadn't heard about that.'

Jill explained, and he looked thoughtful. 'OK,' he said slowly. 'Go on. What else have we got for means and opportunity?'

'We're in the middle of checking ANPR and CCTV footage for all four cases to see if we can get anything else on Mason's car and van, or indeed Mason himself. Nothing so far and it's a slow process,' replied Jill.

'On means, we do have another partial of Mason's plate near one of the sources of wild hemlock on the Broads,' explained Ram. 'And he had been in Atkinson's garage the day before the attack, so he knew where tools were to be found.'

'What about the bike battery at the Newells'?' asked Greg. 'And have we found the weapon used to stab Sharon Jones?'

'Nothing so far on either,' replied Ram, looking downcast. 'And we're running out of possibilities.'

'Hmm,' said Greg, moving to stand by the whiteboards that detailed their progress to date. 'Have you tried the facial recognition software on the CCTV footage you do have on the four cases? That might speed things up. You could set it to look for both Louise Lacon and Dean Mason.'

Ram smacked the side of his head with the palm of his hand. 'I should have thought of that,' he exclaimed. 'I'll get on to it straightaway. Bill and Gray, that makes your search for other CCTV sources even more important. Do another sweep around all four locations, broadening out into surrounding streets, and see what you can find. If we're running it through the facial recognition system, quantity becomes less of an issue.'

'Got it,' said Bill, and nodding to Gray, led the way out of the room.

Greg was still musing by the whiteboards. 'Something's making me uneasy,' he said. 'And I think it's the earbud. Whoever is doing this, if it is just one someone, they've been pretty careful so far. Even to obscuring their plates with stealth spray. But this was careless. It feels more like an attempt to implicate Mason, than an error *by* him.'

He moved over to the board that listed the partial number-plate data and pointed to one of the photos. 'Also,' he said, 'why has the person obscuring the plate hidden the same numbers both front and back? If they'd run out of spray part way through the process, you'd expect one of the plates to be wholly hidden. But it isn't. It's almost,' he said, thinking aloud, 'as though someone wanted us to see part of the plate.

'I think Mason is a red herring,' he said decisively. 'I think he's being set up.'

'By Louise?' asked Ram. 'Apparently, they were briefly in a relationship at one time. Perhaps there's some anger left over.'

'It didn't feel like that,' objected Jill, and then flushed. 'Sorry, sir, I just meant that, whatever the reasons for their breakup, it seemed it was a long time ago, and the relationship now seemed to be one of patient tolerance on her part.'

'And killing off her friends to set Dean up for a prison sentence seems an elaborate way to go about getting revenge for a slight,' said Greg. 'Does she seem to you someone who'd react like that?'

'No,' replied Ram despondently. 'Put it like that and, no, she doesn't. But someone's knocking these folk off!'

There was a long and uncomfortable silence, which Greg eventually broke.

'Perhaps we're looking at this backwards,' he suggested. 'Perhaps Louise Lacon is the victim, not the perpetrator.'

'And someone's aiming for her and missing, over and over again?' Ram was sceptical.

'No. Someone's taking out all her friends and supporters, to leave her isolated,' replied Greg. There was another silence. This one charged with excitement.

'That would fit,' said Ram slowly. 'That would definitely fit. But if so...'

'Then the next victim could be another of her friends. Being around Ms Lacon doesn't seem to be very healthy at the minute,' responded Greg.

'It's a bit off the wall.' Ram was still unconvinced.

' "When you have eliminated all which is impossible, then whatever remains, however improbable, must be the truth" – Sherlock Holmes,' replied Greg. 'It's worth a look. Get Louise

197

in for another chat, with her solicitor, if need be. And Jill, when you're running the video footage through the facial recognition software, see if it can find images common to several locations – even if they're not Louise or Mason.'

32

Personal note 4

Time to review progress. Three down. One hors de combat. *One still in the picture. Resulting in – nothing! I'm still no further forward and time's running out.*

There must be another one somewhere. I don't think it's that pompous old twat Ware. He was a mistake. But someone, somewhere, is still in the way. Time for some research.

First, check her movements. The tag in her car is still active. Impressive battery life, I must say.

Second, check her emails. Bet she still hasn't changed the password.

33

Afternoon of 3 September

Getting hold of Louise Lacon wasn't difficult. She was assiduous in answering her phone, as Jill discovered. Persuading her to come in was another matter.

'So arrest me,' she declared with a dramatic flourish. 'This is all complete balls. You know it and I know it. If you haven't got anything better to do...' Words failed her in a way that made it clear they were failing her as a theatrical ploy. Jill waited patiently for the storm to pass.

'We don't want to arrest you,' she said when a moment presented itself. 'But we really do need to talk to you. With your solicitor is fine. In fact, we'd prefer it. If you haven't one to hand, we'll supply one.' This silenced Louise temporarily, and Jill seized her advantage. 'Look at the facts,' said Jill. 'Your hairdresser, your masseuse and the vicar at your local church have all died recently and in suspicious circumstances. Your mechanic and childhood friend has also been attacked and is still in hospital. OK, this could all be a massive coincidence. But what if it isn't? What if someone is targeting your friends?

How would you live with yourself if you had a chance to put a stop to this and you didn't take it?'

The silence went on while Louise did some hard thinking. 'OK,' she said at last. 'I'll come in. When and where?'

'Can you come to Wymondham?' asked Jill. 'Say, in an hour?'

'OK,' said Louise. 'Provided my solicitor can make it. I'll ring you back if there's a problem. Otherwise, I'll see you in about an hour.'

Jill went to report success to Ram, and found Greg perched on the desk.

'I'm going to do this interview,' announced Greg. 'Jill, as you seem to be building up a rapport with Ms Lacon, you'll be with me. It seems Nick Atkinson is well enough to be interviewed at last, so Ram's going to have a chat with him.'

Jill thought she detected mixed emotions on Ram's face, but all he said to Greg was, 'Catch up with you later.'

***

Louise Lacon and her solicitor from Norwich were admirably prompt. As they sat down in the interview room, Greg noted that while Louise seemed pretty self-possessed, her solicitor was more suspicious.

'Gregson,' he said with his hand held out. 'We've met before, Superintendent Geldard. Congratulations on your promotion, by the way. Is this going to be an interview under caution?'

'That wasn't my plan,' said Greg. 'At this point, we're exploring a rather different angle to the case, and hoping for more information.'

'Then Ms Lacon is free to leave at any moment,' said Gregson.

'Correct,' responded Greg. 'But as it seems it is her friends and associates that are being targeted, I very much hope she'll be minded to help.'

Louise looked at Gregson, who nodded to her. 'But of course, I will intervene if I feel you are overstepping the mark,' said Gregson.

'I'd expect no less,' responded Greg. 'I do hope, though, that you are happy with us recording the interview. It saves such a lot of scribbling.'

Gregson nodded again to indicate his consent, and Jill switched the recording equipment on. Once everyone had identified themselves for the tape, she sat back and looked at Greg.

'The line of enquiry we're exploring,' he said, 'is that these incidents are in fact intended to target you at one remove. Can you think of anyone who would want to do that?'

'No,' said Louise without hesitation. 'No one.' It was the response Greg had anticipated.

'Tell me a bit about yourself,' he invited. 'All I really know about you is that you are a fine amateur actress and work in a florist's.'

'Part-time,' said Louise. 'I work in a florist's part-time, arranging bouquets and such. It's a hobby that grew into a bit of a job. I don't really need the money. Although a bit extra is always handy, isn't it? My parents are both dead and they left me well provided for. And my ex is a rich man, so I got a settlement from him when we divorced. That's about it on practical stuff. Normally, when we aren't in the middle of a pandemic, I spend my time doing the acting and helping out with church coffee mornings and so on. I used to volunteer, helping children learn to read, but that's all stopped now.'

'Any...'Greg wanted to say boyfriends, but the term didn't seem precisely accurate. 'Any close relationships? Significant others?'

Louise flushed slightly and giggled. 'In the plural?' she teased. 'Not at the moment actually. Well, not really.'

Greg noted the 'not really' and decided to come back to it. 'What about your ex?' he asked. 'Was the split amicable? Are you still in contact?'

'As amicable as these things usually are.' She shrugged. 'I don't think he was too pleased at the time, but he got over it. We still exchange news from time to time, and I see him very occasionally.'

'Why did you break up?' asked Jill.

'Just wasn't working,' replied Louise. 'I guess we weren't very compatible after all.'

There was a slight pause, then Greg said, 'Let's take each of the recent tragedies in turn. What I'd like to know is why anyone could think their deaths or injury would hurt you. Leonard Ware, for example. What is your relationship with him?'

'I don't have a relationship with Leonard, at least not offstage, not now,' replied Louise.

'You have in the past?' asked Jill after a nudge from Greg's foot under the table. They'd agreed that if Louise seemed likely to be embarrassed by any of the questioning, Jill would take over.

Louise glanced sidelong at her solicitor and said, 'We were good friends for a while, but it was going nowhere, so it sort of cooled off. It didn't last beyond the end of that particular play.'

'When was that?' asked Jill.

'Spring season 2020. We had a four-day run of *Hello, Dolly*. Leonard was Horace, my love interest,' she explained, as Greg was looking baffled. 'Our *thing*, if you can call it that, ended with the last-night party.'

'Might someone think that it was still going on?' asked Jill.

'Well, I suppose, as we're acting together again in *Kiss Me, Kate*, someone who wasn't part of the cast might think that. But no one who saw us together could possibly imagine...' Words failed her again.

'What about Marie Leakey?' asked Greg. 'You told my colleague DCI Trent that you saw her roughly every two weeks but weren't close friends. Why might someone think that she was important to you?'

'No idea,' responded Louise. 'I'm not gay, if that's what you're thinking!'

'Not what I was thinking at all,' Greg said defensively.

'I suppose I've often told people that I couldn't get by without her massages. I suffer with my back,' she explained. 'I suppose someone could have misinterpreted what I said, but that's genuinely all. Yes, of course we chatted during massages, and I probably confided in her when things weren't going my way, romantically speaking, but that's all.'

It seemed the relationship with her hairdresser, and even her vicar, followed a similar pattern. Greg was left with a picture of a friendly, possibly over-friendly, woman who shared personal details freely with all sorts of acquaintances and got some comfort and support out of the process. 'But it's thin. It's very thin,' he said to Jill later. 'And as for Dean Mason…'

When he'd asked about Dean Mason, Louise had laughed outright.

'Dean,' she said. 'Dean is a joke. He's known as Hands-on Henry in the society. We warn new girls, like Josie, not to get into corners with him, but he's harmless. In fact, I think he does it now because he feels we'd be disappointed if he didn't. I had a brief fling with him years ago,' she said airily, in her woman-of-the-world role. 'But I soon caught on to what he was.'

'Which was?' asked Jill.

'A serial groper, and a bit thick, to be honest,' replied Louise.

'What about now?' Jill had asked right at the end. 'You've been very helpful about your past relationships and friendships,' she said. 'Is there anyone at the moment?'

Louise had blushed a little, glanced sideways at her solicitor and said, 'No. Not as such.' And then refused to be drawn further.

'What did you make of that?' Greg asked Jill. 'Don't tell me she's got her eye on her solicitor!'

Jill grinned. 'Did look like it, didn't it.'

'I hope he's careful,' Greg responded. 'Still, he's had fair warning.' And they both laughed.

***

Over at the Norfolk and Norwich, Ram wasn't adding much to the sum of their evidence. Yes, Nick had spoken to Dean the day before he'd been attacked. And yes, they had their conversation in the garage, where all his tools were on display. But he'd spoken to numerous other people in that exact same place. And no, he had no beef with Dean, other than a slight irritation that he didn't always pay very quickly.

'But he's no worse than most,' said Nick. 'And I'm sorry, but I really can't remember much after that, until I woke up in here.' He gestured round to take in his corner of the ward and the beeping machinery. 'They tell me I can go home soon,' he said. 'My sister's coming over for a few weeks to keep an eye on me.'

'No wife or girlfriend?' asked Ram.

'Not at the moment,' said Nick. 'But here's hoping. If we ever get our social lives back again. Never say never.' And he winked.

Ram rang Greg as he left the hospital but got the Ansaphone. 'Suppose he's interviewing,' he muttered to himself and left a message to say he was whipping over to King's Lynn to catch up with Helena Bell and the Sharon Jones enquiry. Then he headed west.

Greg was on his way home when he picked up his messages. The one from Ram and also one from Louise. He rang Ram on his hands-free.

'Got your message, but also one from Louise Lacon,' he said. 'It seems she was planning to meet someone this evening and he hasn't turned up. Silly cow didn't tell us about this one,' he added with an uncharacteristic burst of irritation. 'Some retired solicitor she met online and has been getting "close to".' If he hadn't had both hands on the wheel, he might have employed air quotes. 'Same company as Gregson, hence the silly sidelong glances Jill and I noticed. I'm on my way to his offices in Great Yarmouth. She says he was either coming from there or from home, and she can't raise him by phone or email. Can you check out his home in Worstead? Or get someone to give it a once-over. Jill is on her way to see "La Lacon".'

'Will do,' said Ram. 'Are you thinking it's another possible victim?'

'I'm thinking we need to check it out,' said Greg grimly. 'It's either that, or he's running scared from the actress in hunting mode. Could be either!'

34

Personal note 5

The car movements were interesting. Especially the drive to Police HQ in Wymondham. But I only caught up with that later. After.

The historical tracking data was useful and the emails even more so. Who would have thought our Louise would have resorted to a dating app! How are the mighty brought low! Still, I suppose lockdown's affected us all. Me more than most!

The lovey-dovey messages are a bit vomit-making. I'd have thought a professional man would've had more pride. More dignity. They gave me some ideas though. And it explains why she hasn't come back to me. Even yet.

35

In Great Yarmouth

Greg arrived on the seafront to find Jill attempting to bring Louise Lacon down from her histrionic heights. The sunset was disappearing behind the hotels that lined the road between the town and the dunes, creating dark shadows across the car park and the rough marram grass. In the distance the offshore turbines were turning slowly but steadily.

Just as he pulled his car up alongside Jill and Louise, a solicitous hotel worker appeared across the road with a chair and a blanket. 'Do I need to call an ambulance?' he asked Jill. 'Your friend seems a little...' He hesitated, presumably seeking a diplomatic yet appropriate expression.

Hysterical would have done, thought Greg as Jill showed the Good Samaritan her warrant card.

'Everything's under control, but thank you,' she said as Louise sank into the proffered chair with a long sigh. Jill wrapped the – entirely unnecessary, given the warmth of the evening – blanket around her shoulders. 'Tell us exactly what the arrangement was,' she said to Louise.

On a gulp, Louise replied, 'To meet here at 6pm, have a drink in the hotel bar and then decide what we wanted to do with our evening. It's usually champagne,' she said miserably.

Greg checked his watch. 'He's only an hour late,' he said. 'Could he have got held up? Or maybe something came up and he couldn't make it.'

'He'd have let me know,' said Louise in an almost shout. 'He's a gentleman. He'd never have stood me up. And he's never late. In fact, I've never known him be anything but early. He's not answering his phone. Or replying to my messages. Or *WhatsApp*. I've tried his landline too, and he's not answering that either.'

'Hospitals?' asked Greg. Jill shook her head, to say no, and to deter him from pursuing that line, given the howl that Louise emitted.

'No reports of any accidents between here and Worstead,' she clarified. Turning to Louise, she added. 'You said semi-retired. Is he likely to be in the office?'

'He goes in quite a bit. Like I said, it's here in Yarmouth,' sobbed Louise. 'Down near the river, where all the solicitors are. But he said he wasn't going into the office today. He was coming here from home.'

'Perhaps his plans changed,' said Greg briskly, keen to get away from all the damp femininity.

'But they're not open. Their Ansaphone says so,' wailed Louise.

'Nonetheless, I'll pop over there and see if I can find anyone. Jill, you stay here with Ms Lacon, just in case he turns up. Ram has got someone checking out the Worstead address. Don't worry, Ms Lacon. We'll soon find out what's going on.' *And there's going to be one embarrassed solicitor, if he's just changed his mind*,' he added to himself.

They were interrupted by Greg's phone ringing. 'It's Ram,' he said to Jill as he answered it. He listened for a moment. 'The house in Worstead is empty and his neighbours say he went into the office today. I'll get over there now.'

36

Personal note 6

I'm a bit surprised a semi-retired solicitor goes into the office as often as he does. Hasn't he heard of working from home? But then, I suppose a partner gets to have a room to himself. The fact that it's handy for the public car park is a bonus. Even if he is parking on the street. Or to be more accurate, on the pavement. I've laid my plans. Now to execute them. I use the term advisedly.

37

The other side of town

It took but minutes to cross town to the North Quay and the junction with Queen Street. At that point Greg discovered that the street itself was one-way, and in the wrong direction at that. He parked across the junction with his blue lights flashing and went up the street on foot, making sure that his car was securely locked as he walked away. This was not a part of town or a time of day when he would want to leave his car unlocked.

There were a couple of cars parked partly in the road and partly on the pavement on his right as he headed up the slight incline towards the Greyfriars car park. He passed both, walking on the narrow bit of pavement left to him and narrowly avoided tripping over a step that protruded from one of the buildings into the path. Looking up, he realised that the third and last car parked in the street was not secured. The driver's door was very slightly ajar.

'Now that is odd,' he said to himself, and walked swiftly over to check the interior. The car was empty. With a prickle of unease running down his back, he pulled on a plastic glove and opened the door more fully. In the mix of illumination that

213

was the last of the sun's rays and the nearby streetlight, he saw a dark stain on the lintel and another on the steering wheel. He looked closer, then got out his radio.

'PNC check, please, on...' He stepped back and read off the number plate. A pause, and then the answer came back: 'Joseph Stephen Andrews, living—'

'In Worstead. Thank you, I know,' he said. 'Alert the Yarmouth station and get them to send a team over to Queen Street. I think there's been an assault connected with an ongoing investigation. Send the crime scene investigators as well. Thank you.'

He rang Jill. 'I've found something,' he said. 'No, not Mr Andrews. His car's here and he's missing. Take Ms Lacon over to the Yarmouth station and get someone checking whatever ANPR cameras we have around North Quay, Queen Street and Yarmouth Way, then outwards from there, looking for the partial number plate we've seen in the past.'

As he was speaking, he was looking round at the buildings surrounding him. He spotted several CCTV cameras over the entrances to what were clearly solicitors' offices, but when he looked closer his heart sank. At least the two nearest appeared to have been vandalised.

Seconds later a squad car appeared at the Greyfriars end of Queen Street and blocked off access to traffic. Two officers got out, pulling on their caps, and walked towards Greg.

'Gather we've got a bit of a problem, sir,' said the first.

'Sergeant Briscoe,' said Greg with relief. 'Good to see you. First job here is to secure the scene. Then check the adjoining buildings to see if there's anyone in, cleaners or security most likely, and get hold of any CCTV footage they may have.' He looked up as an unmarked van pulled up on North Quay, followed by Jill's car.

'Seems like the cavalry are arriving,' he said, and walked down to the new arrivals.

'Suspected assault and possibly abduction,' he said to Jill. 'Check the James Paget just in case he went there under his own steam or, maybe, with the help of a colleague or passerby. If not, then abduction is looking more likely, and time is of the essence.

'Ned, there's what looks to me like blood on the car. I'd welcome your opinion,' he added to the tall man coming up behind.

He stood back to give Ned room to work and noted that crime scene tape now closed the road to all comers, if the cars blocking each end left any room for doubt. His phone rang.

'Geldard,' he said, then listened closely.

'Jill,' he shouted, then turned back to Ned. 'I'm going to leave you here with the A-team,' he said, indicating Sergeant Briscoe and his mate. 'Jill. With me. The ANPR has picked up that partial on North Quay to the north of here, and again on Lawn Avenue.'

He got back in his car and performed a U-turn to head north, checking in his mirror to be sure Jill was following.

As he navigated the big roundabout near the post office, Greg took another phone call.

'Boss,' said Gray's voice, 'I think I've spotted something.'

'Go ahead,' said Greg as he passed the magistrates' court and headed on down the A149.

'The timings on the ANPR... There's a gap between when the plate was photographed on North Quay near Aldi and the sighting on Lawn Avenue near the BP garage. It's too long. There's not much traffic at that time of night.'

'He stopped somewhere,' said Greg, catching on. 'Good spot, Gray. Well done.'

Greg put his hazard lights on and pulled over, getting out of his car as Jill parked behind. Going over to her window, he explained the reason for his sudden stop, outlining Gray's idea. 'In which case, it must be somewhere back along here.'

'Or he turned off and turned back,' said Jill. 'He could have turned down one of the side streets and then back again.'

'True. But in either case, it could have been to hide his abductee or dump a body.'

'There's a parking area back there by the river,' said Jill.

'The one by the old tower,' said Greg. 'Damn. If he's gone in the river, that's end of. Better go and see if there're any signs along there. And the cameras on the magistrates' court might be useful. After that, we can check out the side streets. Come on.'

They both U-turned yet again and headed back. The parking by the old river defences was empty. The pub alongside had apparently not reopened after the Covid closure. Or had closed early that night.

Greg and Jill climbed out and looked around them. Cars passed on the main road and the occasional set of headlights on vehicles coming over the roundabout lit up their surroundings briefly, before moving on. The pub, and the old tower that had once been part of the city's mediaeval defences, cast dark shadows towards the river. Greg pulled covers over his feet, just in case, and walked to the river wall to peer over. He checked downriver, but could see nothing in the swiftly flowing current. It was hard to see anything at ground level either, particularly in this light. The shadows confused everything.

Jill, her shoes similarly protected, was walking towards the old tower and playing her torch beam on its ancient flints and brickwork.

As she turned to shout to Greg, the torchlight swung with her and picked out something odd. Greg squinted in an effort to see more clearly. By the river wall was an old-style signpost with a cast-iron upright. The finger pointing upriver read 'Yacht Station' and the opposite one '1845 GY Suspension Bridge Disaster Memorial'. Greg wondered fleetingly what the disaster had been, but that wasn't what had attracted his attention. Roughly level with the top of the wall, a rope was tied round the post. And it seemed to be under tension.

Telling himself it could be a boat mooring, nonetheless Greg started to run towards it. Jill, startled, spun round again and headed in the same direction. Greg got there first, and hung over the wall, straining to see what was dangling at the end of the taut rope.

At first glance it looked like a bundle of clothes, then the moon came out from behind a cloud and he realised it was a body, apparently hanging head down, the rope tied around its ankles.

'Looks like we're too late,' he gasped. 'Damn. Jill, call it in. I'll see if I can get down there somehow.'

He looked around for one of those convenient ladders folk from the tourist cruisers used to get ashore, but, of course, there wasn't one anywhere near. Nor were there any boats he could use as a platform. As he looked desperately up- and downriver yet again, the rope suddenly jerked, and he thought he heard something.

'It moved!' he exclaimed. 'Jill, hear that?'

'No,' said Jill, her phone pressed to one ear. 'Just traffic noise.'

'I thought...' Greg took hold of the rope. 'It's definitely moving,' he shouted. 'He's still alive. Quick, Jill. Give me a hand.'

He leaned over the wall and bellowed, 'Hang on! We're coming!' Then looked again at the rope. 'We need a lot more help,' he said. 'I can't pull him up on my own.'

'And the tide's coming in,' said Jill.

38

Next steps

At least three possible courses of action ran through Greg's head and were as quickly dismissed as impracticable. He looked again over the wall, to see if they could wait for the fire service or the other help currently being called up by Jill on her phone. As he watched, the rope jerked convulsively, and he realised that the victim's head, or at least hair, was already touching the fast-flowing water beneath.

'Try to keep still,' he shouted. 'I'm going to pull you up.'

'You can't,' said Jill. 'It's impossible.'

'I can try,' responded Greg in a determined tone. 'It's that or stand here and watch him drown.' He looked again at the signpost and the rope, and made up his mind. Stripping off the plastic gloves and discarding them on the ground, he braced a foot against the wall and took a firm hold on the rope. Jill was still hanging over, looking down.

'He's going under,' she reported.

'No pressure then,' grunted Greg. 'He put his other foot on the wall and hung in a curve between his braced feet and his hands on the rope. Then took a deep breath and heaved, using the strength of his legs and back to drag the rope, little by little, over the coarse stonework. He got to the point where his legs were straight, his arms trembling under the strain of the weight on the end of the rope. Then stopped.

'Can't. Get. Further.' he grunted.

Jill still had her head over the wall. 'He's clear of the water,' she reported.

The rope jerked, and Greg hissed through his teeth as it dragged through his hands, taking skin with it.

'Tell. Him. Still.'

'Keep still!' bellowed Jill to the upside-down victim still just clear of the river. 'Help's coming.'

The rope vibrated as Greg's arms and legs shook under the strain.

'Better. Be. Quick.'

'Save your breath, Boss,' said Jill, wishing she could do something more constructive than just offer advice. But there wasn't enough clear rope for her add her weight to the pull, and nowhere she could tie off the small gain Greg had made. To their enormous relief, the sound of sirens became audible.

'Nearly here, Boss,' she said. And Greg, now washed in the eerie glow of multiple blue flashing lights, heard not just the slamming of vehicle doors but the even more welcome sound of running feet.

It was the fire service commander, Bob Fisher, who got there first and took in the situation in one rapid glance. A stream of commands resulted in gloved hands taking the strain on the rope from a much-relieved Greg and equipment being bustled from the nearest tender to the riverbank. The arrival of two ambulances added paramedics to the mix, and with Jill and colleagues from the Great Yarmouth station keeping an eye on things, Greg reluctantly gave in to the paramedic's insistence that he move away.

Apart from shaky legs and sore muscles, he reckoned the worst damage was to his hands, and that he considered minor. 'Just slap some tape on,' he urged the paramedic cleaning the rope burns. 'I need to get back to work.'

'Nothing you can do at the moment,' said a familiar voice over his shoulder.

Greg turned his head sharply to see Ben Asheton, regretted the move as strained muscles complained and turned back again. 'Might have known you'd turn up,' he joked. 'Never one to miss a drama.'

'Certainly not,' said Ben. 'Especially when it involves an old friend with form around rivers. I'm glad you managed to stay out of it this time.'

'Not much point joining him down there,' replied Greg, wincing as the paramedic got heavy with the disinfectant. A sudden flurry over by the river wall announced the arrival of a stretcher-borne body safely onto dry land. Greg stood up to see better, staggered slightly but braced himself on Ben's shoulder. He saw that Jill was hovering closely behind the medics bending over the stretcher and decided he could leave things to her for the moment. As he watched, she turned away from the huddle and came over to him. He sat down again, not entirely voluntarily, on the back of the ambulance and waited.

'He's alive but drifting in and out of consciousness,' Jill reported. 'They're taking him to the Norfolk and Norwich.'

'Not the James Paget?' asked Greg. 'It's nearer.'

'No. Apparently he has a head trauma, and they think he'll be better off at the N&N. Bill just arrived, and I'm sending him in the ambulance. He'll keep an eye on things for now.'

'Have you updated Ram?' asked Greg.

'Yes, and Jim Henning,' responded Jill. 'Jim's due in court again tomorrow, but he thinks he'll be free by late morning. I thought I should keep him posted. Ram says he'll meet the ambulance at the N&N.'

'Good. Well done, Jill. Can you keep an eye on things here? Until the scenes of crime folk have it under control. I'm going to head back to Briscoe in Queen Street and make sure we don't miss anything there. One other thing,' he added. 'Better let Louise Lacon know we've found him alive.'

'You should go home,' said Ben, taking the words from Jill's mouth.

'After Queen Street,' said Greg. 'We can't afford to miss anything this time around.'

'You sure you should be driving, Boss?' asked Jill hesitantly.

Greg flexed his now-taped fingers, winced slightly and looked up with a grin. 'If these won't bend round the steering wheel, I'll borrow one of the locals to drive me,' he replied. 'Go on, Jill. Organise this lot here and let me know what they find. I'm afraid none of us will be home anytime soon.'

***

Bill did not enjoy his ride to Norwich. He had long been of the opinion that in the back of an ambulance was one of the *most* uncomfortable ways to travel, and this trip wasn't doing anything to change his view. Strapped into the seat near the back doors and swaying with every bend as the driver hurled his charge onwards with blue lights flashing, he thought that there were a good deal too many roundabouts between Yarmouth and Norwich. By the time they swung round the last bend to drop off their charge by A&E, Bill was on the point of throwing up. He nodded his thanks to the grinning paramedic who opened the doors, and jumped out, hand firmly clasped to mouth. After a moment in the fresh air and a couple of deep breaths, disaster was narrowly averted and he turned to follow the stretcher into Resus. He took up station outside the bay housing the unfortunate Joseph Andrews, and prepared himself for a long wait as doctors, nurses and specialists of all kinds bustled to and fro with mysterious pieces of kit. And waited.

He was joined by Ram Trent within the hour. 'Any news?' he asked.

'Not yet, sir,' reported Bill. 'Last thing I heard was what the paramedics said when he was hauled from the river. Traumatic brain injury. That's the lot.'

'Yes, I heard that,' said Ram, then interrupted himself as a senior-looking doctor in green scrubs came out of the Resus bay.

'How's Mr Andrews?' asked Ram, waving his warrant card.

'Not well enough to speak to you yet,' the doctor replied. The badge on his chest read *Hello, my name is David Watkins.* 'He'll be going up for an MRI scan shortly, and then on to the ward, but I'm pleased to say it's looking good for him. Mainly because the blow hit him in the front rather than to the side.' Dr Watkins tapped his own head just above his forehead. 'The bone here is a lot thicker than over the ears. Either his assailant missed, or he didn't intend to kill.'

'He hung him head down in the river, so I think he intended to kill,' said Ram grimly.

'Fair point,' said the doctor. 'Either way, I don't think you'll be able to talk to him for a few hours.' He looked at his watch. 'Probably not until the morning,' he said. 'You might as well go home and get some sleep for what's left of the night.'

As the doctor walked away, Ram looked at Bill. 'I'll check in with the Super,' he said. 'Are you OK to stay with Mr Andrews for now. I'll get you relieved in the morning.'

Yes, sir,' said Bill, and sat down again.

Outside in the open air, Ram rang Greg and brought him up to date.

'OK. Not surprising,' said Greg. 'Could have been worse. Ram, you go home, and I'll catch up with you in the morning. I'm going to do the same shortly.'

'Found anything at Queen Street?' asked Ram.

'The SOCOs have crawled over Andrews's car and are taking it into the secure garage for another look in the morning. There were more blood traces in addition to the ones I saw. The whole street is locked down, but we can't get much in the way of CCTV footage until we can get staff in from the surrounding offices. That's a job for the morning too.'

'And at the river?' asked Ram.

'Jill's in charge there. I haven't spoken to her recently.'

'I'll ring,' said Ram. 'See you in the morning, Boss.'

'You mean later in the morning,' said Greg with a tired chuckle, looking at his watch.

Around three thirty, Greg decided to call it a day. He thanked the constable who'd driven him to Queen Street, said a final good night to the uniformed officers securing the scene from the curious, both amateur and professional – the press had begun to gather – and bent his stiff hands round his steering wheel.

It was close to four in the morning when he finally bounced over his rough drive and pulled up outside his cottage. Bobby, returning from a night's hunting, slipped in behind him and curled up on the sofa in the kitchen. Listening closely, he thought he heard a low voice, and sure enough found Chris resettling Jamie in his cot. She put a finger to her mouth to indicate he should keep quiet and shooed him into their bedroom before her.

'Late one,' she remarked. 'How's the victim?'

'Stunned but not dead, according to Ram,' replied Greg, sitting down on the bed. 'Can you give me a hand with these?' He held up his taped hands, which were making undoing shirt buttons a little challenging.

'What happened to you?' Chris exclaimed, sitting down beside him and tackling the cuffs first.

'Rope slid,' said Greg economically. 'Nothing much. Just a nuisance.' He lay back and was asleep before Chris got his clothes off. She sighed, removed shoes and trousers, then pulled the duvet over him. 'Sleep well,' she muttered, and turned the light out again.

39

---

4 September

By seven thirty, after a scant three hours of sleep, Greg was in the shower, ruefully examining the damaged palms of his hands. The hot water stung, and he dried and dressed himself with more than a little care. Chris had helpfully part buttoned his shirt so he could pull it on over his head with minimum hassle. Pushing his feet into loafers, he decided against a tie and descended the stairs, ready for the fray. Chris was in the kitchen, coffee bubbling on the hob, a bacon roll beckoning from the worktop, with his son and heir muttering cheerfully to himself on the activity mat, watched closely by both Bobby and Tally.

'You are a star,' he pronounced. 'I'll drink the coffee and take that with me' – indicating the bacon roll. Chris turned to add a drop of cold water to the piping-hot black coffee, and watched as Greg gulped it down.

'Your hands OK?' she asked.

Greg held up the one not holding the coffee mug. 'They'll be fine,' he said. 'Bit sore but no worse than that. Is the girl in today?' he asked, meaning their childcare arrangement.

LAST ACT

'Yes. She'll be here around nine. Something you need me to do?'

'Can you and Chas see what you can dig up about Louise Lacon's friends and associates? The ones that haven't been attacked, I mean,' he asked. 'She professes herself mystified by these attacks and claims she can't name a likely culprit. But it must be someone in her past or present. We're going to interview her again, but I'd be glad if you'd take a look as well.'

'Will do,' said Chris, dropping a kiss on his mouth and handing him his breakfast. 'Good luck. And try to snatch a nap sometime.'

'Will do,' he said, kissing her back. And whisked himself out the door.

By the time he arrived in Wymondham, Jill was pinning photos on the whiteboard and Ram was on the phone from the hospital.

'Just been told we can speak to Joseph Andrews later this morning,' he said. 'Do you want to be there?'

Greg glanced at his watch. 'I'll meet you there in ninety minutes,' he replied. 'I want to check in with Ned first.'

He went to take the stairs to Ned's office in his usual two-at-a-time manner, then found that a number of muscles were complaining about their ill treatment the day before and slowed to a more sedate ascent. Ned was also in bright and early, notwithstanding his late night. Greg wondered, not for the first time, if the public had any idea how dedicated some of the police team were, and how long and hard they worked to keep people safe.

'Congratulations,' he said to Greg.

'On what?' Greg asked.

227

'On saving a life of course.'

Greg grunted. 'Never mind that,' he responded. 'What do you have for me?'

'A couple of things. Obviously, a lot of results are yet to come back from analysis, but I can tell you there was blood from two different people in that car.'

'Two!' exclaimed Greg. 'Now that is interesting. Suggests Andrews managed to fight back?'

'Looks like it,' agreed Ned. 'The DNA isn't back yet, but, conveniently, the blood is from two different groups: one is A and the other is O. I checked with the hospital, and Andrews is blood group O, so there's a good chance we have some DNA from the attacker. We've also found hair and fibres so, one way or another, once you have a suspect, we should have a means of placing them at the scene.'

'What about down by the tower?' asked Greg. 'Anything to suggest what happened there?'

'No fingerprints on the rope or the signpost. Or, for that matter, in Andrews's car, other than his own, so it's likely the attacker wore gloves. There are some marks on the wall and on the ground near it that suggest Andrews was dragged from a car and levered, rather than lifted, over the wall. I've asked the hospital for a detailed list of the injuries on their patient, but I'm expecting them to find scrapes and grazes that match what I've found.'

'So we're not looking for the Incredible Hulk,' commented Greg. 'To be clear, you think he dragged an unconscious Andrews to the wall, tied his feet together with the rope, then propped him against the wall and pushed him over?'

'First tying the other end of the rope to the signpost. Yes,' agreed Ned. 'He may have tied the rope to his feet before he got him out of the car, but that's how it looks to me.'

'So it's sheer luck that the rope was short enough to keep him dangling clear of the river.'

'Looks like it,' responded Ned. 'Either that, or the attacker had somehow measured the distance to the water and deliberately made sure the rope was too short for him to drown at low tide. Then left him to hang there waiting to die.'

There was a silence while both men contemplated the mind that would devise such a plot.

'Possible, but not probable,' said Greg at last. 'He'd have needed to know not only the length of the drop but also Andrews's height. And he'd have needed to know he'd be conscious after the blow to the head. Otherwise, it was all wasted effort.'

'One other thing,' added Ned. 'The fingerprints we found on the gate at the Newells'... They match a partial we lifted off the earbud. And they're not Mason's.'

***

At Norwich Crown Court, Jim had arrived early to prepare for his final session in the witness box. The Witness Service volunteer on duty that day was a familiar face. In fact, he'd seen her so often she was becoming almost a pal.

'You've time for some breakfast,' was her greeting. 'The defendant isn't here yet. Bit of a hold-up apparently. You might as well get yourself a bacon butty.'

Jim grinned. 'You're getting to know me too well,' he replied. 'Why the delay? I hope he's not playing the Covid card.'

Sylvia, the volunteer, grimaced. 'I don't know the details,' she said. 'I hope not. Too many hearings have been buggered about by people conveniently claiming to have Covid. You pop down to the canteen and I'll let you know if I find anything out.'

Jim did as suggested and headed for the canteen. The bacon tended to be a bit on the flabby side for his taste, but still a lot better than nothing. He was just finishing up the last crumbs when Sylvia put her head round the door, spotted him and came over, her face a mixture of excitement and frustration.

'They've lost him,' she declaimed loudly enough to turn heads.

'They've what?' asked Jim, waving a hand to indicate that a quieter tone might be a good idea.

'Lost him.'

'How do you lose a defendant in a prison?' demanded Jim.

'That lot could lose a sneeze in a pepper factory,' responded Sylvia. 'No idea how, but the fact is, they can't produce him at court.'

Jim was already gathering up his bits and pieces. 'I'd better have a word with the CPS,' he said. 'Thanks, Sylvia.'

He ran Frank to earth without difficulty, as by then Frank was also looking for him. 'It's true,' he said, correctly interpreting Jim's expression. 'Thorne has gone missing. Assumed to have absconded from prison either last night or in the early hours of this morning.'

'Don't they know?' exclaimed Jim. 'When did they last check on him?'

'Around midnight, apparently. No further information at the moment on how exactly he did it. The hue and cry is up, as you can imagine, and the court case temporarily suspended. I'll let you know when I hear anything more.'

'Does Greg know?'

'Not as far as I'm aware. I only found out a little while ago myself.'

'I'll ring him,' said Jim.

But when Jim rang Greg's number, it went to Ansaphone. He tried Chris next.

'He's probably in the hospital, talking to Joseph Andrews,' she advised. 'Leave a message and I'll try again later. If you're free of the court for a while, I think Ram would be glad of your input in the search for Andrews's attacker.'

'I'm on my way to Wymondham now,' Jim assured her.

40

Personal note 7

I decided on a lie-in that morning. It had been a busy and tiring night. I'm not used to that sort of physical work any more. In fact, I almost had to give up. The relative heights of the wall and Andrews had virtually defeated me. And when he started to struggle, that had nearly been the end of it. Luckily that was the moment when gravity tipped in my favour.

So it was particularly disappointing to hear the news. Rescued and survived. Damn. I reassure myself that head trauma almost always means loss of memory. Almost always.

41

At the hospital

Greg had joined Ram in kicking their heels around the waiting area outside the HDU. Luckily, in view of the other pressures on their time, they weren't kept waiting too long. Within a few minutes a nurse popped her head around the door and beckoned them over.

'The doctor says you can see him now, but to keep it short,' she instructed, and pointed down the ward to where Bill was sitting beside a screened bay.

'Bill! I'm surprised you're still here,' said Greg as they got closer.

'My replacement hasn't made it here yet,' said Bill, getting up from the chair to greet his superiors.

Ram looked seriously displeased. 'I'm sorry, Bill,' he said. 'If he's not here in the next ten minutes, stick your head round and I'll sort it. It's just not good enough,' he muttered to Greg as they approached the bed.

Greg nodded to acknowledge the comment and made a mental note to follow it up later. Then turned his attention to the man in the bed, wired up to the usual multiplicity of mysterious machines flashing and clicking.

Joseph Andrews looked like a solicitor was his first thought, even when lying in a hospital bed, in a hospital gown, his normally well-shaved and symmetrical face marred by a huge bruise spreading down his forehead and obscuring his right eye. His hair, what could be seen of it around bandages, had been well cut in a style that made no attempt to hide his receding hairline. A pale mark across the bridge of his nose suggested that he usually wore glasses, and his firm chin bore a pronounced dimple in the centre. His eyes had been closed when they approached, but flickered open as they sat down, one each side of the bed. Greg got out his phone, checked it was on silent and noticed he had a missed call from Jim before he switched it to record.

'Police?' said Mr Andrews in a voice that managed to be both faint and firm. Greg and Ram both leaned nearer to ensure they could hear him clearly over the noise of the machinery and a ward cleaner wielding a mop just beyond the screens.

Greg and Ram introduced themselves, then paused as Andrews reached a shaky hand across for the glass of water on the table over the bed. Ram leaned forwards to pass it to him.

'We're sorry to bother you,' went on Greg, 'but as I'm sure you know, these next few hours are crucial to a successful investigation, and anything you remember about last night, anything at all, will be immeasurably valuable.'

Andrews put the glass down, narrowly avoiding missing the table altogether. 'Oops. Sorry,' he said as Ram caught it. 'My depth perception's shot. Last night...' he went on. 'I remember arranging to meet Louise Lacon. I remember leaving the office. I'm not sure what time, but everyone else had gone. Most are still working from home,' he added. 'I remember getting to my car, opening the door and starting to get in. The next is a bit mixed up, but I think someone pushed me, and when I turned round, they hit me on the head. I think I ducked, but the blow knocked me silly.'

He paused and lay still for a while. It looked like he was gathering his thoughts, so Greg kept quiet.

'I think I might have made a bit of a grab for whoever hit me, but that's all confused. I do remember I still had my car keys in my hand, and I might have lashed out with them. They're on a bundle with my house keys,' he explained. 'I imagine they've gone.'

'No, we found them just under the car,' responded Greg. 'And there was blood on the house keys that isn't yours, so it looks like you gave a good account of yourself.'

A faint smile flickered over the face of the man in the bed. 'That's good to know,' he said. 'I don't remember anything else until I came to, hanging upside down with my head almost in the river. The water was flowing fast, and I think it may have splashed me and helped to bring me round, but that's rationalisation after the event. All I actually remember is the horrible feeling of all the blood rushing to my head, how hard it was to breathe, and the panic. I thought I was going to drown there, and I had so little breath I couldn't properly shout.'

He reached for the glass again, and again Ram handed it to him.

'That's very clear,' said Greg. 'You are an excellent witness.'

The tired smile again, and Andrews said, 'I've been in court enough to know how it's done.'

'Do you know who might have attacked you?' asked Greg. 'Do you know of anyone with a grudge, for example?'

Andrews went to shake his head, thought the better of it and said, 'No.'

'Has anyone made any threats to you?'

'No.'

'Or does your legal practice lay you open to someone developing a grudge?'

'No. I can't think of anyone or any reason,' said Andrews.

The nurse stuck her head round the curtain at this moment, pointed at her watch meaningfully, and left again.

'I think our time's up,' said Greg. 'We'll leave you in peace, but we may need to ask you some more questions soon.'

'Just one more,' said Ram suddenly. 'Did you see anything of the man who attacked you?'

'Not that I can remember,' replied Andrews. 'But I did see someone in the street.'

'Before or after you were attacked?' asked Greg.

'Before,' said Andrews. 'He was walking up from the river when I came out of the office.'

'What do you remember about him?' asked Greg, ignoring the indignant expression on the face of the nurse, who had returned to chivvy them away.

'Just that he was about my height, bald, probably about my age,' said Andrews.

'Skin colour?' asked Greg.

'White.'

'And what was he wearing?'

There was a pause, then Andrews said, 'I'm sorry, I'm not sure. Something dark and fairly smart. I mean, it wasn't a hoodie or anything like that. Perhaps a suit? I'm sorry,' he said, and his eyes closed for a moment.

'We understand you had planned to go out with Louise Lacon last night. How long have you known her?' Greg asked.

'About a month. No, six weeks,' said Andrews. 'We first met for a very well-ventilated and rather chilly lunch on the twenty-ninth of May.'

'How did you meet? Were you introduced by friends?'

'No. We met online,' said Andrews with a faint smile. 'And I bet that surprised you, didn't it?'

'Not really,' said Ram. 'Everyone's doing it these days, and there's a website for every taste.'

'That sounds dodgy,' responded Andrews. 'But you're right. Only the website we met on was for the older customer! No teens or twenties on that site. Just the middle-aged and older looking for friendship, with romance an optional extra.'

'So you met for lunch on the twenty-ninth of May, and clearly you hit it off,' said Greg. 'How often have you met since?'

'At least two or three times a week. And we speak most days. We think alike and like the same sorts of evenings out – quiet drinks, meals and, now things are opening up some more, the occasional theatre visit. You know Louise really is a good actress,' he added. 'She could have been a professional, given the opportunity.'

'Have you met many of her friends and family?' went on Greg.

'Not really. She doesn't have any children or siblings. I've met some of her friends in the Northfolk drama group. That's about it.'

'Have you met anyone who might...' Greg hesitated. '...might target you because of your relationship with Louise?'

'No.' The man in the bed looked startled and raised his head from the pillow. 'You mean, you think I was attacked because of Louise? Is she safe?'

'It's a possibility we're exploring,' said Greg. 'And yes, Louise is safe at home. I have no doubt you're likely to see her very soon.'

'Good,' said Andrews, and closed his eyes. He did look genuinely pleased, Greg noted.

The nurse's foot having been well and truly put down, Greg and Ram retreated. Greg was pleased to note that Bill had, at last, been relieved. He was not at all pleased to note that the late-arriving replacement was DC Waterton. He opened his mouth to make his views plain, then caught a glance from Ram and decided to leave him to discipline the recalcitrant DC.

'I'll leave you to it,' he said to Ram. 'See you back at HQ.' Ram nodded, and Greg headed for the exit.

As he departed, he heard the opening words: 'I hope you have a good reason for being so late,' and smiled to himself.

***

On the road back to Wymondham, Greg decided to use the driving time to catch up on developments. He was less than delighted, therefore, to find that the first news over his Bluetooth connection was the disappearance of Warren Thorne from prison.

'I do not believe it,' he said twice, channelling his inner Victor Meldrew. 'How the hell did that happen? The Bure is meant to be Category C!'

'He wasn't in the Bure last night,' said Jim's voice over the car loudspeaker. 'Because he was mid-trial, they didn't bother returning him to the Bure but parked him in the first convenient cell they came to in Norwich, which is, of course, Category B. The latest guess is that he hid in a delivery truck. They had a food delivery in the early hours of the morning, and they think he might have got into the back while the driver was carting a pallet load of frozen chips into the cold store.'

'Where was the truck going after Norwich?' asked Greg.

'Back to base at a food park outside Great Yarmouth.'

'Any other dropping points?'

'None after the prison.'

'Still, no business of ours,' said Greg. 'Thankfully! I'm more than happy to leave the job of recovering him to others. And in the meantime, we can make good use of you, Jim.'

'I'm already on it,' said Jim. 'Jill and her team have gone through a mound of video, and Chris has been digging about in the Louise Lacon archives. We'll turn something up, no problem.'

Greg hoped his confidence wasn't misplaced and rang off to concentrate on the road.

42

Pulling the threads together

Reaching his office, Greg was greeted by an indignant secretary and a pile of paper.

'Bugger!' he sighed to himself, and tossed his jacket over the chair back as he sat down. Catching sight of the tape still protecting his hands, his secretary's expression softened a little. But only a little.

'Upstairs are chasing for your budget bid, and HR wants to know what happened to the training report and have you signed off DC Graham Clarke's probation yet. And the Chief Constable wants to see you at your earliest convenience. That usually means now,' she translated.

'OK, OK,' he muttered, and flashed her what was meant to be an appeasing smile. Judging from her expression, it wasn't working. 'The budget papers are ready, including my bid for a sergeant in King's Lynn. I'll send them to you now. Tell HR to contact DCI Trent for Gray's probation report, which isn't due for a couple of weeks anyway, and they can have the training report when I'm not dealing with a quartet of murders. I'll check in with the big boss after I've caught up in the incident room. If anyone asks, that's where I'll be for the next hour or so.'

'He meant...'

'Well he should have said what he meant then,' said Greg, losing patience. 'Look, I know all this stuff is important, and that everyone's chasing you, but it's not as urgent as stopping a killer. There's a difference between important and urgent. Tell them that, if they get on your case. And if all else fails, tell them I'm impossible and it's not your fault.'

'I've already told them that,' she told the door swinging to behind him. But she was smiling by then.

Down in the incident room, there was the steady buzz of purposeful activity. Greg instantly felt at home. He joined Jim at the whiteboard, just as Ram came through the door.

'Excellent, we're all here,' said Greg, glancing round. The assembled company included representatives of Norwich, King's Lynn and Forensic Science, he noted, although Bell and Waterton were missing. He clapped his hands together to make sure he had everyone's attention. 'Let's update each other, to make sure we're all on the same page and to identify new leads. I'll start us off with a summary of where I think we've got to.

'We were exploring the possibility that the attacks on Leonard Ware, Marie Leakey, Sharon Jones, Nick Atkinson and Anthony Newell were, in effect, attacks on Louise Lacon at one remove. A sort of Munchausen's murder by proxy, if you'll forgive the phrase.' He pointed at the board behind him. 'These five people are, or were, her actor friend, masseuse, hairdresser, mechanic and childhood friend, and local vicar.

The only link we've been able to find between them was Lacon, and the only common thread we've been able to identify was that they all have been or were confidants of hers. All a bit vague, as I think some of you have pointed out. Then we had the events of last night. A semi-retired solicitor, by the name of Joseph Andrews, was bludgeoned, kidnapped and then hung upside down over the river wall in Great Yarmouth, near the mediaeval watch tower across the road from the magistrates' court. He and Ms Lacon have been in a relationship since May, when they met via an online dating site.

'So, the Lacon link is reinforced. But where does that leave us as regards suspects?' He looked round the room, caught Ram's eye and beckoned him to continue.

'The pool of suspects, as I see it,' said Ram, 'includes Ms Lacon herself, Dean Mason and A N Other. In my view, the latest attack rules out Lacon. First, she was with Jill for much of last night, and while it is theoretically possible for her to have hit Andrews over the head and driven off with him before reporting him missing, the timing would be difficult. More to the point, she would have been physically incapable of lifting him over the river wall.'

'She could have had an accomplice,' objected Jim, playing devil's advocate.

'Hypothetically yes,' agreed Ram. 'But where's the motive? No. I can't see Lacon as a realistic suspect.' He looked at Greg, and receiving a nod, put a line through Lacon. As he did so, the door in the corner of the room opened to admit Chris, who winked at Greg and went to sit next to Jim.

A few seconds later, Greg's phone buzzed in his pocket, and he checked it discreetly: *Jamie with mother. Got new data.*

'Now let's take Dean Mason,' went on Ram. 'A partial car number plate has been recorded at at least three of the locations key to this enquiry: outside Marie Leakey's home, at Barton Broad boardwalk, near a source of hemlock and in Great Yarmouth last night. This number matches part of Dean Mason's car number—'

'Five locations,' interrupted Jill. 'Sorry. That's partly what I wanted to tell you. We've got it on the main road leading into Martham and also on the A47 heading into King's Lynn the night that Sharon Jones was attacked.'

'And we have the earbud with Dean's DNA on it found near the Martham arson attack,' added Ram. 'I'm liking him as our prime suspect.'

Chris stirred in her seat, but Greg was already speaking. 'I can see the attraction, and I agree, he should stay on our list, but it still doesn't sit right with me. The earbud doesn't ring true. It feels like a deliberate red herring. Someone trying to implicate Dean. Moreover, Ned doesn't think the fingerprint on the earbud is Mason's. And he has explanations for where he was during the earlier assaults – not least being onstage with Louise Lacon when the hit-and-run driver went for Leonard Ware. But, in the interests of ruling him out or in, once and for all, three things strike me as priorities. First, we trace his movements last night.'

'Already in hand, and I've sent a uniform team to bring him in,' Ram interpolated.

'Second, we impound his car and get Forensics to check it for any traces of stealth sprays on or around the number plates. And third, have we found out where the lithium bike battery came from? The one implicated in the Martham fire?'

There was a moment's silence, then Jill nodded. 'I'll get on to the car,' she said.

Roberts chipped in. 'And I'll follow up on the battery.'

Chris could be silent no longer. 'And I have another possible suspect for you,' she announced. 'It's what I came here to tell you. Louise Lacon's ex-husband has a number plate that also matches the partial we have on record.'

'Has he indeed?' said Greg. 'Well done, Chris. In that case we need to run the same checks on his car and his whereabouts on the key dates.'

Jim was already getting out of his seat. 'I'll get on to that,' he said. 'Chris, can I have a word?'

Greg turned to Ram but was interrupted by the door opening and his secretary's face peeking round.

Sorry to interrupt, she mouthed, as though the message delivered silently would somehow be less disruptive. *The Chief Constable wants to see you now.* She emphasised 'now', with air quotes.

'Damn. OK,' said Greg. 'On my way. Ram, I'll have to leave this with you for the moment.' And he shot out of the room.

***

Chief Constable Thornfield was clearly not pleased. When Greg was ushered into his office by a disapproving secretary, he was shuffling papers together with unnecessary violence.

'Ah, Superintendent Geldard,' he said. The words *at last* might as well have been voiced, they were so clear. 'I have an urgent job for you. Don't bother to sit down,' he added, 'you won't have time. I assume you know Thorne has escaped. It's all hands to the pump, I'm afraid. Get your team looking for him. ASAP. I don't need to tell you it's important.'

Greg didn't sit, but he made no move to go either.

'I'm sorry, sir, but my whole team are currently fully occupied chasing down a serial killer—'

'I'm aware of what you're up to, Geldard. I'm fully briefed. And I understand the only thing you have connecting the three deaths is part of a number plate that, in Norfolk, is as common as lost pens in a boardroom.'

'And they're all linked to Louise Lacon. Plus, there have been three other serious attacks that haven't resulted in deaths,' protested Greg.

'Tenuous.' Thornfield dismissed the objection. 'I've given you your orders, Geldard. I don't want any more argument. Find Thorne and put him behind bars again. Before the press jubilation at our embarrassment gets any louder. Then you can go back to your hypothetical serial killer.'

Greg took a deep breath, turned on his heel and headed for the door. He contemplated slamming it, then decided a quiet closure would be more dignified.

He took the stairs down rather than the lift, deciding that he needed the extra time to think. And to calm down. When he entered the incident room, it was to a hum of intense activity. As those present took in the expression on his face, the room gradually fell silent.

'I'm sorry, folks,' he said. 'We have another job. It seems we are the only people deemed capable of catching Warren Thorne.'

A host of objections bubbled up, and subsided as quickly, as he raised his hand for silence. 'Believe me, I've said it all,' he said. 'But I've been overruled. This is what we're going to do.

'Ram, you, Chris, Helena and Bill stay on the Lacon case. I'll have to leave it to you how you prioritise the various leads. Bring Helena up to speed, and keep me posted, please. I realise I'm leaving you short of DCs, but it's the best I can do without incurring wrath from above.'

'More wrath, you mean,' muttered Chris. 'He's not going to be pleased, you know.'

Greg ignored the comment. 'Jim and Glyn, you and the rest of the team are with me. Jill, you chase up Waterton and Challinor. Let them know about our new task. Let's start with what we know about the truck it's assumed he used for his escape and take it from there.'

43

After Thorne

Jill made her phone calls while Ram whisked his depleted team from the incident room, then pulled a fresh whiteboard in front of the one already covered with photos and Post-its.

'OK, we start from scratch,' announced Greg. 'Let's list what we know, then check everything.

'Jim. You have the report from Yarmouth?'

'Such as it is,' he said, looking from his laptop. 'It doesn't add a lot to what we know already.

'First, Thorne was dumped in the nearest available cell in Norwich, because the contractors couldn't be ars— er, bothered to take him back to the Bure. For some reason, they were delayed leaving the courts and arrived too late for the evening meal, which peed off all the prisoners no end. Apparently there was a bit of a fuss when they unloaded them at Norwich prison, which partly accounts for the lack of thought about where Thorne was deposited.'

'First thing to check,' interrupted Greg. 'What caused the delay and why? It may have been part of Thorne's escape plan.'

'Once they were all in cells, and apparently the only one housed individually was Thorne, they got a sandwich supper and that was it for the night,' went on Jim.

'Again,' said Greg, 'what drove that decision?'

'The final check was around midnight, and all was well then. When they came to unlock in the morning, Thorne was missing.'

'What about the delivery?' asked Greg. 'What details do we have on that?'

'The delivery was made at four in the morning by a truck from Park Farm food suppliers. They operate out of a trading estate on the edge of Great Yarmouth. Notwithstanding the name, it's essentially a logistical service for foods. They have frozen and chilled storage on site as well as ambient. Manufacturers deliver to them. They make up mixed or single loads and deliver on to hotels, shops, restaurants and, in this case, prisons.'

'What exactly was being delivered to the prison?' asked Greg.

'Frozen food of various sorts. Not just chips, which was what was said in the first place.'

'Only frozen?' Greg asked.

'So they say.'

'Check again,' said Greg. 'It will affect what sort of truck was making the delivery. And who helped unload? I don't suppose it was just the driver.'

Jim scribbled a note. 'And also check who signed the delivery in and out?' he asked.

'Absolutely. OK. After it was all unloaded, signed for – one hopes – and the truck checked. It was checked, I suppose?'

Jim scribbled another note, and Greg sighed. 'Either way, what happened next?'

'The truck returned to Park Farm.'

'Direct?'

'So they say.'

'Definitely no stops on the way?'

'So they say,' said Jim again.

'We check that. I assume we have the truck registration. Check ANPR from the prison to Yarmouth. Make sure it's consistent with a journey straight from one to the other at that time in the morning. Exactly what time did they leave the prison?'

'Recorded as four thirty-eight,' replied Jim.

Jill nodded and added to the details mounting on the whiteboard.

'Do Park Farms have any means of tracking the deliveries?' asked Greg. 'I remember the delivery company involved in a case a couple of years ago. They had trackers on their vehicles and knew exactly where they went and when.'

'There's nothing mentioned here,' said Jim, flicking through screens. 'I'll ask about it.'

'If we take all this at face value, I can see why the investigation so far has been focussing on the Great Yarmouth end,' commented Greg. 'But as far as I know, they haven't found anything yet?'

'No credible reported sightings, nothing on CCTV at Park Farm nor on neighbouring units at the industrial estate. Zilch,' said Jim. 'They're widening their enquiries across Yarmouth, the harbour and the railway station.'

'OK,' said Greg. 'Leave that to them but keep in touch. We'll start as we've said already, checking everything from the courthouse onwards. We need to rule out any diversions early in this apparent breakout before we go wider. You know what we need to do. Get on with it. I'll liaise with Yarmouth and be back here shortly.'

Greg left the incident room, his phone already pressed to his ear. When he reached his office, he closed the door behind him and sat down at his desk.

'Chris, can you talk?' he asked.

'I've got a minute,' she said.

'Anyone with you?'

'No. Ram's preparing for his chat with Mason, Bill's on the phone to Halfords and Helena Bell is, as far as I know, on her way here.'

'That's who I wanted to talk about,' said Greg. 'It only occurred to me in the last few minutes, but when I was trying to persuade him that we had too much on our plate already, the Chief said he had been "fully briefed". Now, who the hell briefed him? It wasn't me or you. It wasn't Ram or Jim, because they were fully engaged in the incident room.'

'It has to have been Helena Bell,' said Chris. 'Yes. I did warn you she didn't like being corrected, and she's never been convinced about the Sharon Jones case.'

'I need to think about that,' said Greg. 'It leaves a nasty taste. Both because she went behind my back and because I'd like to know how a DCI in King's Lynn has such ready access to the Chief Constable's ear.'

'I'll make some discreet enquiries,' said Chris.

'Very discreet,' said Greg, and rang off.

The conversation with Chief Inspector Lake of Great Yarmouth was short, and relatively friendly, considering he would have been within his rights to have taken offence at the high-handed hijacking of his case.

'At the moment we're checking across all the transport hubs in Yarmouth, on the assumption he got here and will now be planning the next stage of his escape,' he said. 'We're covering rail, bus and port options, plus I've got someone checking for any reports of stolen vehicles. But, as I'm sure you know, there are a hundred ways he could have moved on from here.'

'Needle and haystack come to mind,' agreed Greg. 'Is there anything to show that he definitely reached Park Farm?'

'No,' admitted Lake. 'The CCTV coverage at Park Farm is exemplary and there's nothing on any of their cameras. And no missing footage. He was either very lucky, or he knew where the cameras were.'

'Or he had guidance from someone who did,' commented Greg. 'Have you ruled out any conspiracy with the truck driver?'

'First thing we checked,' replied Lake. 'There's no suggestion of any link, and he's got no record apart from a youthful rap over the knuckles for shoplifting. The prison checked him out as well. They didn't turn anything up. He's worked for Park Farm for over three years and they have no complaints. The foreman we spoke to was happy to give him a character reference.'

'The other possibility, of course, is that Thorne never reached Park Farm at all,' remarked Greg.

'The driver swears he didn't stop anywhere between the prison and the depot. I suppose it's possible he stopped at traffic lights and Thorne bailed out, but it's hard to see how he could open the truck doors without the driver being aware. That would only work if he was under the truck rather than in it. And Forensic say there are traces of him inside the truck – hair and suchlike. We're checking CCTV near traffic lights to see if we can pick him up, but that's a backstop. I don't think it's likely. So you can see why we're pinning our efforts on the assumption he ducked out at Park Farm without being spotted and is now somewhere in the Yarmouth or Gorleston area.'

'I need to consider where we can best add value to your efforts, given the Chief is obsessed with all hands to the pump,' said Greg. 'We're starting by checking the conclusion that he reached Yarmouth. I'll get back to you when we have anything.'

Rejoining Jim in the incident room, he immediately noticed that excitement levels had risen.

'Jill's found something already,' said Jim.

She turned round from her screens and nodded. 'There's a time discrepancy,' she said. 'A bit like the one Gray picked up last night. Only this time, it's the truck that took too long to get from Acle to Yarmouth. Whatever the driver says, I think he stopped somewhere.'

'Jim, you and I will go and have another chat with this driver,' said Greg. 'Where's Glyn?'

'Gone to check what happened at the courts to hold up the departure to the prison, and then on to check at the prison itself.'

'Good. Jill, widen your search area and see if you can pick the truck up between Acle and Yarmouth. Check other food businesses, just in case there was another drop that hasn't been declared. Come on, Jim.'

***

Chris and Bill waited as Ram completed his phone conversation with Helena Bell.

'She's on her way,' he said briefly. 'She and Dean Mason should arrive about the same time, so I've asked her to join me for his next interview. A fresh pair of eyes and ears might be helpful. And I've asked Ned to get someone to check his car over for stealth spray. That leaves following up on your latest intelligence, Chris.'

'How about Bill and I do that?' suggested Chris. 'We have a Norwich address on record. Bill and I could call there, get a look at his car and have an initial chat, to see if he's worth a closer look.'

Ram looked hesitant. 'I thought you were supposed to be office-based for the moment,' he said.

'That was then, this is now,' said Chris. 'I'm covered at home for the rest of the day, and given how shorthanded we are...' She left the sentence hanging and Ram decided not to quibble further.

'OK. Let's do it,' he said.

As Chris and Bill headed for the car park, she saw Greg just ahead of them with Jim.

'Hang on, Bill,' she said, 'I'll just bring Chas up to date before we set off.' She got her phone out and dialled, keeping one eye on Greg disappearing round the corner without noticing them.

'Chas,' she said. 'Bill and I are going to check out the lead to Lacon's ex-husband. Have you turned up anything new on him?'

'Not much,' he said. 'He's clearly a wealthy man, judging by his address in Newmarket Road. Given the location, I made a phone call to the golf club and, sure enough, he's a member, although they say he hasn't been playing much recently. I've done the round of the banks and it seems he has accounts at Lloyds and Coutts, but no one will give me any details without more justification than we yet have. That's all I have at the moment.'

'Well done so far,' said Chris. 'Go back to the golf club and check whether his membership dues are up to date. And check his credit rating. A fancy house doesn't always mean solvency.' She was about to ring off when another thought occurred to her. 'Chas,' she said, lowering her voice and checking that the only person who could overhear her was Bill, 'any reason I should know of, why DCI Bell has been seen around the Chief Constable?'

There was a knowing chuckle down the phone. 'Gossip has it that they're good friends,' said Chas. 'But actually, I think it's just that he's a friend of the family. He knew her father.'

'I thought that might be it,' said Chris. 'Thanks, Chas.' She looked at Bill. 'Not a word, not yet,' she said.

By the time they reached her car, she'd already trawled through her contacts and found the number she was looking for. There was no answer, but she was able to leave a message.

'Hi, Margaret. Chris Mathews here. Hope you are enjoying your retirement. Am I right in thinking Helena Bell's father served alongside Ralph Thornfield earlier in his career?'

***

Park Farm belied its name in almost every aspect. Far from the bucolic image the name evoked, it was a spread of commercial storage facilities spaced around a logistical hub and located within a broader trading estate. Its boundary was secured by heavy-duty fencing topped by razor wire, and the single gate in was both manned by security guards and covered by CCTV cameras.

'This place is probably more secure than the prison,' remarked Jim as Greg pulled up to the entrance barrier. The guard on duty in the security hut came out, putting his cap on. He was a heavyset man clad in a navy uniform of drill trousers and polo-shirt top, bearing the logo of N&M Security. He looked like an ex-boxer, even to the broken nose.

'No cars allowed,' was as far as he got before he spotted the warrant card Greg was holding out to him. 'Ah. OK. I thought we'd done with your lot,' he remarked, a little grumpily, and went back into his hut to raise the barrier.

'Jim, pop in there after him and see what sort of records they keep for vehicles coming in and out. I'll see you in the offices.' Greg pointed to a sign that read 'Reception' on the double-height converted-container-style offices in front of them.

Reception was manned by another man who looked remarkably similar to the guard on the gate and was clad in the same regalia.

'DCI, I mean Detective Superintendent Geldard,' said Greg, feeling like a fool and cursing himself for the slip. 'Here to see' – he checked the note on his phone – 'Mr Hurst and Mr Snelling.'

'Both in Mr Hurst's office,' said the man on the desk. He pointed over his shoulder to a door that apparently led into the back rooms.

'And you are?' asked Greg.

'Tim Boyd,' replied the man.

'Does your security firm usually man the reception desk?' asked Greg.

'Usually, yes,' he said. 'It's usually trucks and deliveries we're checking in. Not really a job for a girl, if that's what you were thinking.'

Greg suppressed any comments he might have had about sexist assumptions and asked, 'Who checks what, where? Two checks seem like overkill.'

'The gate checks times in and out and ID. Whoever's in here checks loads and directs them to which storage unit is appropriate. Or if it's a collection, we check the truck ID and send them to the despatch shed. For everything except frozen foods, the mixed orders are put together in the despatch shed.'

'And frozen foods?' asked Greg.

'They go direct from the cold store into refrigerated trucks.'

'OK. Thank you for explaining. This way, I think you said.' And Greg pushed open the door indicated, to find himself in a narrow corridor running to left and right. A door on his left was clearly labelled 'Managing Director', and he chose that one.

Mr Hurst, a well-shaven man in his mid-fifties clad in shirt and tie, was sitting at his desk, surrounded by dockets. The man sitting in one of the two visitor chairs in front of him shot to his feet as Greg came in. Hurst got up in a rather more leisurely fashion and held out his hand.

'I'm Martin Hurst,' he said. 'I gather you want another chat with Snelling here.' He indicated the driver shifting uneasily from foot to foot.

'I've told you everything I know,' burst in Snelling. Greg looked at him, taking in the red nose and watery eyes, which he charitably put down to a cold or hay fever rather than drink. At least, given the man's profession, he hoped so.

'I would indeed,' he said. 'Is there a room we can use? My colleague DI Henning will be joining me as soon as he's finished at the site entrance.'

'You can use this room,' said Hurst, moving round the desk and hooking a jacket from the back of his chair. 'I've one or two things I need to be doing. I'm a bit surprised you're going over this again,' he added. 'Our security here is good, and we've answered all your questions once already. I've said it several times: I don't believe anyone could have got off this site without us knowing. So it follows, he was never on the truck in the first place.' He opened the door to reveal Jim just outside, his hand raised to knock. 'You must be DI Henning,' he said. 'Do come in. I'll be back in an hour or so.' And he left through the door into reception.

Jim looked at the fidgety driver and over at Greg. 'Can I have a word, Boss, before we start here?' he asked.

Greg nodded to Snelling. 'Take a seat, we'll be back in a minute,' he said, and followed Jim into the narrow corridor, closing the door behind him. 'What is it?' he asked, keeping his voice low, in view of the thin walls around them.

'Very interesting,' said Jim. 'I'm quite impressed with their procedures here. It seems Mr Hurst runs a tight ship. Every vehicle moving on- or off-site is recorded: registration number, time and driver. If the driver isn't known on site, for example if it's a delivery in by a driver who hasn't been here before, the man on the gate asks to see their driving licence, and that's recorded too. Now for the interesting bit. The time recorded for Snelling's truck arriving in the early hours is consistent with the data Jill got from the ANPR cameras. But it doesn't match what Snelling said in his statement. The time he gave was half an hour to forty minutes earlier.'

'How did they not notice that?' demanded Greg, referring to the earlier stage of the investigation.

'I'm guessing because Snelling wasn't on hand when they did the initial search of this site. He was in bed, asleep, after his night shift. He made his statement after he was routed out of bed, and no one has put the two bits of info together to expose the discrepancy.'

'This is going to be very interesting,' said Greg grimly. 'Come on, Jim. We're not leaving here until we find out where he spent that missing forty minutes.'

They re-entered Hurst's office. Snelling spun round in his seat so fast he seemed at serious risk of a crick in the neck.

'Don't get up,' said Greg, although the man had shown no signs of doing so. He sat himself down in Hurst's chair, while Jim took the other guest seat, moving it a little way round the desk until he was at right angles to Snelling. 'In light of what we have just learned,' he began, 'I've decided to conduct this interview under caution. This means that you are entitled to legal representation if you want it. If you do, we'll need to move this down to the station in Wymondham. If you're happy to carry on without, then we'll get on here, and finish up as quickly as we can. It's entirely up to you,' he added.

Snelling swallowed and looked at his watch. 'I have to pick my daughter up from school. I promised my wife. Will I be back in time?' he asked.

Greg too looked at his watch. 'I can't make any promises,' he said.

Snelling hesitated, sniffing and wiping his nose on the back of his hand. 'Let's go ahead then,' he said finally. Greg presumed he was more afraid of his wife than he was of them, and made a mental note not to shake hands with the man.

'In that case, Mr Snelling, I need to caution you that you do not have to say anything, but anything you do say...'

As the words of the caution rolled over him, Snelling fidgeted again, looking less than happy with his decision. Jim had set his phone to record and placed it on the desk in front of him.

'Could you confirm for the recording,' said Greg, 'that you have been reminded of your right to have a solicitor present and have declined.'

There was a small hesitation, and Snelling said at last, 'Yes. Let's just get on with it.'

'In that case, Mr Snelling, I have some questions relating to your delivery at Norwich prison last night and your return journey here. In your signed statement it says that you carried out your delivery at the prison between four and four thirty, and everything was normal. Who helped you unload the truck?'

'No one really,' said Snelling. 'The truck has a tail lift, and I have a hand pallet truck on board. Normally I just load up a pallet onto the hand truck, put it on the tail lift to lower it to the ground, and then move it into the cold store. It's only if I need to break down a pallet load that anything has to be done by hand, and that's rare.'

'So, let me get this clear,' said Greg. 'You arrived at the prison and were checked in by their security. You parked in the delivery bay, in the secure compound. You unloaded a pallet or pallets – how many, by the way?' he asked.

'Two,' said Snelling.

'Is that one at a time or both together?' asked Greg.

'One at a time,' replied Snelling.

'Was the truck secured while you delivered the pallets into the prison cold store?'

asked Jim.

'No,' said Snelling. 'But it was under observation by the prison warders the whole time,' he added defensively. He wiped his red nose again on his hand. Greg itched to offer him a box of tissues but there were none on the desk.

'So you delivered the two pallets, one at a time, then returned the hand truck to the back of your vehicle. Was there anything remaining in it at this time?'

'Just one pallet of chips. I think,' said Snelling.

'Oh! Why?' asked Greg. 'You said in your statement that the prison was your last drop. Why was there still a pallet of chips in your truck?'

'Perhaps I'm wrong. No, it must have been empty,' said Snelling. 'Sorry, I'm still tired from my night shift. No, now I think about it, it was empty. Of course it was.'

'So if anyone had been hiding in your truck, it must have been in your cab rather than in the back. Because you'd have seen them in an empty truck, wouldn't you?' asked Greg.

'I suppose,' said Snelling. 'But I didn't. I didn't see anyone. Not in the cab or in the back.'

'Let's turn to your journey back here,' said Greg. 'It was in the early hours of the morning, so presumably the roads were quiet.'

'Yes, that's right,' said Snelling.

Greg looked at Jim.

'Why did it take you so long to get here then?' asked Jim.

Snelling shifted his gaze from Greg to Jim. 'It didn't take all that long. Just the normal time,' he said.

'Not according to the log on the gate,' remarked Jim. 'According to that, you arrived here five minutes past six. Some forty minutes later than you claim in your statement.'

'He must have got it wrong,' protested Snelling with more vehemence than confidence. 'It's easy to get a number wrong on a long night shift.'

'Odd,' said Jim. 'Because we have your truck logged by ANPR camera on the A1064 near Caister at a time that is consistent with you arriving here just after six.'

'Which raises two questions,' said Greg, taking over. 'Why were you on the A1064 at all, rather than on the Acle Straight? And what were you doing for the missing half an hour or more?'

There was a pause, then, 'No comment,' said Snelling.

'OK,' said Greg. 'We'll continue this at the station. Unless you'd like to reconsider your last answer.'

'No comment,' said Snelling stubbornly. 'And I'm not going anywhere. I told you, I have to pick my daughter up.'

'Mr Snelling, I'm arresting you on suspicion of perverting the cause of justice,' said Greg, losing patience. 'Jim, caution him and put him in the car.'

Mr Hurst returned to the offices as Jim was hustling the driver through the reception area, under the fascinated gaze of the guard on duty.

'Where're you taking him? What's the problem?' he asked.

'To our HQ at Wymondham for further questioning,' replied Greg. 'And if I were you, I'd do a stocktake. I suspect there've been some shenanigans going on involving unauthorised deliveries.'

44

Newmarket Road

Chris and Bill were sitting in his car just a few yards from the entrance to what, by any standards, was a very impressive house. A broad sweep of drive led from the busy main road to a half-timbered, gable-fronted construction that wouldn't have looked out of place surrounded by acres of parkland. As it was, the garden between the wall that fronted the road and the pillared porch was mainly dusty shrubbery.

'Around the one to two million mark, I'd guess,' said Bill.

'Interesting the way people's minds work,' replied Chris. 'I was thinking that it didn't look like he was paying a gardener. Come on, let's go in.'

'Hang on a tick, Boss,' said Bill, shifting in the driver's seat. 'Shouldn't we do something about backup? If this chap's done what we think he's done, he's poisoned, stabbed and bludgeoned to death, to name but three. I'm not sure we should just rush in.'

'We're not rushing in. We're two police officers undertaking a considered approach to a possible suspect. And we're armed.

At least, I assume you have a taser. I certainly do. And pepper spray,' she added. 'What's the problem?'

'The boss, Boss,' said Bill, getting tangled in his bosses. 'I mean the big boss. I don't think he's going to be happy about this.' *And I couldn't help but notice you made sure he didn't know,* he added to himself.

'Greg fusses,' said Chris dismissively. 'If he doesn't know, he won't worry.' Bill muttered something. 'What was that?' she asked irritably. 'Speak up if you have something to say.'

'I said,' repeated Bill, gathering his courage with both hands. 'I hope I have indemnity insurance, because if anything happens to you on my watch, I'm for it.'

'You'll be fine,' she replied. 'Don't worry, Greg will know who to blame. And nothing's going to happen anyway. You watch my back, and I'll watch yours. Come on, drive us in and park in front of the garage. That way, he can't make a run for it. At least not in his car.'

Bill did as he was told, and the two of them climbed out of his car in the drive near the double garage. It was surprisingly quiet, much of the traffic noise being muted by the wall and the shrubs. Chris surveyed the garage doors. They were of the up-and-over type, and firmly closed, as she discovered when she rattled the one nearest.

'Can I help you?' said a voice behind them.

Chris and Bill whirled round to confront a man who had appeared round the corner of the garage block. He was heavily built, about six foot tall and probably in his early sixties, Chris estimated. As he came towards them, she amended her estimate slightly to *late fifties but not wearing well*. His hair was greying, thin and even a bit patchy where he wasn't completely bald, and she wondered if he had alopecia. She held out her warrant card and introduced them.

'Good day. I'm Detective Inspector Mathews, and this is Detective Constable Street. We would like a few words, please.'

'You'd better come in,' he said and started past them to lead the way to the front door.

'Before we do, I wonder if we might have a look at your car,' said Chris on impulse.

'Why?' He raised an interrogative eyebrow. Or what would have been an eyebrow had there been a decent sprinkling of hairs. Chris realised they too were sparse and amended her thoughts about age to wonder about ill health and chemotherapy.

'Our investigation involves an incident involving a car. It would be useful to rule yours out of our enquiries,' she replied.

'Well you may, but I can't open the doors without the zapper, so you'd better come in and ask your questions first.' He went to the front door and pushed it open with a gesture that said argument was not going to be tolerated, and led the way in.

'Clearly the front door isn't locked,' Chris muttered to Bill as she passed him.

Bill nodded and followed her into the house. He still wasn't happy.

'I take it you are Mr Reginald Coleman,' Chris said as she followed their host through a tiled hall and into a chilly lounge.

He waved at a pair of sofas that faced each other across a would-be baronial fireplace. 'Take a seat,' he said. 'What can I do for you?' He waited for them to sit on one of the sofas, then sat on the one opposite.

Bill, mindful of the possible need for a swift exit, had chosen the one nearest the door, and perched himself at the end nearest the fire, leaving Chris to sit on his right. Left-handed Bill wanted his left hand clear to grab for his taser. Chris, fully aware of his thinking, suppressed a smile and got out her notebook, it seeming less threatening than a recorder.

'I am Coleman,' answered the man in response to the earlier question. It was clear that offers of refreshment were not going to be forthcoming. 'What can I do for you?' he asked again.

'And you are the ex-husband of Louise Lacon?'

'Louise Coleman, as she was then,' said the man. 'Yes, that's right.'

'When did you last see your ex-wife?' asked Chris.

'Oh, I don't know exactly. Around a week or two ago, I suppose,' he replied, leaning back into the sofa cushions in what Chris immediately thought was an exaggerated demonstration of relaxation.

She reminded herself not to be prejudiced by assumptions, then wondered why the prejudice had arisen. *What has he done to raise my hackles?* Unconsciously, her eyes narrowed as she sharpened her focus on the man lounging opposite, and he straightened in his seat as he too read the body language in the room.

'I needed to hand over some papers, so I met her at one of her rehearsals. We're still on good terms,' he added, 'notwithstanding the divorce. It should never have happened really. Think of us as the middle-class version of Prince Andrew and Fergie,' he said with a smile that went no further than his mouth.

Chris thought he could have chosen a more appealing parallel and moved on to her next question. 'How often would you normally meet her?' she asked.

'Every week or so,' he replied. 'Covid rules permitting, of course.'

'Where were you last night?' she asked.

If Coleman was surprised by the sudden change in direction, he didn't show it. 'Here,' he said, 'reading and watching TV.'

'Can anyone corroborate that?' asked Chris.

'I doubt it,' he said. 'I live alone, and I'm not exactly overlooked by neighbours.'

'What did you watch?' asked Bill.

'An old film I found on Netflix,' he said, and named an elderly war film. 'But after a bit I got tired of it and returned to my book.' He reached an arm out to the coffee table in front of him and showed them a battered copy of *The Two Towers* with a bookmark prominent halfway through the text. 'I've read it before of course, but it stands a lot of re-reading.'

Bill reflected that it must have been a lot easier to establish if someone was watching TV at home alone when there were only a few channels and no streaming. Coleman could have watched that film anytime. And the fact the TV was tuned to Netflix, which he had no doubt it would have been, was no guarantee anyone was actually watching it.

'And the evening of the twenty-eighth of July?' asked Chris.

'Very probably the same,' he responded. 'I haven't been in good health, and I don't go out a lot. Except when I'm meeting Louise. Or playing golf.'

One by one, Chris went through all the dates and times when the six victims had been attacked. It was no surprise that he produced the same, uncheckable, alibi each time. *He's smart. An alibi that can't be proven also can't be unproven. And at present, we have very little more than a suspicion to go on.*

'Perhaps we can take a look at your car now,' she said, and stood up. For the first time, she thought he looked a little disconcerted.

'I suppose so,' he said slowly. 'I'll just get the zapper.' He left the room, and they could hear his footsteps disappearing across the tiled hall and towards the back of the house.

'I'd love a look round this place,' said Chris softly. 'Not least to check out his kitchen for hemlock and his kitchen knives to see if they match the wound on Sharon Jones.'

'Come back with a warrant?' asked Bill.

'We don't have enough for one so far,' she replied, then shut up as the footsteps came back across the hall.

'Got it. This way,' he said, leading them back out of the front door and to the double garage at the side of the house.

As they approached, he pressed the zapper: first the button on the right and then the one on the left. First one door, then the other, emitted a whining noise, shuddered, and wound slowly up. The garage on the left was empty except for an old freezer on one wall and a stack of what looked like garden stakes. The one on the right contained a dark grey Mercedes with a number plate beginning AO20. Bill took a surreptitious photo with his phone as Chris distracted the owner with a question.

'The car doesn't look that old,' she remarked, referring to the registration plate. 'Mind if I take a closer look?' And without waiting for an answer, she walked up to the car.

'It's a personal plate,' replied Coleman. The car had been reversed into the garage, so was facing outward.

Ready for a quick getaway, Chris thought. Then castigated herself for paranoia. She bent to examine the number plate close up, then started to walk around the car to examine the one on the back.

'That'll do,' said Coleman suddenly. As Chris stopped and turned, he beckoned her out of the garage. 'I think that's enough,' he said. 'I've tolerated your unannounced visit and your questions, and even you poking round my car, but enough is enough. You can come back with a warrant and speak to me with my solicitor present, or not at all.' He pointed firmly towards their car. 'Please leave. Now.'

Chris exchanged a look with Bill. He nodded, just a fraction, and they got back into the car. As Chris buckled up she asked, 'Got the photo?'

'I took a couple,' he replied, putting the car into gear and driving towards the exit on to the main road. He glanced in the rear-view mirror and noted that the garage doors were already closing, and Coleman was walking back towards his front door.

'And?' she asked.

'I couldn't tell,' he replied. 'I'll need to take a closer look on screen. And the lab boys may need to enhance the image.'

'They can take a look at this as well,' said Chris, and held out the small white hankie in her hand, its pristine surface marred by a smear. 'I managed a quick swipe. It won't be valid in court, but it may tell us if we're barking up the right tree.'

45

Later that day

By the time Snelling was lawyered up – he'd refused one of the duty solicitors on the grounds he preferred his wife's cousin's best friend – it was getting late. 'At least the delay let me get on top of the blasted paperwork,' Greg said to Jim as they strolled down the corridor to the interview suite. 'And that's got HR off my back, for now. Any news from Ram?'

'Last thing I heard, he'd interviewed Mason, checked his alibi for last night and he's apparently in the clear. Moreover, Forensics have run a fine-tooth comb over his car and found no trace of stealth spray. I believe Ram and his crew are now chasing the possibility Chris brought up.'

'Well at least ruling Mason out is a step forward,' said Greg. 'I'll catch up with Ram after we see this chap.'

Snelling and his brief both looked equally uncomfortable, sitting side by side at the table facing the door.

'I'm Henry Fell,' said the solicitor.

'Pleased to meet you,' responded Greg. He'd already been told that Mr Fell was not a regular around the Norfolk courts.

This was confirmed as Fell went on to explain. 'This isn't my usual area of expertise, but Mr Snelling has insisted I represent him.'

Greg guessed Mr Fell was usually involved in conveyancing property or writing wills, judging by the level of discomfort he was exhibiting. 'Well I hope this won't take too long,' he said. 'It needn't, provided your client is willing to cooperate.'

Jim turned the recording equipment on, they all identified themselves and Greg administered the caution. Then a silence fell. After a spell that allowed the sounds of summer to enter the room through the narrow window high in the wall: a combination of birdsong and lawnmowers, Greg said, 'I'm going to be plain with you, Mr Snelling. We have clear evidence that your truck did not take the most direct route from Norwich to Great Yarmouth on your return journey from the prison to the Park Farm depot.' He fanned out the printout showing the truck number caught on ANPR and pointed to the time signature. 'It is equally clear that there is at least half an hour to forty minutes unaccounted for. Long enough for you to make an additional, unauthorised delivery somewhere between here and here.' He placed a map on the table between them and pointed to two locations: the first the ANPR camera near the roundabout at Acle, the second near the Caister bypass.

'Now, quite frankly, Mr Snelling, I don't give a monkey's what you were delivering to where or why. That's a matter for your employer, and if you've been stealing from him, he's free to take it up with our uniformed colleagues.'

Both Snelling and Fell stirred in their seats, but neither said anything.

'What I do care about, very much, is that you've let an allegedly homicidal maniac loose on the community.' He fanned out some photos on top of the map. One was of a body in a ditch, a bicycle resting on top of it. A second was of a young man lying crumpled under a tree. The third was of DC Hall, the hatchet in his neck clearly visible. Snelling turned green and coughed into his hand. Fell didn't look much better.

Greg stabbed his forefinger onto the last photo with an abruptness that made them both jump. 'Now, in fairness to the law, I should say that the allegations relating to the other two deaths have not yet been proven in court. The case is still ongoing. But...' He stabbed his finger down again, for emphasis. 'I can assure you that Warren Thorne did, without a shadow of a doubt, kill my officer Steve Hall. I was there at the time. I witnessed the act. I had Steve's blood all over my hands when I tried to stop the bleeding.' He held up his hands and both Snelling and Fell stared at them, fascinated as though by a snake.

'I really, really don't want to be in that position again,' he said. 'So, for God's sake, Mr Snelling, tell me where you stopped and where Warren Thorne left your truck. Or the blood of who knows how many will be on your hands.'

He sat back in his chair and waited. The silence dragged. Fell didn't say a word. Jim stirred, but after a look from Greg, he remained silent too. Just when it seemed it wasn't going to work, Snelling spoke up.

'It was here,' he said dully, pointing on the map. 'Filby. I was dropping stuff off to a mate who runs a fish and chip van. I don't suppose you can keep this from my boss,' he added without much hope. 'I won't do it again, I promise.'

'I rather think he'll have worked it out for himself,' replied Greg, 'once he's carried out the stocktake I recommended. What action he takes next is up to him. The exact address you stopped, please?'

'22a Thrigby Lane,' he replied.

'And what did you see of Thorne when you opened the truck?'

'Not much,' said Snelling. 'I pulled up at my mate's. His lights were on, so I knew he'd be out in a minute. I opened the doors at the back, then as he hadn't arrived I went round to his garden gate to see if he was on his way. When I turned back, I saw a shadow slipping away from my truck down the road towards Thrigby. I didn't shout because I didn't want to attract any attention. I went and looked in the back, in case someone had been thieving, but it all looked OK. Next thing, my mate was at my elbow. We unloaded – it was only a few boxes – and then I was on my way again.'

'Thank you, Mr Snelling. Better late than never I suppose, although it would have been better if you'd told me this when we spoke in Yarmouth. Thorne's now had another few hours to further his escape. If he attacks anyone, I hope you can live with yourself. This will all be written up into a statement for you to sign. Then you can go,' Greg added, pre-empting Mr Fell's next, and only, question.

Back in the incident room, Jim sat down to start phoning. 'Door to door in Thrigby Lane?' he said, eyebrows raised.

'That's where we start,' agreed Greg. 'Looking at the map, there's not a lot of transport possibilities around there. Either he hitched a lift, was picked up by a mate, or he's still in the vicinity.'

***

Chris had spent the first part of the afternoon in the forensic laboratories, chivvying action on Bill's photos and her, somewhat irregular, smear from Mr Coleman's car number plate. For all the fussing, the end results were not entirely satisfactory.

'I'm sorry, but that's it,' said Yvonne, Ned's highly competent deputy. 'There's no clear evidence of stealth spray on either your handkerchief or Bill's photo. To be certain, we'd need to take a proper look at the car.'

'But no evidence of paint isn't evidence of no paint,' remarked Chris, undeterred. 'OK. Bill, we need more data before we can get a warrant, so let's see what we can find.'

As it happened, she reached this point just as Ram returned from his fruitless conversation with Dean Mason.

'Chris, great,' he said. 'Can you join us?'

She squeezed into Ram's small office along with Bill. 'Where's Helena Bell?' she asked Ram. 'I thought she was with you, interviewing Mason.'

'She was. Now she's gone back to the Sharon Jones case,' he replied. 'She's got the local uniforms doing another door to door along the street where Jones was stabbed, mainly to see if she can track down the murder weapon. It seems the last door to door tended to focus on possible witnesses and any CCTV footage, since they were still working on the assumption it was a mugging. I gather you didn't get very far with Lacon's ex. What's his name?'

'Reginald Coleman. No, we didn't get very far. He's a well-to-do man of apparently independent means with very little social life, apart from golf and his ex. He has bank accounts at Lloyds and Coutts. The mere existence of the latter argues for a certain level of wealth, but they won't share any details with us at the moment. He has unverifiable alibis for the dates in question and refused to let us have a close look around his car. I've got Chas doing some more checking, but that's about it for now.' Chris put her notebook away.

'In that case, our main leads are still the bike battery used in the vicarage fire, and the rope used on Joseph Andrews. As the rest of our team are currently doing other people's jobs for them by hunting Warren Thorne, I've begged a return favour in the shape of some manpower to check out possible sources for the rope and the battery. Chris and Bill, can you get that organised, please?' Correctly interpreting Chris's raised eyebrow, he added, 'I'm off to have another chat with Louise Lacon, following up on my conversation with Joseph Andrews.'

Chris and Bill headed for the incident room, found it humming with people working the Thorne case and, much in the way a dog will make space for itself on its owner's bed, gradually appropriated a corner for themselves.

'Did you get anything off Halfords?' asked Chris.

'Mainly a promise of information to come,' said Bill. 'They said they sold lots of batteries, and if we could be more precise about the exact make and model, they could look up their records. I got a distinct impression they might cooperate faster if I stood over them.'

'OK, Bill. I'll leave you to follow up with them. But first, check out all the possible battery and rope sources and sort them into localities,' instructed Chris. 'In view of the possible involvement of Coleman, don't neglect Norwich.'

'I assume I include both climbing suppliers and yacht chandlers in the rope search,' said Bill, making notes. 'Bike shops, obviously, for the battery. What about second-hand options?'

'As far as the rope is concerned,' replied Chris, already picking up her phone, 'Forensics thought it looked new, and if you check their report, I think you'll find they thought it was more mooring rope than the climbing type. But you've given me another idea. I'll get Chas to check for any reports of stolen electric bikes and/or bike batteries in the last few weeks. It may have been nicked not bought.'

'Then, of course,' added Bill, still pursuing his own line of thought, 'there are the online options.'

'Bugger. Of course there are,' said Chris, her phone call temporarily suspended. 'If we could get a warrant, we could check his online activity…'

'But we need the evidence for a warrant,' said Bill. 'Bit of a catch 22 going on here.'

'Let's try the local suppliers first, and keep our fingers crossed,' said Chris, turning back to her phone. 'I'm going to find out what officers we have available, and sort them into teams.'

By dint of a lot of ringing round and calling in of favours, Chris eventually lined up a team: two from the hard-pressed Yarmouth station, two from Broads Beat willing to do a round of the yacht chandlers and two more from Norwich. Bill had a list of possible suppliers, and they sat down to divvy them up. Norwich and its suburbs had way too many possible bike shops for the team of two, and Bill heaved a mock heavy sigh as Chris's cursor hovered over the list on her screen.

'Which shall I do?' he asked resignedly. 'I'll start with Halfords, shall I?'

With all the searchers underway with strict instructions to report every result, negative or positive, to her asap, Chris headed for home. Before leaving, she poked her head round Greg's office door but was unsurprised to find it empty except for his secretary.

'Still interviewing,' she said to Chris, glancing at the clock. 'I expect he'll be finished soon. Do you want me to give him a message?'

'Just say I called in and I'm on my way back home,' said Chris. 'Thanks.'

***

In fact, Greg hadn't gone back to his office at all. After the bombshell from Snelling, he'd wasted little time hitting the road east for the village of Filby. Only two phone calls had delayed his departure: one to the dog teams, the second to the armed response unit. Then leaving Jill to update Rick Lake in Yarmouth, he headed out.

By the time he reached Filby, by some alchemy of phone calls and emails Jill had also 'borrowed' the village hall for a control centre and lined up a meeting between Greg and the parish council chairman.

'George Winner.' He held out a gnarled hand for Greg to shake. 'How worried do we need to be?'

Greg waved him to a chair and sat opposite. 'I'll be frank with you,' he replied after a moment to take thought. 'This man Thorne is dangerous, violent and unstable. He is being tried for several murders, and I know for a fact that he killed one of my officers because I witnessed him do it. Having said that, we now know precisely where he got out of the back of a truck and took off on foot. I have a dog team on the way,' – he didn't mention the armed police – 'and it's only a matter of time before we catch him. The best way your residents can help is to let my officers know if they have seen or heard anything suspicious over the last twelve hours, and, as far as possible, to secure their homes and stay away from lonely or isolated spaces. He was a tree surgeon by profession and he seems to have a natural affinity for woodland.'

'OK. I'll get the message out,' responded Winner. 'But I should warn you, we have a lot of woodland round here, not to mention the wildlife park.'

'Noted,' said Greg. 'I'll let you know if there are any developments,' he promised. 'Now, I must check in with my team.'

Winner took the hint and moved away towards a small office at the back of the hall, where he picked up a phone, stared earnestly at a list of phone numbers pinned to the wall and started dialling.

By the time Greg got outside, a small group of uniformed officers was already piling out of a minivan, adjusting their PPE and checking they had torches, tasers, batons and radios at the ready. They were joined by more from a couple of patrol cars, also parked in front of the village hall. Sergeant Briscoe from Yarmouth was liaising with Glyn Roberts as they split the available force into three teams. Greg noted that Glyn had posted DC Waterton and DC Challinor to two different teams and himself to a third, spreading the detective resource as best he could.

Jim broke off from his conversation with Inspector Lake, newly arrived from Yarmouth, and turned to Greg. 'We're about ready to go,' he reported. 'Inspector Lake is going to stay here and mastermind the search up and down Filby main street with the teams organised by Briscoe. I'm going to head off down Thrigby Lane, outwards from the village, with Glyn and his teams.'

'So far, so good,' Greg approved. 'Is everyone warned to be on their guard? And to call on the armed response team the moment they have a sighting? When is the dog team arriving?'

'Everyone's been briefed about the dangers, and the dogs should be here in five or ten minutes,' Jim replied. 'Then they'll come with us to where Snelling saw Thorne get out of the truck.'

'And armed response?'

'On their way. They'll come here to the hall and wait in reserve until we've narrowed down the search.'

'OK. I'll wait here for Jill and armed response to arrive.'

Jim nodded and started to turn away to his car but was interrupted by the arrival of a small van marked 'Police Dogs'.

'Dogs are here,' said Greg. The man driving the van was new to him, but he thought he recognised the fair-haired woman in the passenger seat. 'Good to have you with us,' he said. 'We meet again, PC Scouller.' He remembered her name in the nick of time. 'I assume you've been briefed.'

'Prison escape, likely to be very violent, competent woodsman,' the driver summarised. 'I gather Scouller here has already had dealings with him. I'm Rogers. Good to meet you, sir. We've been told you know where he left the delivery truck.'

'Filby Lane,' Greg confirmed. 'DI Henning will take you to the location.'

'Fine. But we have control until the man is located,' he responded. 'Which means all these' – he waved – 'need to keep out of our way.'

'Of course.' Greg nodded. 'Let's get going, shall we?' He got into Jim's car. The van drove off down Thrigby Lane, followed by Jim and his teams of searchers.

46

Early evening

By the time Ram Trent and Helena Bell caught up with Louise Lacon, she had left for her evening's rehearsal of *Kiss Me, Kate*, back at the Garage in Norwich. The mere sight of them entering the rehearsal hall caused the self-styled Aubrey to smack himself on the forehead with the back of a dramatic hand.

'Nooo,' he wailed. 'Not *again*!' There was such emphasis on the last word, even the legendary Dame Edith Evans would have been envious.

'DCI Trent,' said Ram, unmoved by the histrionics.

'I can see *that*,' exclaimed Aubrey, still channelling Lady Bracknell.

'Hilda Bracket's off again,' Myrtle mischievously muttered to Josie. Josie snorted, causing Aubrey to bend a minatory glare in her direction.

'And DCI Bell,' said Helena.

'We need a few words with Louise Lacon,' went on Ram, glancing round. Louise was onstage with Leonard Ware but headed for the steps up into the audience seating as Aubrey sighed heavily again.

'Just take it out there, will you,' he said, pointing to the exit. 'Bill, Lois, let's take your duet instead.'

Ram and Helena retreated to the silent canteen, followed by Louise and, to their surprise, Myrtle.

'Do you have some new information for us?' Ram asked Myrtle politely. 'Because if not, we need a private word with Ms Lacon.'

'You need a word with me,' Myrtle corrected him. 'We've all heard about poor old Joseph Andrews, and Louise told us your theory about her friends being targeted. So you need to talk to me, as an unbiased observer.'

'Observer of what?' asked Helena while Louise showed distinct signs of exasperation.

'Myrtle, I told you to leave it,' she said in an indignant undertone. 'You've got it wrong.'

'No I haven't. You're just blind where he's concerned. I've told you before. In fact, I told you right at the start, before you married him. And I was right, wasn't I?'

Louise threw her hands up in exasperation – Ram couldn't help but reflect that the entire company seemed to be heavy on dramatic gestures – and stalked over to a corner before hurling herself into an uncomfortable canteen chair.

'You'd better let her have her say,' she said to Ram. 'We'll have no peace until she does.'

Ram sat down at the nearest table and nodded to Helena to join him. 'Perhaps you'd like to tell me what you know,' he said to Myrtle. 'And start with your proper name – I only know you as "Hattie".'

Myrtle took the seat opposite. 'Myrtle Harris. And I wanted to talk to you about her ex,' she said, jerking a thumb over her shoulder at Louise, who snorted audibly in response. 'She thinks he can do no wrong, even after all the hassle that led to the divorce, but let me tell you, he's nasty, vindictive, controlling and devious. If anyone's been targeting Louise's friends, I guarantee you it'll be him. It's right up his street.'

'We're talking about Reginald Coleman, are we?' asked Ram.

'Who else? She hasn't any other ex-husbands that I'm aware of,' responded Myrtle.

'I am still here, you know,' intervened Louise. 'And I *can* hear every word you're saying.'

'Then you're not hearing anything I haven't said before, umpteen times,' said Myrtle. 'Look,' she added, turning again to Ram. 'When they were together, he was controlling to the point that she stopped seeing all her friends and even gave up the theatre. He undermined her confidence and bullied her. She was a shadow of her real self. And after she escaped, after she did *at last* see the real him and got the divorce, he started again. He's got in the way of every relationship she's had since. And he keeps showing up, even at rehearsals sometimes, with spurious bits of paper she simply has to see.'

'I told you, Myrtle, he's changed. He's only looking out for me,' protested Louise. 'And I don't think he's very well.'

Myrtle cast her eyes to heaven. 'See what I mean?' she demanded.

Ram turned his gaze to Louise. 'How long ago did you divorce?' he asked.

'Must be seven years now,' replied Myrtle. 'That's right, isn't it, Louise?'

'If you wouldn't mind letting Ms Lacon reply for herself,' said Ram.

'She's right,' replied Louise, getting up and joining them at the table. 'It was just over seven years ago.'

'And the grounds for the divorce?' asked Helena.

Louise hesitated, then said reluctantly, 'Unreasonable behaviour.'

'In that case, and bearing in mind you must have convinced a judge of the truth of that, I assume you do, at heart, agree with Myrtle's description of your marriage,' commented Ram.

Louise played with the end of her belt for a moment, then admitted, 'He was then, yes.'

'And now?' asked Ram. 'If I were to tell you that we think we have his car on camera close to several of the recent incidents, would you really be surprised?'

There was a long pause, then Louise said, 'Yes. No. I don't know. Honestly, I really don't.'

'Can you think of any reason why he might want to see you isolated and alone?' asked Ram.

'I don't know,' said Louise again.

Myrtle could keep quiet no longer. 'Oh for goodness' sake, girl,' she snapped. 'Use the brains you were born with! Because he wants you under his thumb and isolated from any other support, just like before. It's the same pattern of behaviour all over again, only then some. Can you really not see it, Lou? He wants you back, and he doesn't want to share you.'

***

Out on Thrigby Lane, police cordons had closed the road to traffic where it met Filby High Street and, at the other end, just past the turning to Thrigby Hall. PC Scouller had released the first of the dogs, Nell, from the back of the van. The second, another German shepherd whom Greg was informed was PD Digby, was held in reserve on his lead. Nell was shown a soiled grey tracksuit top, which had been brought from the prison, then set to quartering the road near 22a Thrigby Lane. Under instructions from Rogers, everyone else was kept out of the dog's way.

It seemed but a matter of minutes before Nell signalled and then, with her handler, set off in a purposeful manner down the road towards the high street. Barely a hundred yards along, she faltered, cast about a bit and then turned to follow an apparent scent back in the opposite direction but on the other side of the road. This time she went on past 22a and down into the darker reaches of the lane, where it left the immediate environs of Filby.

'Seems he doubled back,' muttered Greg to Jim. 'I wonder why? He was heading towards his old place in Ormesby, but now he's headed away.'

'Perhaps he saw something in the high street that spooked him, and he chose to head back to the woods,' suggested Jim. They realised that in their eagerness they were starting to overtake the dog team. A glare from Scouller warned them off, and they fell back a little.

Nell led them along the hedge line, paused where a pile of paper and cans lay on the verge, then turned with renewed enthusiasm towards the entrance to Thrigby Hall car park, where she turned left. Rogers stopped and turned to speak to Greg.

'We may have a problem here,' he said. 'I know this place, not least from days out with the kids. The car park is huge. It's not just the hardstanding here.' He gestured to the gravelled area in front of them. 'There's also a lot of grassed car parking space further back and over to the right.'

'So what's the problem?' asked Greg.

'No problem as far as the parking areas are concerned, but a difficulty if our target has headed off into the main wildlife areas. I'm sure we'll get a lot of resistance from the management, and to be honest, I'd agree with them. This isn't a good environment for a dog search. There are risks, both for the collection and for the dogs.'

'I'm not familiar with the place, but surely whatever animals they have here are in secure enclosures,' objected Greg. 'I can see they wouldn't want us creating a noise and fuss, but no one ever wants that and sometimes they just have to lump it while we do our jobs. But what's the issue for the dogs?'

'The pens are mainly designed to keep the animals in, not to keep a determined criminal out. If he takes refuge inside a pen, I can't send the dogs in after him. My recommendation is that we track as far as we safely can, and not too close to any wildlife. If he's moved into an enclosure or any other area I deem unsafe, I'll move the dogs downwind and attempt to windscent.'

'You mean the dogs can work at a distance?' Greg was a little sceptical.

'These dogs' – Rogers indicated the two German shepherds waiting calmly, but alertly at their handlers' sides – 'trained as they are, they'll react at some considerable distance to a human scent by lifting their noses and whining or straining to get at him. We should be able to narrow down the suspect to quite a small area, then you can send armed response in to get him. And if he makes a run for it, the dogs will have him,' he added. It was clearly his preferred option.

'Brilliant!' exclaimed Greg. 'Let's do it. Start with the car park and the boundaries. If you establish he moved on from here, then we follow. If necessary, I'll try for a police helicopter – but don't hold your breath. I believe they're responding to less than ten per cent of callouts. If you find he entered the park itself, then we follow the procedure you've just outlined. But we need a word with their management, and I must bring Inspector Lake up to speed as well.'

He spoke to Rick Lake first. 'I know the Thrigby team,' was his immediate response. 'I'll have a word with them, and I think Roger's judgement is spot on.'

'From the map, I understand there's a cafe and an old hall with a souvenir shop and so on,' said Greg. 'They might be a magnet for a man on the run looking for supplies. Tell them we're going to use dogs in the car park, and possibly in the cafe and hall. If we find he's gone into the wildlife areas, we'll use the dogs at long distance to narrow down our search area and continue with men. It would be helpful if some of their staff could meet us on site.

'Also, alert the armed response team now and send them down here. I'm not taking risks with this chap. Not this time.'

An hour later and he was assimilating the unwelcome, but not unexpected, intelligence that the dogs were unanimously certain their quarry had entered the main site near the Cockatoo Cafe.

'As I feared,' he said. 'Probably after food supplies. Jim, check both buildings for forced entry and get men stationed by the entrances and exits. Rogers, we'll need the dogs to check these two buildings. If we're lucky, they'll find him in one of them and our task is done. If not, then, as we agreed, you'll take the dogs downwind and guide our search from there.'

'Get the armed team over here to back up the dogs,' he said to Jill, and turned back to survey the vista of oddly shaped buildings, trees and fences that obscured the skyline. 'Let's hope he's pigging out on sausage rolls in the cafe,' he said, half to himself.

***

Bill was chuffed. He stared at the database entry being pointed out to him by Halfords' resident computer nerd, a thin lad with glasses that kept slipping down his nose. He pushed them up again with one finger and remarked to Bill, 'That is what you wanted, isn't it?'

'It looks like it,' responded Bill. He made a note of the model number listed alongside an entry that said the battery had been bought on 9 June 2021 by a Mr Reginald Coleman and paid for by Lloyds Bank credit card. 'Is there any other ID on the battery?' he asked. 'Apart from the model number, I mean?'

'There would be a maker's mark – in this case Apollo,' the lad replied. 'It's one of our cheaper batteries; although none of them are exactly cheap,' he added. 'This one retails at three hundred and thirty pounds.'

Bill wasn't listening any more. He had already speed-dialled Chris.

'Let me check those details with the list from Forensics,' she was saying. And a few seconds later he was almost deafened by a full-throated 'Eureka!'

'Enough for a warrant?' he asked.

'I'd say so,' she replied. 'I'll brief Ram then get back to you. Well done, Bill.'

'Any news on the rope?' he asked.

'Unfortunately not. According to the latest report, the rope Greg took off Joseph Andrews was almost certainly a climbing rope, not a mooring rope as we assumed at first. Apparently, the tensile strength of the core is different in a climbing rope. Maybe he did get it off the internet rather than a physical shop. But they're still looking at the moment.'

Twenty minutes later she was on the phone to Ram. 'A complete blank so far on the rope,' she reported. 'Which means he probably got it on the internet. The battery, however, he bought at Halfords in Norwich, only a few weeks ago. And was rash enough to pay for it by credit card. I hope we can get a search warrant now, and I think we'll find enough to convict him when we check out his house, bank statements, etc.'

47

That night

Jim swiftly deployed men to the front and back of both the cafe and the old hall, with strict instructions to call for backup if they spotted anyone leaving either building and on no account to engage closely unless the target obeyed a command to lie down on the ground.

'We've checked for forced entry,' he said to Greg. 'Unfortunately, neither building is secure. The cafe has a storeroom window ajar and the old hall has an open hatch to what I assume is a cellar.'

Rogers and Scouller were waiting patiently with Nell and Digby. 'Over to us then,' said Rogers. 'Behind me, please,' he added as Greg headed for the cafe entrance, 'sir.'

Greg acknowledged his mistake and stepped to the rear as instructed.

'Oh, and make sure none of the lone rangers take a pot shot at our dogs,' added Scouller. Grinning at the recurrence of inter-team rivalry, Greg followed the leashed dogs and handlers into the cafe.

Indicator lights from chiller cabinets provided spots of colour in the darkness and the only sound, apart from the eager panting of the two dogs, was the humming of numerous electrical motors. Rogers slipped his thermal imaging goggles down over his eyes and surveyed the room.

'Can't see anything other than the warmth coming off the equipment,' he muttered over his shoulder to Greg. Glancing sideways at his partner wearing similar goggles, he said, 'Let's go.'

The first dog, Nell, was released and bounded down the cafe. It was a matter of moments before she returned, having found nothing and disturbed no one.

'Good dog,' said Rogers, patting her. 'Next space.'

He carried out a final check at the far end of the cafe, then led the German shepherd behind the serving counters to the door into the kitchen. The same procedure was repeated in the kitchen, then Scouller let Digby take a turn in the storage areas beyond. At last Rogers returned to Greg, waiting as instructed by the door. Both dog handlers pushed their goggles up, and Scouller reached sideways to flick down the bank of switches by the door. Strip lights from one end of the cafe to the other flickered then steadied. Greg and everyone else blinked at the sudden change in light.

'Clear, sir,' Rogers reported. 'Let's move on to the old hall. That's going to take a bit longer.'

Outside in the open again, Greg thought he detected a hint of rain in the air, and the breeze had freshened, making the trees whisper. There was a quiet murmur of voices from the dark group of armed police, and Greg was surprised to hear what seemed to be dogs barking from the centre of the park. He turned to look at Rogers.

'Nothing to do with us,' he said, correctly interpreting the look. 'I'd guess it's one of the wild animals. Perhaps a wild dog or wolf?'

Jim joined them in the wide space before the hall, accompanied by a stranger in dark overalls.

'Red pandas,' said the man. 'That's one of our red pandas. They do sound a bit dog-like.'

'This is Bert Granger, head keeper,' said Jim. 'He's got more staff on hand, but I asked them to stay in the car park for now, since we know that's clear. I've explained the dangers of the man we're looking for.'

'I realise you have a problem,' said Bert. 'I'm obviously worried about your dogs and indeed the threat of firearms within the park. But I don't think you'll find your man in any of our enclosures. They're pretty secure. If he's here at all, which, forgive me, I hope he's not, he'll be in one of the public spaces.'

'Noted,' said Greg. 'And I hope you're right. The cafe's clear,' he said to Jim. 'Any movement out here?'

'Only our chaps,' replied Jim. 'And Bert's night watchman, but I've asked him to keep back for now too. As for the hall, I've officers stationed front and back, so if he was in there, he's still there.'

'OK, let's do it,' said Greg, turning to Rogers. But he and Scouller were already on their way to the front door. Greg hurried to catch up and, followed by Glyn with a couple of uniformed officers, entered the silent old building.

The ground floor housed the souvenir shop and offices. According to the map Greg had been given, there were more offices and storage spaces on the floors above. Goggles down, Rogers checked the visible areas of the shop, and Nell was off her lead again, doing her duty with every evidence of enthusiasm.

Nothing.

The team moved on through the whole of the ground floor, with the same result.

'What about the cellars?' asked Scouller.

'According to the map, there's only one door into the ground floor and I've a man standing by it,' replied Greg.

She looked at Rogers. 'Let's check the upper floors first,' he said, leading the way to the stairs.

The rooms on the second floor were smaller and led off a central corridor. At a nod from Greg, Glyn Roberts stationed officers at the top of the stairs while the dog teams started down the east corridor, clearing pairs of rooms on each side as they went – first left then right, the two dogs deployed in turn. They reached the far end and turned to come back.

'Clear so f—' said Rogers.

He was interrupted by shouts from the back of the building. He rushed into one of the rear-facing rooms that had already been cleared. Greg was about to follow when his radio crackled and Jim's voice said, 'Fire visible from the west end of the hall – looks like second floor.'

Scouller and Digby took the stairs two at a time, followed closely by Greg and Glyn's team. Rogers made to follow, then, realising that they still hadn't cleared the west end of the first floor, stayed where he was. Outside, the men guarding the front and back of the building ran to where they could see flames reflected in a second-floor window. Bert started for the front door, but was held back by Jim.

'Call the fire brigade. And leave this to us for now.'

Bert nodded, hauled his phone out and dialled 999. As he did so, the armed team came up the drive at a trot.

Jim ran around the building to get a better view of what was happening at the back, and as he rounded the corner, he saw a shadow jump the last few feet to the ground, apparently having shinned down a drainpipe, and run off into the centre of the park.

***

Ram was relieved that getting hold of a magistrate had proved surprisingly easy. And even happier that the warrant had been granted with little argument. Mentally surveying his available assets, he realised it came down to himself, Helena, Bill and Chris, who was already at home.

Cursing the incompetence of those who had let a prisoner escape, and thus bugger up his investigation, he stuck his head round the door of the incident room. Helena was also heading home, judging by the look she gave him when he beckoned to her and Bill with a terse, 'With me, please. We've got the warrant and we're going to execute it now. Yvonne Berry is meeting us there.'

'I was...' started Helena, then let it trail off as she realised the futility of protest. 'OK,' she said and picked up her bag.

Bill was already halfway across the room. 'What about Chris?' he said to Ram. 'She'll want to know.'

'I'll ring her from my car,' said Ram.

When he got through, Chris seemed unsurprised. 'Good. Great in fact,' she said. 'I've already organised cover here. I'll meet you in Newmarket Road.'

'You won't,' said Ram. 'You're on admin duties, remember?'

'I've already interviewed Coleman,' she reminded him. 'I'll meet you there – you'll need me.'

He gave way with suspicious alacrity, and Chris grinned to herself. She rather thought that was precisely the outcome he had anticipated. Especially as Greg was busy elsewhere. Returning to the kitchen, she smiled at her mother currently cuddling her grandson.

'He's meant to be left to sleep in his cot,' she reminded her.

'A bit of a cuddle never hurt anyone,' Jane Mathews retorted, nuzzling her face into Jamie's head. 'Besides, they smell so good at this age.'

'I'm so grateful for this,' Chris went on. 'Thanks, Mum.'

'Just you look after yourself, and don't forget to tell Greg this was your idea not mine. I don't want him on my case,' said her mother.

Chris rang Greg as she bounced her little car down their rutted drive and turned towards Norwich. There was no answer from his phone, so she left a message and concentrated on her driving. She reckoned she should arrive in Newmarket Road about the same time as the teams from Wymondham.

She was right. As she turned off the A47 and down the A11, a car behind her flashed its lights twice, and she recognised

Bill's slightly dilapidated old Ford Escort. At the same moment her phone lit up and the hands-free indicated an incoming call. It was Ram.

'We're behind you,' he said. 'And Yvonne Berry isn't far behind. We'll go straight in when we arrive at Coleman's. Best not to give him chance to make a break for it.'

'Got it,' said Chris. And in a matter of moments, four police cars and a van were choking the generous spaces of Reginald Coleman's circular drive. In addition to the detective contingent, Ram had managed to rustle up from Norwich a couple of uniformed staff very happy to swop a tedious evening rounding up drunks for something more interesting.

A few swift words from Chris, whom they knew well – everyone in Norfolk knew Chris – and they were deployed, one to the back door and the other to stand by the garage. Ram nodded his thanks and rapped a brisk tattoo on the door.

'Mr Reginald Coleman?' said Ram to the man who answered the door. 'I am DCI Trent. Under the powers provided by the Police and Criminal Evidence Act 1984, I have a warrant to search this property and seize any items relevant to our investigation of the murders of Marie Leakey, Sharon Jones and Anthony Newell and the attempted murders of Nick Atkinson and Joseph Andrews.' He handed a copy of the warrant to Coleman and stepped forwards, forcing the householder to step back. 'You have the right to remain silent,' went on Ram. 'And you do, of course, have the right to legal representation.' He was followed in by Helena and Chris after a slight, and unspoken, vying for priority in the doorway. Bill, behind them, suppressed a smile and silently put his money on Chris as ultimate winner.

Coleman was scrutinising the warrant under the hall light, then turned to Ram.

'I protest this invasion of my home in the strongest possible terms,' he said in a voice that trembled slightly – whether with rage or fear, Ram was unable to say. 'I shall ring my solicitor immediately.' Coleman headed for the sitting room, followed by Ram, who turned in the doorway to speak to Chris and Helena.

'Get Yvonne and her team in here asap,' he said. 'I'll stay with Coleman and start asking a few more questions. Chris, you with me, please. Helena, can you keep an eye on the search? Let us know if they turn anything up.'

Helena didn't look best pleased by the arrangements but nodded her assent.

'I'll see to the garage and the car, shall I?' Bill asked her. She agreed, and he headed for the front door. He was back in moments. 'We need the zapper,' he said.

'Try this,' said Helena, holding up an evidence bag containing a couple of zappers. 'They were in the kitchen.'

'Great. Looks like the very thing.' And Bill returned to the drive.

In the sitting room, Reginald Coleman was sitting on one of his sofas, holding his phone. 'My solicitor will be here shortly,' he snapped. 'He says I'm to say nothing until he gets here.'

'Fair enough,' said Ram. 'We'll just wait. Impressive service at this time of night,' he added. 'I don't know all that many solicitors with an emergency service. Or perhaps you were expecting a visit from us?'

'Know him from the golf club,' muttered Coleman. Then fell silent again.

Through the open door, Ram and Chris could hear the sounds of the search proceeding, upstairs and down. Looking around them, if only for something to do while they waited, Chris spotted something sticking out from under a sofa cushion near Coleman. She stood up and moving swiftly, leaned forwards to pick it up. It was a laptop. Coleman stretched for it and got a hand on it.

'Now don't turn this into a tug of war,' said Chris reprovingly. 'You'll only lose. I have the weight of the law on my side.' She heaved sharply, and the laptop was in her hands. As she sat down with it, Coleman stood up, and Ram hurriedly got between them.

'Sit down, Mr Coleman, and wait for your solicitor,' he recommended.

'I. Want. My. Laptop. Back,' he snarled. 'She has no right.'

'She does have the right, as granted under the warrant, which I've already given you,' said Ram. 'Sit down.' He emphasised his command with a gentle push on Coleman's chest, which was, nonetheless, adequate to precipitate him into the sofa cushions.

Chris had opened the laptop and discovered, to her delight, that it was not password-protected. 'Very careless,' she observed.

'Rubbish. I have nothing to hide,' retorted Coleman.

'Then you won't mind me looking.' As Ram looked up, she added, 'Just a quick look now, then I'll hand it over to the forensic experts. But as Mr Coleman is sufficiently reckless, or perhaps blameless, that he hasn't password-protected the appliance, it seems likely that I'll find something interesting without getting too technical.' Noting that Coleman looked uneasy, she added, 'It would be consistent with him using his credit card to buy the lithium battery in Halfords.'

Now an expression of panic did cross Coleman's face before he managed to reassume the deadpan. Chris left him to stew on that thought, while she trawled through his emails.

'Very interesting,' she said. 'At least, I find it interesting that you apparently have access to your ex-wife's email account. That must be unusual!' She looked up, and Coleman scowled but said nothing. Knowing her skills didn't extend to researching in depth, she was about to hand the laptop over to Yvonne Berry when something occurred to her. She checked Safari and found that Amazon was open. A few clicks and she found that not only were his passwords all saved to the laptop, but his order history was plain to see. She whistled quietly to herself, and Ram came over to see what she had found.

'Now that is *very* interesting,' he said. 'Very interesting.' He looked up. 'Mr Coleman, why did you buy a climbing rope just two weeks ago? And where is it?'

'No comment,' said Coleman. But his face was now white, verging on green.

At a nod from Ram, Chris extricated herself from the depths of her sofa and went into the hall to give Yvonne Berry the laptop. She was explaining, in an undertone, what she had found, when the front door was pushed open by the constable standing guard.

'Someone's just arrived. I think it's the solicitor,' he called.

Everyone was distracted by this announcement. In the sitting room, Ram moved over to the window overlooking the drive. Helena turned back from the kitchen doorway, where she was keeping an eye on the search, and came towards the front door.

It seemed Coleman's nerve had cracked. He seized the apparent opportunity and bolted for the front door, pushing Helena out of the way so violently she fell across the bottom of the stairs and gave her head a nasty crack on the banisters on the way down. Chris shoved the laptop into Yvonne's hands, turned, and as Coleman passed her, quietly stuck out a foot.

When the solicitor entered the hall, the sight that met his astonished eyes was of a young woman on the stairs, dazedly rubbing her head, his client prone on the tiled floor and with a triumphant Chris sitting on his back.

Ram came through from the sitting room, and Yvonne caught his eye with a nod.

'Reginald Coleman, I am arresting you for the murders of Marie Leakey, Sharon Jones and Anthony Newell. And the attempted murder of Joseph Andrews. Other charges may follow. Chris, caution him and put him in the car. We'll take him to the station in Norwich for interview.'

48

Last Act 1

As Chris hustled the now unresisting Coleman from the house, Ram followed Yvonne back into the kitchen.

'What have you got?' he asked.

'First,' she said, 'I've rung the lab and the spec of the climbing rope he bought from Amazon matches the one that was used to hang Joseph Andrews over the river wall.'

'They're sure?' asked Ram. 'I mean, sorry, I'm not doubting their expertise, but to me, a rope is a rope.'

'It's definitely the same spec,' Yvonne confirmed. 'Both mooring ropes and climbing ropes have an outer cover wrapped round an inner core, but in the case of a climbing rope, it's designed to cope with sudden increases in tension. For example, it needs to cope with holding and stretching under the sudden weight of a climber falling off. A mooring rope, by contrast, isn't expected to stretch much or cope with sudden increases in tension. This is identical to the one bought online. What I can't say yet is whether it's the same one, but now we have a suspect, DNA analysis might give us that link.

'But what I wanted to show you is what we've found in the bottom of the freezer.' She pointed to a small package in a plastic bag, now filmed with condensation as the frozen contents began to defrost. 'I'm ninety per cent sure this is wild hemlock. We'll take a closer look back at the lab, but I'm confident.'

As they spoke, an assistant was bagging all the knives from the knife block on the granite worktop behind them. Ram turned to watch. 'Any of those a candidate for the weapon used on Sharon Jones?' he asked.

'I think so, yes,' confirmed Yvonne. 'We're taking them all just in case. But we'll have a close look, and there's one I think Dr Paisley will want to compare to the wounds on Jones.'

'What about the bike battery?' he asked. 'I know you said it was the same type, but was anything recovered that would help with identification?'

'Not much,' admitted Yvonne. 'When thermal runaway occurs, the intense heat causes the battery contents to decompose and explode. So the interior vanishes. On the other hand, fragments of the outer layer were thrown across the hall. Some of them carried lettering that identified the precise make and model, and they match some of the details Bill got from Halfords. We'll have another look now.'

By the time Ram reached the drive, an ambulance had arrived, its blue lights adding to the lurid glow already provided by the police cars. Chris joined him on the steps, wiping her hands down her jeans.

'I've sent Coleman off under the supervision of a couple of uniforms, and his brief is following behind,' she reported.

'And the ambulance?'

'For Helena. She got quite a crack on the head. They'll probably take her in for checks.'

'Right. In that case, Chris, are you OK to come and interview Coleman with me?'

'Try and stop me,' she said with a flashing smile.

***

By the time he arrived at the police station, tucked away behind the town hall, Ram was having second thoughts. As he parked round the corner, he tried a phone call to Greg to update him on developments and, in the process, check that he was happy with his fiancée's sudden return to active duty. But there was no answer. He left a message that didn't mention Chris's role and hurried into the station.

Chris, as well known here as in most police stations across the county, was already in possession of two mugs of coffee and a plate of biscuits. 'I thought this would be a good idea,' she said. 'Thanks, Robin,' she added to the stout sergeant behind the desk. 'How do you want us to play this?' she asked as she handed Ram one of the mugs.

'It's going to be a late one,' he replied, looking at her through the steam from his coffee. 'Are you sure you're OK with that, what with things at home and so on?'

'If by "*things at home*" you mean my son,' she said slightly tartly, 'my mother is staying the night. I'm OK to do this.'

'OK.' Ram decided that facing Greg was something he'd worry about later. 'I assume his brief is with him now?'

'Yes. Went straight in. So, are we going to ask questions across all the cases, or focus on one?'

'Let's start with his relationship with his ex-wife, as that's at the heart of this matter. Then we'll pick up on the hemlock and... Damn,' he said suddenly. 'I forgot to ask about his car and the stealth spray.'

'No worries,' said Chris. 'I'll ring Bill. He's still at the scene. If they haven't looked already, I'm sure he'll get Yvonne's lot to give it the once-over. Just give me a minute.'

'I'll go and get the preliminaries out of the way,' said Ram. 'Join us when you've got the answer on the car.'

When Chris entered the interview room, she gave Ram a discreet nod and sat down beside him as he said, 'DI Chris Mathews has entered the room.' He glanced at the piece of paper she pushed in front of him as he went on. 'Mr Coleman, you were explaining to me why you and Louise Lacon got divorced. I think you were blaming interference from other parties.'

Coleman was scowling and, unlike most interviewees, was glaring straight into Ram's eyes as though seeking to intimidate him. 'I *said*,' he repeated with emphasis, 'that we were perfectly happy until certain so-called friends of hers started to suggest I was being unreasonable. Just because I wanted her with me rather than always off *acting*.' If the final word had been 'debt collecting', it couldn't have been delivered with more disdain.

'You didn't admire Louise's acting talents then?' asked Ram.

'In my view, she was wasting her time,' replied Coleman.

'So you put your foot down, stopped her spending time doing what she loved and seeing the friends she'd known for years. And the end result was she left you altogether,' observed Chris. 'Not a great result from your perspective, Mr Coleman.' She noted with interest that he ignored her completely, even to keeping his focus on Ram's eyes.

'What do you want from Louise now?' asked Ram.

'I can't see what relevance this has,' objected the solicitor, but was ignored by his client.

'I want her home of course,' said Coleman. 'Where she should be.'

'And was that why you sought to remove all her emotional props?' asked Ram. 'Everyone she confided in or leaned on, or was getting close to?'

Coleman scowled some more but remained silent. Ram watched him for a moment, debating with himself what his next move should be. He was getting a strong impression of a supremely self-confident and arrogant man. *What would provoke him most? Undermining his self-belief or reinforcing it?*

Glancing again at the piece of paper Chris had placed before him, he said, 'One thing did impress me. And that's your use of stealth spray.'

The solicitor looked puzzled, and Ram explained. 'If you haven't done a lot of criminal work, Mr Hempstall, you may not be familiar with this particular product. Sprayed on a car number plate, it reflects light in such a way that it's difficult for an enforcement camera, such as a speed camera or ANPR, to take a clear picture. Its use is, of course, illegal. But it's fairly readily obtainable. We found a part-used can in Mr Coleman's garage – with his fingerprints on it.

'But what was really clever about Mr Coleman's use of it, was that he didn't spray the whole plate. Oh no. He sprayed only part of each plate, front and back, such that the numbers and letters that were captured on camera were those that matched part of Dean Mason's registration number.

'It worked for a while,' he admitted. 'We spent too much time chasing that particular red herring. Well done, Mr Coleman. But you made two mistakes. I've already mentioned one: your fingerprints on the can. You really should have worn gloves. Or even better, got rid of the can. The other mistake was obscuring the exact same numbers on both the front and back plates. The chances of that happening by accident were very small. That's what first put us on to your subterfuge.

'Good word that,' he added reflectively. 'Subterfuge. You've used a few, haven't you, Mr Coleman. And every time you've made at least one fundamental error. I often say that the main reason we catch criminals is that they're stupid. But in your case, I don't think you're stupid, Mr Coleman. But you have made stupid mistakes. Mainly out of arrogance. Or hubris. Now that's another really good word, isn't it?'

Coleman added audible teeth grinding to his signs of rage, and Ram concluded he was on the right lines.

'So let's turn to another stupid mistake, shall we? The bike battery. I admit that using the thermal runaway property of a lithium cell battery to kick-start an arson attack was creative. But buying the battery in person, and with your credit card? Now that was stupid. Especially as you don't even have an e-bike.

'And then there's the rope. Hanging Joseph Andrews upside down over the river wall was creative too. Were you lucky with the tides, by the way, or had you already checked the time of low tide? But buying the rope online was risky; while failing to password-protect your laptop... Well, words fail me.

'As for leaving hemlock in your freezer—'

Reginald Coleman hurling himself over the table and grabbed for Ram's throat. As his weight hit, Ram's chair went over backwards and both men sprawled on the floor. For the second time in one evening, Chris intervened to grab Coleman's right arm and twist it up behind his back. She was joined in short order by the constable who had been standing by the door, and between them they subdued Coleman, removed him from Ram and sat him in a chair.

'Shut up,' ordered Chris as he spouted a bunch of unspeakably racist insults in Ram's direction. 'Shut up or I'll arrest you for a hate crime as well as assaulting a police officer.'

'What'd he say?' asked Ram, who had been understandably distracted. He returned his chair to the upright position and sat on it.

'Believe me, you don't want to know,' said Chris grimly. 'Although, I suppose it'll be on the tape anyway.'

Ram got his breath back and looked at Coleman. 'What I don't understand,' he said after a moment, 'is what you wanted to achieve.'

'To get her back. She needs to come back and look after me,' responded Coleman in a tone that could almost be described as triumphant. 'And there's nothing you can do about it,' he added.

His solicitor attempted to intervene, to tell him to keep quiet, to say no more, but Coleman brushed him away.

'It's too late and there's nothing they can do,' he repeated. 'I'm dying. Cancer. Given the current inefficiency of the justice system, I'll be dead before they get me into court. So stuff that in your pipe,' he snarled.

49

Last Act 2

In Thrigby, Greg was deep in discussion with the firearms team commander. The latter had spread a map of the site on the bonnet of the nearest car. His team, Greg, Jim, Rogers and the Thrigby head keeper, all crowded round as best they could.

'At the risk of sounding like an old joke,' he said to Greg, 'if I was mounting a search, I wouldn't be doing it here! This is not the place for an armed shoot-out.'

'Dead right,' said the head keeper, with considerable emphasis. 'Our animals are valuable, rare or both. And the level of disturbance they've already been subjected to tonight is enough to put some of them off breeding. This is derailing years of carefully planned breeding programmes.'

'I get that,' said the commander. 'Although, given the man we're hunting, my main concern is safety. He's violent and unstable, but not as stupid as I'd like. He knows perfectly well the limitations we will be operating under. He knows, for example, that there are multiple lines of sight where it will be difficult or dangerous to take a shot. He used to live not far from here, so I guess he's also familiar with the layout of the place.

'My strong advice, sir,' he said to Greg, 'is that we don't even attempt to catch him while he's in these grounds. That we herd him out of here and set up an ambush in an area we can control.

'Look, the dogs have told us he's somewhere in this triangle here.' He pointed to the map. 'My plan is that we pressure him to move in this direction, and we leave a gap in our lines that, with luck, he'll take advantage of. That will move him this way, over the hall boundary and towards the old church here. Then we corner him.'

'Once you get him away from the wildlife, we can send the dogs in,' Rogers pointed out. 'That way, we may not need to start shooting.'

Greg looked at the map again, looked up at the animal pens in front of him and nodded. 'Agreed,' he said. 'Let's do it. Just one thing,' he added. 'Remind everyone they're hunting a tree surgeon. He's very competent at height and he climbs like a cat. They need to remember to look up.'

While the commander turned to his unit and the dog teams retreated back towards the boundary, Greg took the opportunity to check his phone. A bland update from Ram Trent got a nod. Then, scrolling further back, he found the message from Chris. It was immediately clear to him that she had returned to active service. Indignation and worry warred for his attention. Greg pushed both to the back of his mind, to allow him to focus on the present. By the time his attention was, once again, on the armed response team, it was clear each man knew what he was to do. Everyone checked their watches.

Two of the armed officers quietly peeled off to set up by the church. The rest moved left and right, spreading along the paths and avenues between the animal enclosures.

'You and your men can come with me, sir,' said the commander to Greg. 'But keep behind me.'

As they too moved off down the main avenue, two constables emerged from the old hall, sweaty, breathless and slightly sooty. 'Fire's out, sir,' one of them reported. 'It was only a pile of paper. It was sitting on an old metal desk, and that limited its spread. A couple of fire extinguishers sorted it.'

The head keeper heaved a sigh of relief. 'I'll have another word with the fire service,' he said. 'They'll probably still want to come and check things over, just to make sure, but they won't need to come mob-handed now. Thank you. Good job.' He took his phone out again, and was left behind as the police contingent moved on past the turning to the lake and up the hill.

Just as they reached the lime-tree walk, a radio crackled. Greg was close enough to hear the message.

'Target spotted. Due east from your current position. In the trees by the tiger enclosure.'

The commander stopped dead and looked around for cover. There was little in their immediate vicinity, but he moved off the road to take advantage of a patch of deeper shadow, beckoning Greg and Jim to follow him.

'Move towards the aviary,' he ordered his sharpshooter. 'Keep out of sight but make a bit of a clatter. Push him away from the lime avenue, towards the church.'

'Roger,' said the radio. Then: 'Target gone the other way. Over the tiger enclosure.'

A new sound obtruded itself into the rustling whispers of a Norfolk night, and every other animal fell silent. It was the cough-like roar of a Sumatran tiger.

Everyone froze. This was England in the twenty-first century, but every man present reacted exactly as would his primaeval ancestors. Muscles in skin contracted to raise hairs that would have formed an aggressive ruff, pupils dilated to improve sight of the threat and heart rates accelerated to prime the owner for flight or fight. Greg certainly felt the effects of the massive adrenaline rush. So did the officers holding firearms.

The man in the tree, who had alerted the rightful occupant of the space below to the presence of an intruder, was not immune. An increased heart rate and suddenly clammy hands loosened his grip on the branches. He slipped. And the tiger roared again.

THE END – FOR NOW

HUNGRY FOR MORE?

follow Greg into Norfolk Mystery Book 10 – to be published February 2026

FINAL CUT

Norfolk, Autumn 2021. Greg is wrestling with problems in his team and at home, when a decomposed body turns up in a derelict farmhouse—bound, masked, and posed in front of a camera that hasn't rolled in years. What begins as a suspected sex crime quickly unravels into something far more disturbing.

Greg Geldard is no stranger to the depravity people inflict on each other—but this case leads him into the darkest recesses of the internet, where violent fantasies blur with reality and where the line between performer and victim vanishes.

As more footage surfaces, each more disturbing than the last, Geldard and his team must confront a horrifying question:
What if the worst part isn't what's on the tape?

Prologue: Norfolk, September 2021

The tiger roared again. There was a rustle as armed police moved stealthily through the wildlife park, along the paths normally traversed by happy holidaymakers. They were trying, and failing, to get a better view of what was happening in the enclosure before them. Detective Superintendent Greg Geldard moved closer to the armed response commander.

'Any sign?' he hissed.

Commander Leaming shook his head and held up a hand for silence, apparently listening intently to a message in his earpiece. After a moment he turned to Greg.

'We can't see him in the pen,' he said softly. 'We can see the tiger is stressed…' As if to emphasise the point, there was another roar. 'But as far as we know the target's still in the trees overhead. There's a heat source where there shouldn't be. Up there.' He indicated the row of lime trees that circled the tiger enclosure in the wildlife park. 'Keep back sir. We're going to try to herd him towards the boundary.'

The dark clad officers melted away to left and right. Greg did as he was told, and turned towards the old hall, keeping to the shadows. '*There are times to take the lead, and times to stand back,*' he told himself, itching to get into the action but knowing better. His interference would just destabilise a well-trained team.

The sound of dogs snarling and excited yelps broke out over to his right, where the park boundary met the old churchyard. His radio crackled and he lifted it to his ear.

'Rogers sir', said the quiet voice of the lead dog-handler. 'The dogs have picked up his scent. Over by the old church.'

'You're sure?' asked Greg.

'*They're* sure,' said Rogers with emphasis, just as a couple of the armed response team came running back down the hill towards Greg and the exit.

Printed in Dunstable, United Kingdom